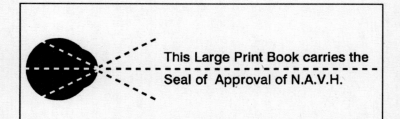

This Large Print Book carries the
Seal of Approval of N.A.V.H.

THE SQUARE ROOT OF MURDER

ADA MADISON

WHEELER PUBLISHING
A part of Gale, Cengage Learning

GALE
CENGAGE Learning®

Detroit • New York • San Francisco • New Haven, Conn • Waterville, Maine • London

GALE
CENGAGE Learning®

LIBRARY OF CONGRESS CATALOGING-IN-PUBLICATION DATA

Madison, Ada.
  The square root of murder / by Ada Madison. — Large print ed.
    p. cm. — (Wheeler publishing large print cozy mystery)
  "A Professor Sophie Knowles Mystery."
  ISBN-13: 978-1-4104-4393-9(softcover)
  ISBN-10: 1-4104-4393-0(softcover)
  1. Women college teachers—Fiction. 2. Murder—Investigation—Fiction.
3. College stories. 4. Large type books. I. Title.
PS3613.A28447S68 2012
813'.6—dc23   2011039265

Published in 2012 by arrangement with The Berkley Publishing Group, a member of Penguin Group (USA) Inc.

Printed in the United States of America
  1 2 3 4 5   16 15 14 13 12

FD026

*This book is dedicated
to my former agent,
the late Elaine Koster,
who saw me through fourteen books.*

ACKNOWLEDGMENTS

Thanks as always to my dream critique team: mystery authors Jonnie Jacobs, Rita Lakin, and Margaret Lucke.

I can't say enough good things about Dr. Jeanne Trubek, mathematics chairwoman at Emmanuel College in Boston. Jeanne, an amazing teacher, allowed me to attend her class, answered many questions, read a draft manuscript, and is still talking to me. I hope the final product is worthy of her input.

Thanks also to Dr. Sally Dias, woman of many titles at Emmanuel, including vice president, who welcomed me back to my alma mater and has been a constant resource as well as a friend.

A special word about my good friend and medevac pilot Mark Ramos. Mark submitted to interviews straight from twelve-hour shifts. He fielded my questions, no matter how "obvious" the answers should have been, and toured me through his Northern

California facility. Mark introduced me to a whole crew of generous coworkers who shared fascinating stories. In particular, I'd like to thank Ernie Acebo and Sim Mason. Flight nurse Acebo was especially helpful with details of the story. No one at the facility is responsible for my errors or literary license.

Thanks also to the extraordinary Inspector Chris Lux for continued advice on police procedure. My interpretation of his counsel should not be held against him.

Thanks to the many writers and friends who offered critique, information, brainstorming, and inspiration; in particular: Gail and David Abbate, Judy Barnett, Sara Bly, Margaret Hamilton, Eileen Hotte, Peg McPartland, Suzanne Monaco, Ann Parker, Mary Solon, Sue Stephenson, Jean Stokowski, Karen and Mark Streich, and Ellen Twaddell.

My deepest gratitude goes to my husband, Dick Rufer, the best there is. I can't imagine working without his support. He's my dedicated webmaster (www.minichino.com), layout specialist, and on-call IT department.

Finally, how lucky can I be? I'm working with a special and dedicated editor, Michelle Vega.

HENLEY COLLEGE

CLARA BARTON DORM

NATHANIEL HAWTHORNE DORM

PAUL REVERE DORM

GYM / STUDENT UNION

COFFEE SHOP

TENNIS COURTS

ADMINISTRATION BUILDING

BENJAMIN FRANKLIN HALL

EMILY DICKINSON LIBRARY

HENLEY BOULEVARD

Sometimes it is useful to know how large your zero is.

— AUTHOR UNKNOWN

1

Who thought summer school was a good idea? Especially in Massachusetts, where the humidity can take your breath away, never mind frizz up your hair.

I loved teaching in one of the oldest buildings on the beautiful campus of Henley College. Today, however, with the temperature hovering around ninety-five degrees, I'd have been willing to give up the magnificent collegiate architecture of Benjamin Franklin Hall for a sleek, modern, air-conditioned building.

But I had only myself to blame for the fact that I was teaching on a wretched Thursday morning in July. I'd persuaded the dean to fund a learning center in Franklin, the building that housed Henley's mathematics and science departments.

I was the go-to person for a program that provided tutoring sessions, online problem sets, videos, and classes in special topics for students at every level of achievement in math. The program, plus a twice-a-week seminar in applied statistics, kept me in a hot, stuffy classroom for many more hours than I liked.

By noon today I'd spent three hours using math games to help incoming freshmen who had declared themselves victims of math anxiety. I waved a sheaf of practice sets in front of my face, creating a warm breeze, and declared the session on graphing calculators over.

Students filed by, picking up a tip sheet for overcoming their fear of math as they left the room, hopefully for cooler realms.

"I just can't do retro," I overheard one young women say to another.

"I totally get it," said her companion.

"Is there an algorithm you don't get?" I asked, unable to resist.

"No, we're talking about clothes, Dr. Knowles," the first woman said.

"I knew that."

Rachel Wheeler, my assistant, stayed behind to walk me out. Rachel was everyone's assistant, in fact; a post-graduate student helping out in all the math and science labs.

"Do you have a minute, Dr. Knowles?" Rachel asked. Her narrow face was somber, her usual animated personality subdued. I hoped it was simply the nasty July heat that gave her a bedraggled look.

"As long as we walk while we talk," I said, eager to leave the stifling, musty building. "We might be able to catch a breeze."

No such luck. We walked in stagnant air down the imposing exterior steps that led from Franklin's clock tower to the lush campus below, and headed for the parking lot.

I envied the small group of scantily clothed students in front of the gym, frolicking in the fountain that surrounded a statue of our esteemed founder. I hoped our humorless dean wasn't looking out the window of her administration building office. The simple caper could generate a long memo from her about decorum taking precedence over the possibility of heat stroke.

"Thanks for setting up the measurements lab for tomorrow," I said to Rachel. "I don't know what I'd do without you."

"I'm thinking of quitting." Rachel's head was down; her eyes seemed focused on her red patent sandals.

I'd heard this threat all summer, and it wasn't about the math labs or converting from inches to centimeters. Rachel's thesis work in chemistry had not been going well.

15

"Did the metric system finally get to you?" I asked, a weak joke, an attempt at lightening the mood for someone who'd been tutoring metric since her freshman year. I was sorry Rachel was having such a hard time with her key project.

We shuffled past the tennis courts, where the asphalt seemed to be sending up plumes of steam. A few yards later, Rachel stopped in front of the campus coffee shop. Ordinarily the smell of Huey's dark roast would draw us in, but I could tell Rachel needed more than an iced cuppa.

"I mean it this time," she said.

"He's been that bad?"

Anyone in the Henley academic family who was listening would have known we were referring to Dr. Keith Appleton. He was Rachel's thesis adviser and the chemistry teacher known not fondly as *Apep,* after the Egyptian god of darkness and chaos, the destroyer of dreams.

Rachel's big dream was to do this extra year of study and research at Henley and then enter med school in Boston. She needed Apep's help and recommendation to make it all come true.

"He told me my data is crappy."

"He used that word?"

"No, he'd never use that word, but that's

what he meant. He said everything I've done so far is worthless." Rachel bent over double and blew out her breath, as if she'd just finished running the Boston Marathon and couldn't take another step.

I reached down and rubbed Rachel's narrow shoulders, helping set her upright at the same time. I thought how young she seemed sometimes, young enough to be my daughter, if I'd taken that path. On hot days like this she tied her long many-shades-of-blond hair into a ponytail, taking another four or five years off her age.

"He can't mean it," I said. "You've been working day and night on those — what are they again?"

"Proteins," Rachel said, coming back to life at the mention of her passion. "I'm purifying proteins. It's just a matter of separating the different types of proteins that exist in a mixture, so —"

"Right." I was at my limit of understanding Rachel's biochemical specialty. In my mind, numbers were already pure, thus eliminating a lot of complicated chemical processes.

"Sorry," Rachel said. "I can get carried away."

"No, no. Someone has to do it." I glanced at the hot, clear sky. "God knows, those proteins need purifying." I got the smile I wanted and pushed ahead to ease Rachel's mind. "Maybe Dr. Appleton was just in one of his moods," I suggested.

"Or maybe I'm not cut out for graduate work, let alone making it through med school."

"Of course you are."

I held back the diatribe that was on the tip of my tongue. Keith Appleton was the only Henley faculty member who didn't command my utmost respect. He seemed to thrive on making his students' lives as difficult as possible, considering it a great achievement when the majority of his class failed his midterm. And he didn't stop at students. His record of supporting faculty rights was dismal.

"Also, I did something stupid."

"Which was?"

"I sent him an email right after he made those comments. I should have waited until I cooled down."

Always a good idea. "What did you say in the email?"

"I kind of told him he shouldn't even be teaching."

Never a good idea. "In those words?"

"Maybe even worse. I can't remember exactly. After I wrote it, I decided not to send it, but I hit *send* accidentally. I couldn't believe it whooshed off and there was nothing I could do."

"Let's hope it doesn't come across to him as harshly as you meant it."

"Would you talk to him?" Rachel asked as we continued on to the parking lot. "You know, professor to professor. Pretend I didn't tell you anything and try to find out what he really thinks of me and my work." Rachel stopped again and put her hands to her ring-laden ears, a minimum of six silver baubles on each. "No, wait. I don't want to hear it."

I looped my arm in Rachel's, glad to see that she'd kept a sense of humor about her situation. "I'll give it a try, but we're not exactly best friends."

"If Dr. Appleton had any friends at all, you'd be it."

"Ouch. I'm not sure I like that distinction."

"He always says how you're the only one who remembers his birthday."

"That's because it's the same day as Lamarck's, August 1."

"How do you do that? Remember dates? Like for some eighteenth-century biologist?"

"For Lamarck and Dr. Appleton, I make

the association that both of them developed theories that don't work."

"I like that. Dr. Appleton's theory is that if you torture your students, they'll learn better," Rachel said.

"And Lamarck's is that if you keep frowning, the lines on your forehead will deepen and your kids will inherit deep frown marks."

Rachel gave me a broad smile that smoothed out her forehead. "I get it."

"Much better," I said.

When we arrived at my car, Rachel turned to me. "If you don't feel comfortable talking to him, don't worry. I'll be okay." She gave me a reassuring grin. "If I don't make it to med school, well, doctors don't make the money they used to, anyway."

"And we all know that's what matters most to you."

I gave Rachel a playful nudge, and waved good-bye from the front seat of my smoke-stone metallic Fusion. Strange name for a color, but today the interior felt like I imagined a smoking stone would. I could barely turn the key in the ignition, very hot to my touch. I cranked the A/C to max.

I couldn't let Rachel down, but I didn't look forward to talking to Keith Appleton either. He was my age, mid-forties, yet he had a way of making me feel unimportant and inexperienced. There was no telling whether my interceding on Rachel's behalf would help or hurt her chances of gaining his approval of her thesis.

My fondest hope was that somehow the situation would resolve itself before I had a chance to contact him.

Fifteen minutes late for my beading class, I tried to sneak in through the back door of A Hill of Beads, the shop owned by my best friend since high school, Ariana Volens. She and I had gone off to different colleges, on the West Coast and in Boston, respectively, but reunited as soon as we moved back to town.

I breathed in the scent of Tibetan incense. Sweet jasmine this time, Ariana's latest favorite for calming the mind. I tiptoed to a seat at the end of a long table where six other women had gathered, but I should have known Ariana wouldn't let me get away with a quiet entrance.

She stopped mid-demonstration and swung her long, graceful arm in my direction. "And, finally, our eminent Dr. Sophie Knowles joins us," Ariana said, a big smile on her face. She knew she'd pay later for this drama.

Ariana's platinum blond hair was streaked with strands of red and blue, her eye-catching, patriotic design of choice for the summer. My hair, on the other hand, won compliments without my even trying. My short dark locks were graying in a design of their own choosing — a jagged stripe of white hair about an inch wide had grown out on one side of my head. I'd learned to simply say, "Thank you" when people complimented me on my artistry.

I'd been talked into beading by Ariana.

"You need a hobby," she'd told me a month ago.

"I already have one."

"Making up puzzles and brainteasers doesn't count. It's too much like math," she'd said. "You might as well be talking square roots."

"You say that like it's a bad thing."

Ariana had rolled her eyes.

I agreed to try a hobby, partly to keep Ariana quiet. It came down to beading or handwriting analysis, Ariana's new passion, and the latter seemed a bit too woo-woo for me. I couldn't see myself making judgments about someone's personality based on how she drew a capital S. I, myself, wrote it differently every time, no matter what Ariana claimed.

Beading seemed innocuous and apolitical enough.

I had to admit, Ariana had a point in wanting me to expand my horizons by meeting Henley townsfolk who weren't part of the college community. With a full load of classes, plus office hours, faculty meetings, and research, sometimes it was hard to get off campus until late in the evening. Bruce Granville, my dark-eyed boyfriend, kept even stranger hours. A former Air Force pilot, now flying a medevac helicopter, he worked seven days on, from nine to nine, and then had seven days off. We'd settled into a routine that excluded nearly everyone except my students, a few colleagues, and Ariana.

"Your world is too small," Ariana often told me. On those occasions, invariably, she'd form a circle — a planet, I figured — with her arms. "You need to get out more. And even if you don't fall in love with everyone in the beading class, you'll end up with something useful," she'd added, appealing to my multitasking, goal-oriented personality. She'd held up, in turn, a beaded basket, a bead-fringed bookmark, and a ballpoint pen covered with multicolored seed beads. I thought it was a stretch to call them all *useful.*

After a couple of classes I found I liked the craft and the crafters more than I'd expected. All the other stresses in my life disappeared when our conversation focused on the best gauge wire to use for each kind of bead. Or when I had to concentrate on picking up tiny beads with a needle and thread and keeping them from rolling off the other end. I was a novice at the hobby, however, and doubted I'd ever be as good at it as I was at making and solving puzzles.

Ariana wasn't finished with me this afternoon. As the six other women, all more advanced beaders than I was, turned in my direction, Ariana asked, "Were you engaged in some high-level mathematics, Professor? Or were you tied up in the backseat of a helicopter with a Colin Farrell lookalike?"

I felt my face turn red, in spite of the comfortably air-conditioned shop. I was consoled by the fact that Bruce wasn't around to hear the innuendo, though he was unlikely to blush the way I had. He'd probably be flattered at being compared to one of his favorite actors. Or was Colin only on *my* favorites list?

The beader in the seat next to me, an older, graceful Indian woman, patted my hand and said, "She's just trying to make you feel at home, dear."

I smiled at her and my other classmates and gave Ariana a look that said we'd settle this score later.

Today's workshop was not going well for me, in spite of my dipping often into one of the many small bowls of candy on the worktable. Ariana could never go too long without a sweet treat, and chocolate always had a prime spot wherever she held forth.

I let out an aggravated grunt, annoyed at how fumble-fingered I was, trying to attach a short beaded string to a jump ring to make a key chain. When my cell phone vibrated on the table in front of me, I was glad for the break.

Until I saw the caller ID number. Courtney, the young administrative assistant in the academic dean's office.

I was pretty sure I wasn't being notified of a raise in salary or a reduced class schedule, which would allow me more time for research. I was nearly positive that Dean Underwood had another complaint to lodge against me. I wouldn't have been surprised if she was ready to blame me for encouraging the sprites dancing in the water fountain.

I clicked my phone on and said "Hello" to Courtney, at the same time walking outside into the back alley, where a blast of heat assaulted my face.

"She wants to see you," Courtney said, sounding apologetic.

It wasn't Courtney's fault the dean spent her days thinking of ways to annoy the Henley faculty. Especially me.

I'd forgotten to take my sunglasses from my purse when I exited the shop. I squinted against the intense sunlight and entertained ugly thoughts about Dean Underwood. First Keith Appleton, and now the dean was upsetting my day. Maybe I was the problem. Maybe I should try to earn a living making beaded key chains. Beads didn't talk back or try to cramp my style.

"Is it urgent?" I asked.

"Isn't it always?" Courtney asked.

I sighed, slightly resigned. There was also my puzzle work to fall back on for income, I thought. Ever since I was a college student, I'd been submitting puzzles and brainteasers on a regular basis to games and variety magazines. But while it was fun coming up with number play and logic puzzles, the pay was hardly enough to pay the bills. I realized Courtney was still on the line. "So, she wants to see me today?" I asked.

"Yesterday. I'm sorry, Dr. Knowles," said Courtney, whose temperament did not match her flaming red hair.

"I'll have to change my clothes," I said, glancing down at my flowered crop pants and bright green sandals.

"It's not about your clothes this time." Courtney paused, as if considering whether to say more. She filled in with a nice offer. "Oh, I have your favorite lemon zinger tea in stock, Dr. Knowles. I'll have a tall, cold glass waiting."

At least I related well with the younger generation. I thought also of my wonderful friends on the Henley faculty and of the richly diverse student body I got to work with every term.

Maybe I wouldn't turn in my Henley College ID card just yet.

Maybe I could get Keith and the dean to turn in theirs.

2

As promised, Courtney had left a pitcher of iced tea on a small table in Dean Phyllis Underwood's outer office. A note said, "Keep cool." If the dean had seen it, I wondered if she knew how many meanings Courtney had in mind.

I poured a glass of lemon zinger and took a seat on the wooden bench outside the main office. The handsome leather briefcase my mother gave me when I received my doctorate rested on my lap. I wrapped one arm around it and thought of Mom. It had been just the two of us since I was a toddler, when my father died. My fingers traced the outline of the metal lock; my mind wandered to Mom's last days and to our last puzzle together.

Never one to be left behind, Margaret (at her request, I'd used her given name since I was in high school, so she wouldn't "feel so old") had joined the sudoku craze. We had an ongoing match: each took on the challenge of creating a sudoku that would be declared "impossible" by the other. She completed one of my challenge sudokus two days before she died.

"Too many backtracks this time, though," she'd said, honest to the end.

The finished puzzle hung on my office wall next to a photograph of the two of us on Cape Cod with the Sandy Neck Lighthouse as a backdrop.

Lemon zinger tea had also been Margaret's favorite. I raised my glass to her and took a sip.

In spite of the urgency of the dean's request and Courtney's assurance, I'd made a quick trip home and changed to a more respectable outfit than the summery pants I'd taught in that morning. Nothing said *professional* more than close-toed shoes.

The last time I'd been summoned here had been about my "classroom appearance."

"Your attire is much too casual, Dr. Knowles," the dean had told me one snowy day, taking in my tasteful slacks, boots, and corduroy jacket in one sweeping, reproachful gaze. "You know we like to keep a dress code at Henley, no matter what the weather, and certainly no matter what the trends of the day may be."

I'd been tempted to ask why the academic dean didn't have more to do than monitor faculty wardrobes. Wasn't there curriculum to watch over? The northeastern colleges' accreditation committee to worry about? And it wasn't as if I'd been showing cleavage. Not that I had any to speak of.

Like most of my faculty friends, I'd already caved on the clothing issue. The dean had met us halfway by allowing an exception for hot days during summer school and blizzard-like days in the winter.

So today's call was definitely not about fashion. What, then?

I tapped the soles of my uncomfortable pumps on the cracked marble floor of the old administration building, a grand Gothic structure that, sadly, had had its marvelous interior chopped up to accommodate more offices than originally planned. Here and there a bulky air-conditioning unit had been wedged into an arched window, entering into an odd pairing with the radiator, and interrupting a lovely recursive pattern of gray stone rosettes.

As the minutes ticked away, I reminded myself that I was forty-four, not sixteen years old. This was not high school, when the principal had caught Ariana and me and two friends cutting class to take the subway to downtown Boston for a shopping spree.

I treated my back to a yoga stretch and took a deep breath, giving up on guessing what the dean wanted with me on a scorching Thursday afternoon. Too bad her recommendation was essential if I wanted to make full professor this year. True, I was relatively young for the title, but there was a rumor that a whopping four slots in math and science were open at Henley, and I wanted a place in line for one of them. Badly.

I'd paid my dues as assistant professor for six years, then associate professor for eight more. I had a decent list of publications on my differential equations research in nationally recognized journals and was often sought out as a speaker at conferences. I'd taken my turn as Mathematics Department Chair and served on a countable infinity of faculty committees. Plus — a big concession on my part — I'd yielded to Dean Underwood's request that I write my puzzles and brainteasers under a pen name, though I bristled at her reasoning.

"We wouldn't want anything frivolous to appear on Henley's faculty publication record," she'd clucked.

After fourteen years, I was finally used to being addressed as Margaret Stone, my mother's maiden name, when a puzzler fan emailed me.

Now here I was wearing pumps and what could pass for a suit, with a dark brown skirt and an almost-matching jacket, hoping to please the person who held my career in her wrinkled old hands. The thought produced another wave of perspiration and new, sweaty smudges on my leather briefcase. I wasn't this nervous sitting next to Bruce in his helicopter, even when he surprised me with a new stunt.

To calm myself, I took a newly purchased cube puzzle from my briefcase, this one with six images of Tiffany windows, and set the case down on the immaculate floor.

Dr. Underwood was too old for the job, I decided, fingering the smaller blocks that made up the colorful cube. The academic dean seemed to have come with this building. I loved hundred-year-old buildings, but not the antiquated customs that sometimes accompanied them.

I knew that Dr. Underwood was upset for reasons bigger than me. Her side had lost the great debate about whether Henley College should follow the trend of the day and admit male students.

"Coed?" she'd exclaimed at meetings when the issue was first raised.

She'd made the word sound profane. The dean and her allies had fought the idea long and hard, citing the history of Henley, founded in the early part of the twentieth century as an academy for "young ladies." There had been plenty of boys at the all-male schools a stone's throw away to invite to mixers. If that model worked a hundred years ago, it could work now, the dean said in so many words, skipping past the fact that there wasn't a single all-male school left in New England.

Times had changed and demanded creative ways of maintaining a large enough student body for our college to survive. The reality was "coed or no ed" as the pro-coed side — my side — warned.

It took the board of trustees and the faculty senate another two years to seal the deal. This fall was to mark the debut of men on campus. The undergraduate enrollment had climbed to more than double what it was last year.

"More men in your life? Should I be worried?" Bruce had asked me.

I let him think so.

The old clock chimed three fifteen. The sound echoed down the empty hallway. During the summer, no classes were held in the administration building. The only people around were the admin staff, and whomever the deans summoned. Today that privilege seemed to be mine alone.

I worked the Tiffany puzzle, clicking the dogwood, the grapevine, and the hibiscus into their slots on the different faces of the cube. I checked the other sides. The views of Oyster Bay, the magnolias, and the autumn landscape were lined up correctly. Stunning, but too easy.

"Good afternoon, Sophie." A statement cum greeting.

I looked up to see Keith Appleton walk toward me. He'd just come through the door from the dean's office. The not unreasonable thought went through my head that Keith was involved in why I was waiting for the dean right now instead of beading.

"Hey, Keith," I said, in part to aggravate him. He hated when we faculty took on the slang and tone of the students.

Having made that point, I decided I wouldn't follow up right now with a request to talk to him about Rachel's thesis. I needed to time my battles more carefully.

"Did you have a chance to look over the amendment I proposed to the Distinguished Professor bylaws?" he asked.

"Yeah, about that. The change would eliminate several women on the faculty."

Keith gave me a quizzical look. "Is that a problem?"

"We'd be penalizing women for taking maternity leave."

He shrugged his shoulders. "Again, is that a problem?"

"Keith, how can you —"

The tune of *Come Fly With Me* rang in my purse.

My cell phone. I smiled when I heard it and saw the ID for MAstar, the nonprofit medevac company Bruce worked for. And just in time to prevent me from an irreversible setback in my so-called friendship with Keith.

"We'll talk later," Keith said, turning on his heels, clearly too important a man to be standing around waiting for me to take a call.

"And a good day to you, too," I said to Keith's back, but not loud enough for him to hear me.

"Huh?" Bruce, who did hear me, asked.

"Not you," I said.

"Come on out and visit me," Bruce said.

How tempting. Not just to see my guy, but because the temperature at the airfield was always about fifteen degrees cooler than in town.

"I'm outside the dean's office." I whispered, though I was sure no sound penetrated the thick door between me and my superior.

"Uh-oh."

"You said it."

"Any idea what she wants this time?"

"Not a clue, but Keith just walked out of the office."

"Uh-oh squared."

"I love when you talk math." I looked at the big clock. "Up from your nap?"

"Starting to think about dinner," he said.

Bruce kept a pretty predictable routine on the days he worked. He'd have an early dinner, relax for a while, and then go into work for his twelve-hour shift as an EMS helicopter pilot. "Officially, it means Emergency Medical Services," he'd say. "Unofficially, it means Earn Money Sleeping." It was Bruce's way of trying to convince me that his job of touching down at crash scenes amid telephone poles and power lines wasn't as dangerous as it sounded, simply because he could sleep or watch movies between heart-pounding incidents.

I started when the dean's office door opened. I clicked the phone shut with a soft, hasty, "Gotta go. Love you," to Bruce.

Dr. Underwood, in a legitimate navy suit with a mid-calf hemline, filled the doorway.

I was annoyed at the shiver that rippled down my spine. So what if the dean was at least six inches taller than my five feet three inches? I was about twenty years younger.

But this wasn't a physical contest, and Dr. Underwood's folded arms and serious expression wielded a lot of psychological power. I stuffed my phone and my puzzle cube into my briefcase as if I'd been reading comic books instead of doing my homework.

After what seemed too long a time, the dean unfolded her arms and indicated the path I should follow. "Come in, Dr. Knowles." The invitation fell somewhere between those of an oral surgeon and a serial killer.

"Good afternoon, Dr. Underwood," I said, through dry lips. No "Hey, dean" from me. I took my place across from the dean at the wide, dark oak desk that dominated the office. *How bad can it be? What? Was I too noisy in class?*

"You've been very noisy," the dean said. I could barely suppress a smile. But Dr. Underwood's tone was somber. "I have complaints that your gatherings in Benjamin Franklin Hall are getting out of hand."

I raised my eyebrows. This was what the urgent summons was about? "I'm sorry?

You've had complaints?"

The dean nodded and let out a heavy sigh, perhaps in memory of an earlier time when only sweet young girls and sedate faculty populated the seventeen-acre campus. "Apparently you had an exceptionally loud and disruptive party in the faculty lounge of your building last Friday afternoon."

I wanted to point out that it wasn't my building, though I had a great fondness for it. Benjamin Franklin Hall and its lounge were shared by the departments of mathematics, physics, biology, and chemistry, in ascending order, up through the four floors. Some said the top floor was specifically designed for chemistry — in the event of an explosion, the roof might blow off, but at least the other departments would survive.

The complaint had to have come from Keith Appleton, the least social and the biggest snob in the building, if not on campus, if not in the state of Massachusetts.

"Friday was Tesla's birthday," I said, with great restraint.

"Whose birthday?"

"The physics department chose the theme for July. They selected Nicola Tesla. He was born on July 10. Well, at midnight on July 9, so it could go either way."

"Tesla?" the dean asked.

I nodded. "I'm sure you've heard of his work in electricity." I pointed to the lovely Victorian-style lamp on the dean's desk, as if it were an example of Tesla's great genius. I thought what a nice jigsaw puzzle the lampshade would make.

I'd deliberately spoken as if I assumed science and mathematics literacy on the part of anyone who deemed herself liberally educated. Or anyone who was a dean at a liberal arts college.

"He was there? At your party?"

I grunted — inaudibly, I hoped — though Dr. Underwood's severe lack of appreciation for math and science was familiar to me. "No, he, uh, died about seventy years ago." I fantasized Dean Underwood's name on my class roster and marked it with a failing grade.

"Of course he did." Dean Underwood's pointy nose seemed to take off on its own, now with flaring nostrils, now curling upward toward her frown lines.

I wasn't proud of this little tactic — putting someone in her place by trying to sound smarter. The truth was that, given the right teacher, anyone could learn mathematics. One of my greatest missions in life was to help students over hurdles that kept them thinking that there was a certain "science brain" or that only a select few had a "knack for math."

I bristled as I recalled a report from Bruce's niece, Melanie, that her fourth-grade teacher had promised, "If you behave yourselves this morning, boys and girls, we won't have to do math this afternoon."

Grrr. I could have gone on forever on this topic, even with no audience, but the dean was back on track, having straightened out her face.

"The complaint mentioned, in particular, bolts of lightning and fireworks."

An image of Tesla came to me. Today we would have called him an *outside-the-box thinker.* One day he'd be experimenting with electromagnetism as a route to time travel, and the next he'd ply himself with enough current to discharge sparks that would make the crackling at our little Franklin party seem hardly worth the trouble.

I called up last Friday in my mind. Almost a week ago. We didn't have fireworks exactly, but we did create a healthy display of static electricity. On my phone, I had a photo of one student with her long red hair standing out straight from her head. I thought it best not to show the dean.

"The physics majors put together a demonstration of one of Tesla's experiments. It was spectacular, but harmless, really," I told the dean.

I spent the next few minutes explaining our custom of monthly parties honoring mathematicians and scientists. I'd been through this description a number of times. Did this dean not listen? Was she too busy being the fashion police? Or did Dean Underwood simply have a short memory for practices she didn't like?

I gave it my best, final shot. "There's more to these gatherings than cake and loud noises. The science and math majors research the scientist or mathematician with the birthday of the month and present reports and demonstrations." I waited for a response. There was none. "I guess this month's meeting was especially animated," I added.

I hoped for a compliment on what had been my own inspired idea. I could trace it back to my parents, who'd named me after the eighteenth century French mathematician, Sophie Germain. Sophie and I shared a birthday — April first. We celebrated together every year. How could we not share a love of mathematics?

"Try to keep a measure of decorum, Dr. Knowles," the dean said finally, sending a loud, agonized breath my way. She stood up and I followed suit.

I wondered who shared a birthday with Dean Underwood. Someone with no sense of humor, I supposed.

On the way to my Ford Fusion, I thought of several brilliant responses I should have made to the dean's reprimand. For one thing, I wished I'd invited her to the August seventeenth party, for Pierre de Fermat's birthday. My math majors were preparing a skit about Fermat's Last Theorem, which he had declared "remarkable," but never proved. I'd been warned by my students that there was a limerick involved in their interpretation.

I knew I should have been relieved that I hadn't crossed the line into sarcasm the dean might recognize. After all, my ranking was at stake. Still, it would have been fun to tell her she didn't have to bring a present for Fermat. He wouldn't be showing up.

I'd also neglected to mention to the dean that the next party wasn't that far off. Tomorrow, in fact, the four Franklin Hall departments would be celebrating a brand new doctoral degree. Hal Bartholomew, the students' favorite physics instructor, had completed all the requirements and would graduate at the end of the year from Massachusetts University.

It was common knowledge that Hal's thesis had been rejected twice before by MU's faculty committee. He'd been burdened with an uncooperative crystal to study and had had difficulty acquiring spectral data. He was also balancing his research time with his full teaching load and family life.

As I understood it, delays in collecting data occurred often to those in experimental physics. And anyone who'd ever been in grad school in any field sympathized with the setbacks on the way to an advanced degree.

Anyone except Keith Appleton, that is.

Keith took every opportunity to make a snide remark about Hal's struggle. I'd never forget his comment when Hal sneezed at Henley's baccalaureate dinner in June.

"Stay well, Hal," Keith had said. "After waiting so long and after all those false starts, you don't want to miss your graduation ceremony."

To his credit, Hal smiled at the remark and ignored the chance to respond in kind. Gil, his wife, found a way to make a point, however: She put her arm around her husband's shoulders and said, "Hal will be fine. He has me to take care of him."

And you, Keith, those in earshot added silently, have no one.

Cheers for Gillian Bartholomew.

As I drove home I amused myself by conjuring ways to get even with Keith for not telling me himself that our Tesla party disrupted his . . . what? His quiet time? His life? Keith brought out the worst in me.

Then I remembered I'd promised to approach him, nicely, on Rachel's behalf.

I wished there was a way to banish Keith Appleton from Franklin Hall. And Dean Underwood from the entire Henley campus.

3

Let it be said: math and science majors know how to party.

To coincide with Hal's research field, the physics majors had decorated the lounge with a sepia-colored poster featuring Nobelists in physics for the last fifty years, and another with a collage of pioneers in spectroscopy. They'd ordered the largest sheet cake they could afford from the local bakery — I recognized only a few of the equations written in blue icing just under the three-dimensional balloons in multicolored frosting. A nice touch.

My own math majors from my first year of teaching had contributed the gold lamé tablecloth that had graced every Franklin Hall party since. There were always so many drinks, bowls of snacks, and platters of dessert that the accumulated stains from previous parties were easily covered up.

Hal examined a greatly enlarged photograph of himself, looking at least a decade younger and situated on the wall between Albert Einstein and Isaac Newton. "Where did you ever find this?" he asked, scratching his prematurely balding scalp.

"On Google," Liz Harrison and Pam Noonan, inseparable roommates and chemistry majors, said in unison.

"It's from a loooong time ago," Pam added.

"You sound like my son," Hal laughed.

Most of us had spent many department picnics and holiday parties with Hal's five-year-old son, Timothy, and Hal's wife, Gillian, a flight nurse who worked at MAstar, Bruce's employer. Ben Franklin Hall was nothing if not family friendly.

As usual when two or more were gathered, I'd placed copies of a draft brainteaser around the room. I counted myself very lucky that my students and colleagues enjoyed being beta testers as I, or rather, Margaret Stone, developed new puzzles for my magazine editors.

"Too many layers," Rachel said of a word puzzle I'd devised. "If I even understand it. First you have to identify a bunch of images, make an appropriate anagram, take the last letters and add one, line up the initial letters" — She threw up her hands —

"I'd give up in, like, three minutes."

I frowned, never one to take criticism easily. "You're exaggerating," I said. "And, besides, it's supposed to be a category five challenge." Was that me whining?

"I agree with Rachel," Fran Emerson, my department head said.

"Copy that," came from Hal and a chorus of students.

More boos came from Robert Michaels, chemistry department chair and Judith Donohue, head of biology.

My public had spoken. I crumpled the sheet in my hand. Back to the drawing board.

The summer faculty crew was small in Franklin Hall, and the department heads' representation down one. Hal's physics department chair had arranged to spend six weeks doing research on a particle collider in Switzerland, prompting me to wish that differential equations — my field of mathematics — was more equipment-based. He'd sent greetings to Hal in the morning via Skype but didn't guarantee he'd be free to electronically attend the party later.

Fran took on the responsibility of making the congratulatory speech to the gathering.

"I'm going to wait until Gil gets here," Fran told us.

47

"She'll be, like, a hundred years late," Rachel muttered.

Apparently Rachel's nasty mood hadn't improved with a night's sleep.

Gil Bartholomew arrived well within the century mark, toting a large basket of sunflowers, tiger lilies, and the reddest bee balm I'd ever seen. At one time or another, we were all the beneficiaries of Gil's extraordinary gardening talent. She moved aside platters of sweets and placed the basket on the center of the table.

"That's better, isn't it? Sorry I'm late, guys."

After some talk of bad traffic and worse weather, Fran called us to order.

I was impressed that Fran had dressed up for the occasion — Dean Underwood would have been pleased. Fran was tall enough to pull off the long, flowing outfit: a pale blue silk pantsuit with a matching scarf that would have dragged on the floor if I'd been wearing it. She praised Hal's excellent teaching record, hard work, and affable personality.

She ended with, "It gives me great pleasure to announce the promotion of Dr. Harold Bartholomew from instructor to assistant professor." Fran's voice carried a deep ring of authority, though the official announcement from the dean wouldn't come until the first faculty meeting in the fall semester.

"Let's make some noise here," she said.

I cringed at first, thinking of the dean, but then clapped loudly.

The cheers that followed from about thirty students and faculty members were a tribute to the popularity and the high regard Hal enjoyed.

Rachel came up to me and handed me a fresh bottle of sparkling water. "You're next for a promotion," she said.

"Could be," I said, casting my eyes down in fake modesty.

"I'll take care of the cake that day. I can see it now. 'PROFESSOR KNOWLES' in lavender icing, all caps," Rachel said.

If I knew birthdays, Rachel knew everyone's color preferences.

In fact, I'd already allowed myself the fantasy of hearing my own name mentioned in the rolls of faculty promotions this year: *Dr. Sophie Knowles from associate professor to full professor,* I fantasized. After yesterday's meeting with Dean Underwood I wondered if the dream would become reality. I might be able to manage to keep the noise level down at Franklin Hall parties, but who knew what else stood in the way of my promotion. I was never any good at academic politics. All I knew was that if I wanted to reach the next level of recognition in my field, I couldn't spend another year as an associate professor.

"Where's Keith?" Fran asked me.

I heard, "Who cares?" from someone in a nearby cluster of students. Rachel?

It hadn't been lost on me that Keith was missing from the festivities. Maybe a higher power (I pictured an exponent in the sky) had heeded my wish, that Keith Appleton be banished from Franklin Hall.

"We haven't seen him at all today, but his Beemer's here," Pam said, gesturing toward the parking lot next to the tennis courts.

"Apep is probably upstairs being antisocial as usual," Casey Tremel said. She folded her bracelet-laden hands, prayerlike. "Gazing at that new Fellow award on his wall." Casey had her own problems with Keith. She was a scholarship student, the one with the neon green "Used" sticker on all her texts. She needed a B to keep her standing; a looming D in organic chemistry could derail the funding for her education.

"Maybe he ran out of rude comments about Dr. Bartholomew," said Liz.

"Who wants him at a party anyway?" Rachel's voice. No doubt this time.

I pulled Rachel aside, unobtrusively, I hoped. "This is not like you at all, Rachel. You need to dial it back. We're at a gathering of the Franklin Hall family and that kind of disrespect is not appropriate."

"Everyone's insulting him, not just me," Rachel said, with a slight pout that was unbecoming a teaching assistant.

"These are undergraduates. You're supposed to be modeling professional behavior, among other things. It's one thing to complain to me, but I can't support this lack of self-control."

I knew I sounded like a scolding parent or a grade school teacher, but I didn't see another way to get through to Rachel.

Rachel looked contrite. "I'm really sorry, Dr. Knowles. You're totally right."

"Did someone say 'Dr. Bartholomew?' I like the sound of that," Gil said, giving her husband a kiss on his cheek.

I was glad she'd found a way to diffuse the awkwardness of Rachel's incivility, as well as all the other anti-Appleton remarks.

I glanced around the room. Fran had maintained a neutral expression, notwithstanding her beef with Keith over the set of amended bylaws he'd proposed for Distinguished Professor status. Robert and Judith also behaved themselves, as befitted department chairs, though I knew them to have been overpowered and outvoted more than once by Keith. Lucy Bronson, a new instructor hired for one chemistry class this summer, with a full load in the fall, looked from one to the other of us, understandably distressed, apparently unprepared for the invective that disrupted the party atmosphere. She was too new to have been crushed by Apep.

Much to my relief, all the other faculty who were present refrained from joining in on the heckling of the absent chemistry professor, and it soon came to a halt. I was especially conscious of returning to good behavior so Lucy wouldn't regret her decision to come to Henley College.

I found myself feeling sorry for Keith and forced myself to remember something good about him. I came up with an occasion last winter when he rushed to my rescue with jumper cables to start my car. So what if he chose that moment to point out my inadequacies, and those of all women, as mechanics.

"What if I take a piece of cake and a drink up to him?" Rachel whispered to me, not needing to specify who "him" was.

I was proud of her for coming around so quickly. "Very good idea," I said, giving her a thumbs-up.

Anything to keep him upstairs, I thought. For the sake of the party, and for his own protection.

By two o'clock, the party had ended. There was a limit to the amount of togetherness students and faculty could enjoy before starting their weekend.

With Bruce on duty at the airfield fifteen miles away, and Ariana at her book club, I was on my own for the evening.

"You should join the club," Ariana had told me. "We read all kinds of books. Mystery, romance, science fiction, inspirational." She'd ticked off enough genres to use most of her fingers.

"Have you ever met a group you didn't like?" I'd asked her.

"I guess that's a 'no' on the book club from you and a 'no' on your question from me."

With all her running around — to her beading classes, yoga group, book club, and volunteer work at a shelter, Ariana still seemed to have time for her friends, including three exes. I felt like a slug next to her.

For me a couple of quiet nights at home every week were a must. The days were given over to my students and colleagues, often until early evening; I never stinted there. Bruce's schedule suited me fine. I could count on seven nights in a row to myself if I so chose.

I enjoyed my small, three-bedroom cottage, the home I'd grown up in. When my mother became ill, I'd moved back until it became necessary to place her where she'd have professional care. That day had been one of the hardest in my life. Margaret, who'd been an independent widow most of her adult life, seemed to take the enormous change better than I did, adjusting to assisted living and claiming that it was enough to know that I was now enjoying the family home. I didn't see the point in telling her it could never be that easy for me.

People who visited me here for the first time were surprised at the cozy atmosphere, expecting a high-tech look to match my image as a modern-day mathematician. But I liked the contrast: the latest computer and peripherals in my office at Henley, and a claw-foot tub and gingham quilts at home.

On tonight's list was work on my research, class prep for the rest of the summer session, assignments to post on the web, and journals to read. A periodical with a cover story on nonlinear wave equations was at the top of my pile. I also had puzzles to solve, math games to create, and even a key chain to bead if I was in the mood. I didn't need to belong to a group for any of these activities.

I made up a plate with oranges and grapes, three kinds of cheese, and plain crackers. I called it a meal; Bruce would have called it the first round of appetizers before the prime rib. Bruce claimed I wasn't being true to my country kitchen décor with such insubstantial menus.

"You should make some meatballs," he'd said on his last day off.

"Excuse me? Meatballs?"

"You know, like that scene in *Goodfellas,* where the wiseguys are making an Italian dinner in prison?" Bruce tended to bring everything back to a favorite movie.

"Funny, that scene doesn't stand out for me," I'd answered.

"How about the potato soup and quail in *My Dinner With Andre*?"

The only way to stop Bruce at times like that was to force-feed him the most convenient snack, often involving high salt content.

There was no question tonight that I needed to finish up my latest journal article. Publish or perish was still an operative phrase in academia. Full professorship was contingent on a substantial publication record, and my clips from puzzle magazines didn't count. I had a respectable list of peer-reviewed articles, but one could never have too many when one's dean had an eagle eye out for maintaining Henley College's accreditation. And mine.

I took care of the one additional reference I needed to round out my article on traveling waves of the mathematical kind. I printed and signed my cover letter and prepared the package for mailing on Monday to the antiquated press that didn't take email attachments. They'd still have it long before Labor Day, and I could add the note to my resume by the official opening of the fall semester and the first meeting of the promotions committee.

I could now check off Lofty Academic Responsibilities and turn to my latest puzzle, which was calling to me loudly. I couldn't stand that no one at the party had liked it. I picked up a copy of the brainteaser that had been ix-nayed by the Ben Franklin group this afternoon. Too tough, eh? What did they want? Simple word-in-word puzzles, like figuring out that CHIMADENA is "MADE in CHINA," or that O ER T O is a "PAIN-less operation?"

Maybe I should heed the second loudest

call instead. I put the puzzle aside and took out my bead case. I'd invested in a portable cabinet organizer that Ariana had recommended as a starter piece.

"Starter?" I'd exclaimed. Equipped with fifteen clear jars, three sliding storage boxes and many dividers, the cabinet seemed sufficient to last a lifetime of beading.

"You'll see," Ariana had warned.

She was right. I was already thinking of buying extra canisters to accommodate the charms I'd bought to add to key chains and bookmarks. Once into a hobby, I did tend to go all out.

I looked around at the ragged piles of books and journals scattered throughout my kitchen and den, and the overflowing briefcase I used for school. Beading was now the most organized area of my life.

I settled on a saddle stool at my large kitchen island, one of my favorite spots in the house. I pushed aside an issue of Bruce's *Rotor* magazine and a copy of an article from the Mathematical Association of America to make room for one of my bead drawers. The light was good in the spacious, cheery yellow room, and I was comfortable with my food and my work, overlapping them in some spots.

A section of orange in one hand, I sifted

through my collection of silver charms with the other. I picked out a few that I'd decided to use for my next projects. A tiny airplane charm for Bruce, since I hadn't found a helicopter yet; a cupcake for Ariana, whose sweet tooth was legendary; and an old-fashioned telephone for my aunt in Florida who was once a switchboard operator.

Rrring. Rrring. Rrring.

Speaking of which . . . I should have unplugged the phone when I started working. Too late now, since I could never let a phone keep ringing.

My screen told me the call was from a private party. I grimaced. I liked the option of knowing who was on the other end. More inconsistencies in my life. My cottage kitchen had an antique glass-front corner cupboard on one side and the latest phone system on the other. Of course my purse hosted a smartphone.

Since I wasn't fully in the beading zone yet, I picked up quickly.

"Dr. Knowles?"

I heard Rachel, sounding distraught, even more than yesterday when she'd talked of abandoning her research. Rachel didn't block her phone numbers, so she must be in distress somewhere remote.

"What's wrong, Rachel?"

"It's Dr. Appleton."

"Is he on your case again?" And after-hours at that.

"No." I waited while Rachel took deep, audible breaths, as if she'd just come up for air after nearly drowning. "He's dead."

"He's . . . ?" I switched ears as if that would send the message into a parallel mathematical plane where *Dr. Appleton is not dead.*

4

A strange feeling overtook my mind and my body. In a matter of seconds, I'd become light-headed and shivery and a wave of sorrow and guilt surged through me, as if my awful thoughts had caused Keith to have a heart attack and die.

I turned my attention to Rachel, on the other end of the line. "When did this happen?"

"Woody found him in his office," Rachel said, sobbing now. It might not have been the first thing she'd uttered while I'd been trying to mentally undo the deed. I pictured our poor old janitor coming upon a body, and of someone he knew. I heard Rachel take some breaths. "I guess it was some time around four o'clock when Woody started his rounds on the chem floor."

"What happened? A heart attack?" I gulped, not wanting to hear that a strong, nasty wish from a mathematician had knocked Keith off course.

"They told me he was poisoned." Rachel's voice was weaker with each utterance.

"Food poisoning?" I shot a look at my fruit, crackers, and cheese and lost my appetite on the spot.

I remembered partaking generously of the big spread at the celebration in Hal's honor. I put my hand to my throat. Was I alive because I'd resisted a second piece of cake? I carried the phone to my patio doors and looked out on my lawn. Who else of the attendees might be sick? Or dead? I paused to check the status of my own system: no stomachache, no headache, no dizziness, no queasy feeling other than my response to this news. I was suddenly grateful for my roses, my crab apple tree, and even my new lawn chairs.

Maybe something I hadn't eaten was tainted, like the onion dip or the store-bought pie.

"Was there something in the food at the party?" I asked Rachel, while my kitchen spun around. A serious solid of revolution.

"He was . . . they're saying Dr. Appleton was murdered, Dr. Knowles."

A whole new set of shivers and waves of unrest came over me and seemed to push me back into the kitchen and onto the ladder-back chair in the corner. Suddenly the room was too bright; the many tones of blue in the braided rug under my feet were too gaudy. I shaded my eyes and tried to process what I was hearing.

I'd wished Keith Appleton would leave Franklin Hall, not the land of the living. Hadn't I? Really, I just wanted him to be civil, I explained to the universe around me. My mind raced to undo Keith's demise. *If I make my intentions clearer,* I thought, *Keith will spring back to life.*

"Who told you all this, Rachel?"

A long, nerve-racking pause. "The police. They came to my house and brought me down here and they questioned me, for, like, hours."

Down here? I remembered the lack of caller ID readout. "Are you at the police station?"

"Yeah."

"Did they" — I could hardly get the word out — "arrest you?" I almost said, "like, arrest you." I was that rattled.

"No, no. But they just let me go a minute ago; I wanted to call you right away. Believe it or not, there's a pay phone here."

"Did they confiscate your cell?"

I didn't know where I got that idea, except perhaps from seeing hardened criminals

62

give up their possessions on television crime dramas. I also didn't know why it mattered. I was simply thrashing around trying to make sense of the last few minutes. I knew if Bruce were here, he'd recite the titles of a dozen movies where the star winds back time and redoes the past.

"No, they didn't take it," Rachel said, but I'd lost track of the question.

"I'm sorry, what?"

"I still have my cell. But I didn't want to use it. What if they're bugging it or something? And I know once I get home, I won't be able to call you. It will be awful. My mom is a wreck and all her sisters will be showing up."

"So you're free and they haven't charged you or anything?"

"Yeah, I'm free, but they told me not to leave Henley."

I breathed more easily. "They must be questioning everyone, Rachel."

"They said they were but I don't see anyone else from school around here. I'm sure they think I did it, Dr. Knowles. They think I poisoned Dr. Appleton." Rachel's voice faded away and then came back. "Dr. Knowles?"

"Why in the world would they think you killed him?"

"I don't want to talk about it on the phone. Will you meet me somewhere tomorrow?"

"Of course."

"The police interview room was stifling and I feel like I haven't had a shower in a week."

I did a quick calculation of the timeline. It was now eight o'clock. If Woody called the police after four, by the time they arrived, questioned Woody, put things together, and decided to question Rachel, it would have been at least six. That meant the longest Rachel could have been at the station was a couple of hours. I had no trouble believing that two or three hours in adversarial interrogation by the police could seem like a week.

"Just one thing, Rachel. Was Dr. Appleton okay when you went upstairs to give him the cake and drink from the party?"

A long pause while I sat down and drummed my fingers on my knee.

"I didn't see him. I knocked, you know, lightly. He doesn't like to be disturbed if his door is closed. That's the code for all his students. If he doesn't answer a light *tap, tap, tap,* we just go away."

I couldn't recall Rachel's coming back down to the lounge with the food and drink, but neither had I been tracking her movements. I wondered if she was a suspect simply because she tried to deliver a treat. Had Woody seen her, perhaps, and assumed she'd gone in and . . . I couldn't imagine.

"You should be home with your family," I said. A pittance of advice but I wanted her out of what must have been a depressing environment, though I had no experience to confirm it. I imagined the police had one set of rooms for casual visitors and another, more dismal setup for suspects.

"I guess I should get home. Can I call you tomorrow to set up a time to meet?"

"Absolutely."

Once we hung up, I sat with the phone on my lap. I had so many questions. Did Rachel have a lawyer? Were there any other suspects? There should be. So many people had it in for Keith Appleton.

But who hated him so much they would kill him? No one I could think of.

Rachel's thinly veiled plea for help rang in my head. I hadn't a clue how to assist a murder suspect, but my faith in her innocence was unshaken. For all her whining and complaining about Keith, I couldn't recall ever seeing her angry. Certainly not angry enough to hurt someone. When she was upset, as she'd been yesterday, she tended to cry or withdraw. Rachel would rather quit than fight.

I thought I was ready for more sustenance. I headed for the cheese plate, but still couldn't bring myself to eat. None of the food in my house had been at the party, but what was to say that the person who poisoned Keith hadn't snuck into my home and injected the contents of my fridge with whatever substance killed him?

The realization that this fear was irrational didn't stop me from emptying my food into the sink. I flushed it down the disposal, holding my nose against the odor of shredding apple and cheddar cheese.

For some reason, they smelled of death.

It took a while for me to collect myself enough to take some action. Finally, I picked up the phone. I had one and only one contact in the Henley PD, and it was once removed at that.

I punched in the speed dial number for Bruce. I usually waited for him to call me when he was on duty, to avoid waking him from a nap or catching him mid-flight to an accident scene. Or in the middle of a serious poker game, as I had a couple of times.

"I know you're not calling to tell me you love me," he said. "Pretty awful what happened, huh?"

"You've already heard about Keith Appleton?"

"I'm not best friends with a homicide detective for nothing, Soph."

Bruce had known Virgil Mitchell, of the small but very effective Henley Police Department, since college. I hoped to capitalize on that friendship for Rachel's benefit.

"Why didn't you call to let me know?" I asked.

"I was going to, as soon as I finished my second doughnut."

I laughed in spite of the gravity of the moment. I pictured Bruce lying on his cot, flight suit on the floor at the ready, in one of the tiny bedrooms in the company trailer. He'd be heedless of how his steel-toed boots were sullying the quilted bedspread I'd given him, purchased at a crafts fair Ariana had dragged me to. "Doughnuts," I echoed. "You try so hard to be a cliché."

"But a well-informed one."

I heard the sounds of explosions in the background and hoped it was coming from the television set in the den and not from outside his window. If Bruce had his way, he'd keep the facility's media cabinet stocked with old movies and cult films, but, alas, most of his colleagues preferred contemporary action flicks.

"How much do you know about all this, Bruce? Rachel called me, but she wasn't very forthcoming beyond that she thinks she's a murder suspect, if you can believe that."

I wasn't happy about the silence that followed. I'd expected an immediate and hearty, "No way."

"Bruce? Is there something I should know?"

"Maybe you should talk to Virge."

My heart sank. "Can you set it up?"

"Matter of fact, he's on the way."

"What a guy. You knew I'd want to talk to him."

"Just go easy on him, okay?"

"Of course."

Whatever that meant.

While it was very handy to have a personal "in" with a cop, I tried not to abuse the privilege.

Only one other time had I needed to call on Virgil about a police matter, shortly after he'd left the Boston PD to sign on in Henley. One of my students had been caught with a small stash of drugs, but not a small enough one to escape police notice. When

Jessie, who'd been clean for more than a year, told me her former associates had set her up, I believed her. I'd enlisted Virgil's help and he'd come through for her, investigating personally and having the charges dismissed. Jessie was now a successful businesswoman and hadn't had a substance abuse problem since.

Now Virgil would be investigating my assistant and friend for the murder of a colleague. I hoped there would be a similar happy ending — justice for Keith Appleton, and exoneration for Rachel Wheeler.

When I thought of poor Keith, I wondered what his last moments were like, whether he knew he'd been poisoned and even suspected or knew who his killer was. Or maybe he simply felt sick or thought he was having a heart attack.

It struck me that the police had determined the cause of Keith's death rather quickly. Didn't it take many complicated tests to determine that someone died of poison? I'd read that unless you knew exactly what you were looking for, the famous "tox screens" of crime dramas revealed very little right away. Had I misunderstood Rachel? Time would tell.

Poor Keith. Poor Keith. I couldn't erase that refrain from my mind. I knew very little about how a person's body reacted to poisons and I had many questions. Without answers, my imagination took over. I tried to shake away all the horrible images that flooded my mind.

Not many murders had been committed in Henley — I couldn't remember the last time I'd heard or read of one — and certainly there were none in the history of the college. I was sure this case was taxing the resources of the small police department. I knew Virgil had more to do tonight than visit his good buddy's fretting girlfriend. But I believed in Rachel as much as I'd believed in Jessie, and I knew I had to do my best for her.

While I waited for Virgil, I paced the rooms of my house — leaving the bright kitchen; walking into and around my dark-toned, comfortable den; stepping out the door to the hallway, lined with photos; weaving first into my modern home office; then into my spacious lavender-colored and lavender-smelling bedroom; and then into the whiter-than-white guest bedroom; rambling back down the hallway to the kitchen.

Along the route, I managed to take calming respites for puzzle solving. I always had a crossword, a jigsaw puzzle, several cubes, and metal and wood puzzles and games laid out strategically in different rooms of my house. I was never far from a mindbender of one kind or another, some bought, some made by me. I encouraged my guests to participate. Bruce, my most frequent guest, hardly ever did, citing his need to reduce stress when he was off the job. He tried in vain to get through to me that solving puzzles wasn't everyone's idea of relaxation.

When the phone rang, I was in my bedroom, leaning on my dresser to work a complex eye twister in a book I'd purchased, trying to determine which figures had been made with one continuous line and which had been constructed of two or more lines.

I checked the screen on the landline next to my bed and saw a Mansfield number. I picked up the headset and greeted Fran Emerson, my department chair.

Why hadn't I thought to call her? Or anyone? It seemed I'd gone into a completely passive state, puttering around my house.

"Can you believe it, Sophie?" she asked. Her voice was muffled against a background of unintelligible sounds. I guessed I was hearing Fran's grandchildren, visiting for the summer from out of state. "I feel so bad now, the way we were talking about him this afternoon."

I knew what she meant. "You didn't say anything mean, Fran," I offered. Unlike me, who had wished the man off the campus.

I carried the phone to the den and sank into the corner of my couch. On the low antique coffee table in front of me was a beautiful cherry wood frame, four inches square, containing eight L-shaped wooden pieces and one rectangular piece in a different shade of wood. Bruce had given it to me a few weeks ago and it remained unsolved. The idea was to fit all the pieces in the frame, with no space left over. The L-shaped pieces interlocked nicely in the area, leaving only small triangles of space to fit the lone rectangle.

As I'd done many times before, I fiddled with L-shaped pieces, moving them around to create a space the rectangle could occupy — without chopping it into pieces, that is. Tonight, in only three moves, I met the challenge. I looked at the design, neatly in place.

Maybe it was a good sign. Or, simply, all my nervous energy had focused itself on the puzzle.

I heard Fran shush someone, presumably a small someone. I wasn't sure where we'd left off.

"Still," she said, "I certainly had mean thoughts about Keith." She paused and I imagined her cataloging her uncharitable, if unspoken, words. "I suppose we should be thinking of holding a memorial service. Probably our dear Dean Phyllis is already working on it. Or the president, I'll bet. I don't even know where Keith's family lives. Do you?"

"He doesn't have many relatives that he keeps up with. Just one cousin that I know of, Elteen Kirsch, in the Chicago area. Keith spends holidays with her and her family. The police may already have notified her, but I have her name and address if they need it."

I made a note to offer that bit of information to Virgil as a paltry gesture to assist the police, from whom I was about to ask a lot.

"I didn't realize you two were that close," Fran said.

"We're not. Keith called me from her home on spring break once and wanted me to overnight a package he'd left on his desk." Not that I was being defensive.

"Well, that makes you closer than anyone I can think of," Fran said.

I had the fleeting thought that maybe Rachel was right, that if Keith had any friends at all, I was it. The notion only made me feel worse about the negative vibes I'd been sending his way, practically until the moment he died.

My usually comfortable home seemed unbearably warm tonight. I carried the phone into the kitchen, poured a glass of ice water from a pitcher in the fridge, and adjusted the thermostat down a notch.

A call-waiting beep saved me from further explaining to Fran the nature of my friendship, or lack thereof, with the deceased.

I clicked my tongue. "I'd better take this call," I told Fran, though I didn't recognize the ID. "We'll talk soon."

I pushed a button to hear chem major Pam Noonan. "Oh, my God, Dr. Knowles," she said, making one word out of the first three. "Did you hear?"

"There are cops at all the doors." Liz Harrison's voice now, with the hollow sound of a speakerphone. "And this big TV truck."

Without waiting for my answer, Pam had apparently yielded the mic to her roomie, who sounded as excited as Pam. "I can't believe it," Liz said. "We're sitting here and, oh, my God. Franklin Hall is a crime scene."

"You're in Franklin Hall?"

"No, no, we're sitting in my dorm room." A new voice.

"Who is this?" I asked.

"Casey," she said, as if she was insulted that I didn't recognize her voice. But I knew

74

Casey Tremel only because she was close to Pam and Liz. "They made everyone go home who lived near enough and then they closed Nathaniel Hawthorne and Clara Barton and put the rest of us into Paul Revere, which is where I live anyway."

Campus-speak was always flavored with the greats of Massachusetts history. I assumed the big shake-up in the dorms was to make security easier.

"But first the cops interviewed us all, like on TV," Pam said.

"They wanted to know where you were, did you see anything strange, and all that," Liz said.

"We walked over to Franklin, but they wouldn't let us into the building." Pam's voice again.

"I guess they're done with us," said someone.

"They're using that yellow and black tape just like on TV and there are cops at all the doors. A lot of good they did at Franklin today. So much for Henley's security department, huh?" said someone else.

I taught these girls in my summer statistics class. How come my students had so much time to watch television? I'd have to step up the homework assignments. And were they calling all their teachers tonight, or was I the only lucky one? Maybe the word had spread that, as Rachel had judged, I was Keith Appleton's only friend on campus.

I tapped the mic in my phone. "Ooh, sorry, girls, I have another call. You three take care of yourselves and try to put all this out of your minds. We'll talk later." I was sure I'd be getting a call back soon.

Not wanting to appear to gossip about a colleague, I was equally abrupt with the next several callers. Collecting and analyzing data was an occupational hazard for me — I couldn't help noting that the science majors, who had Keith in many classes, seemed less sad about their professor's death than they were excited about a campus drama. I found myself listening for clues to Keith's killer, as if the pool of suspects were restricted to those who called me, his alleged best friend. I ticked them off, teachers and students alike: Pam, Liz, Casey, Fran. I added all who were at the party this afternoon. Lucy, Robert, Judith, and nearly a dozen others. Anyone but Rachel.

Through a curious philosophy of what constituted a mathematics or science major, Henley College required its science majors to take math classes, but not vice versa. Thus, few of my own math majors had taken Keith's classes. I hated to think that

that was why they seemed more inclined to express sympathy over his death. I liked to think they were more sensitive, living on a higher plane and all.

I could hear Bruce's loud guffaw in my ears, from times past when I'd expressed a similar observation. I heard the same from Ariana.

Another round of communication came through emails, to and from Hal and other faculty members, and even from Gillian Bartholomew, from the MAstar computer.

I was struck by how rapidly the news had traveled. The entire City of Henley emergency services staff and equipment must have reported to the campus to answer Woody's nine-one-one call. I had an image of the neatly manicured campus lawns and walkways crowded with larger-than-life vehicles, sirens blaring. No medevac helicopter, but everything else — fire truck, police cars, ambulance. And, of course, the local press.

I tried to read an article on reducing the order of a differential equation, but I couldn't concentrate. I couldn't find a cube or twisted metal puzzle to engage me, and beading seemed too frivolous an activity to take up with Keith Appleton in Henley's morgue.

I settled again on the sofa in the den. I ran my hand over the thick fabric, a rich burgundy chosen to match the old chair across from me, which had come from my grandmother's home. I picked away at a new acrostic. I'd been disappointed that the puzzle in last Sunday's *New York Times* had been trivial and I'd quickly replaced it on my clipboard with one from an anthology. This one wasn't all that challenging either, but I had a moment of enjoyment figuring out that for the clue "L" the answer was "the bottom of the barrel" and for "H" it was "the middle of nowhere."

The satisfying moment passed quickly and thoughts of a murdered colleague rushed to claim my full attention.

Rrring. Rrring. Rrring.

My landline. From the way I jumped, you'd think this was the first call of the evening. The evening that wouldn't end.

Bruce was calling to check on me, sweetie that he is.

"Is Virge still there?" he asked.

"He hasn't even arrived yet, but I'm sure he's up to his ears right now."

"Do you need anything? All we're doing is watching DVDs. I can get Bodie to come in for me."

Double sweetie. "Thanks, but I'm fine.

You know me, bouncing from phone to email to puzzle and back. Just hanging out."

"Like us. It's very cloudy, so we really can't take a call. Two minutes ago, we refused one, in fact. A young guy fell off his motorcycle at that busy intersection near the high school. But the ceiling is way too low, so, no go." A nanosecond pause. "Hey, a rhyme. Remember that movie quiz where you had to figure out a title from something that rhymed with it, like Sandra Bullock in *Read* turned out to be *Speed,* and —"

"I get it."

I used to worry about what happened to patients or accident victims when the ceiling was so low that the helicopter team couldn't get to them, but Bruce had cleared it up for me.

"They have to resort to calling an ambulance," he'd told me, making it sound as if that were only marginally better than a wagon train.

I promised Bruce I'd call if I needed him. In any case, I knew he'd come by after nine in the morning when his shift was over. Then, I paced some more and made a comfort — for me — call to Ariana, who promised to send positive thoughts to all of us and to bring me a good vibrations basket tomorrow. She'd scheduled a beading class

79

at my home at noon, as part of her "rotating settings" theory of inspiration. Plus, it was cooler in my home than in the back room of her shop.

"I could change the venue for tomorrow," she offered.

"Not necessary." I had hopes that by tomorrow, everything would be cleared up to my satisfaction and that of Rachel, and of those who presided over criminal justice. "Straightening up and setting out snacks will be a welcome distraction," I assured her.

I entered my home office to check my email for the tenth time since I'd heard the news and this time found one from the college president, Dr. Olivia Aldridge, the driving force behind Henley's new coeducational status. She'd been appointed only four years ago, but I found her very well suited to the college, seeming to understand its traditions while being in tune with its needs for the future.

Oops — that was something I read in the latest recruiting brochure. Still, I was among the seventy-five percent of faculty who approved of the president's performance, the other twenty-five percent being those who wanted Henley to remain a women's college.

The subject of President Aldridge's message this evening was Henley College's great loss. The text, as I expected, included a tribute to "one of our finest professors." Also as expected, there was no mention of a murder on campus, simply "an unfortunate tragedy" and a "sad occasion for the entire Henley family."

There would be no more classes for the summer session, which had another week to go. Instead, President Aldridge encouraged faculty to hold department meetings and to contact our summer students to work out a smooth ending to the term and a mutually agreeable grading procedure. She called for a full faculty meeting on campus on Monday morning at ten.

I was sure the president's decision to cancel the last week of summer classes was due in part to the designation of Benjamin Franklin Hall, one of its major buildings, as a crime scene, temporary as it was. It seemed a good plan to keep the area clear until questions were answered. As much as I hoped that things would be resolved in record time, I was glad there was still a month before the fall term started, which would give everyone time to gain equilibrium and get things in order. And hopefully have closure on what had happened to one of our finest professors.

A knock on the door came, finally, at eleven thirty.

Detective Virgil Mitchell, all six feet and two hundred and fifty pounds of him, give or take, filled my doorway. He scuffed his shoes on the welcome mat as if he'd just come in from a blustery storm of rain, snow, or sleet. I had a flash of an unpleasant image: who knew where his shoes had been?

More important, why was the detective whom I was counting on to help me clear Rachel's name looking so dour?

5

Tonight Virgil and I skipped a high five, our usual greeting. Instead he gave me a hug that nearly brought me to tears, though I hadn't been moved to cry before that moment.

"I'm sorry about your colleague," he said, resulting in a full outpouring from my eyes.

It wasn't only Keith Appleton's death that I was weeping over. Every loss, big or small, for whatever reason, reminded me of so many other losses, other deaths.

Virgil patted my back then let me leave to collect myself. When I got back I was glad to see he'd helped himself to a beer.

"Technically, I'm off duty," he said. His wink told me he knew it was an unnecessary explanation.

"You forget my in with Internal Affairs," I said, coming back to normal now.

Virgil unbuttoned his collar and loosened his tie. He'd already flung his jacket on a kitchen chair. I sympathized. Who else other than priests had to wear a tight collar even in hot weather? And in New England, the summer months were hot twenty-four seven. Period. No cooling off at night. You could be up all night and not feel a breeze or relief from the humidity. I tried to keep from staring at the large dark circles around Virgil's armpits.

"You must be exhausted," I said. And unbearably hot.

He saluted me with his beer. "You got that right."

I led Virgil to the den, the coolest room in the house, where we took seats across from each other. He reached over and picked up an L-shaped piece from the wood puzzle, which I'd emptied onto the table as soon as I'd solved it. He looked at the frame, frowned, then put the piece down and gave it a pat.

"This is me giving up," he said.

I smiled, remembering what a little humor felt like.

Virgil's hairline made a deep V on his forehead, much like Bruce's widow's peak. I'd often teased that there must have been something in the water at Camp Sturbridge where they'd met as teenagers. Bruce would then rattle off a list of famous people who shared their hairline, including Leonardo DiCaprio and Mikhail Baryshnikov. Only once did I throw in a mention of Hannibal Lecter's V hairline.

All other physical resemblances between Virgil and Bruce ended at the hairline, however, as Bruce was shorter by three inches and lighter by about ninety pounds.

"Appreciate this," Virgil said, between swigs of his beer.

I'd put out a bowl of pretzels. They were gone in a flash. I was sorry I'd dumped my cheese and fruit dinner down the disposal but that wasn't the fare Virgil would have liked anyway. I couldn't think of any more tasks or small talk to skirt the conversation I'd ostensibly been waiting up for and looking forward to.

It occurred to me that I didn't know exactly what I wanted from Virgil. Why hadn't I made notes? I'd had all evening and how had I used the time? Doing puzzles, making and taking calls, emailing. I'd actually thought of beading instead of drawing up a plan for this meeting. I was usually so prepared for an interview, a class, a seminar, even for the toast I'd made a month ago at a college friend's wedding.

Now, tasked with assuming a role in a murder investigation, I had nothing. Did I think I'd just say "Please consider Rachel Wheeler not guilty?" Or raise my hand and recite, "I vouch for your number one suspect, Rachel Wheeler," and that would be that?

Virgil sat back, crossed one leg over the other as far as it would go with the heft around his middle. Letting me take my time. I looked at the sole of his shoe and imagined I saw blood and brains. Never mind that Keith had been poisoned, not blown apart. Amazing what happened when a violent act entered the psyche.

My biggest conundrum, and one I should have thought through during the last four hours, was whether to mention Rachel at all. For all I knew the police had another suspect in tow, the real killer, and Virgil came to deliver the news in person.

I saw *LOL* in big text-messaging letters in the air in front of me.

"Virgil," I began, the single word sending my lips into a desert of dryness.

Virgil uncrossed his legs and leaned his bulk forward. "You probably want to know what's what with your assistant."

I could have kissed him for rescuing me. "She's my friend," I said, as if that should make a difference.

Virgil shrugged his shoulders and held up

his hands, palms out. "Your friend."

"I didn't mean to —"

"It's okay. It's a tense situation. Let me set the scene for you," he said, taking a small notebook from his shirt pocket.

I took a deep breath and sat back. "Okay."

"A call comes in at sixteen hundred and ten hours from a male with a report of a nonresponsive victim in Benjamin Franklin Hall, northwest corner of Henley College campus. Uniforms are dispatched. They get to the building where a janitor, later self-identified as the nine-one-one caller, greets them at the door and leads them to an office on the fourth floor."

I nodded. "The chemistry floor," I said, wanting to keep everything neat and correct.

"Chemistry. Thanks. Professor Keith Appleton, determined to be deceased, is ID'd by the janitor."

"He's not . . ." I stopped in time, holding myself back from another irrelevant correction — technically speaking, Keith was not a full professor yet, though most people used the term to mean simply college teacher. "Never mind."

Virgil picked up his thread again. "The first officers on the scene report that the victim is on the floor behind his desk in a position that appears he fell or was pushed from his chair. His shirt collar appears to have been torn open, by himself or another. The victim's face and neck exhibit a pink discoloration." Virgil ran his finger down the page and turned the leaf before he continued. Trying to spare me unpleasant details? Or keeping some matters confidential? Both, probably. "Some things are knocked over. A clock —"

"That's his distinguished alumnus clock from Harvard," I said, swallowing a gulp. "He was extremely proud of that."

Virgil nodded and appeared to appreciate the information. "A photograph —"

"Keith with Senator Kennedy, right? He loved that picture. The only one in his office. It was taken at a special fund-raiser only weeks before the senator died."

"Thanks again," Virgil said.

I nodded. "Uh-huh."

Why were my nerves so rattled? I felt like clamping my hand across my mouth. I looked around the den to find something calming. I settled on a poster, rolled up in the corner, waiting for me to take it to a shop for mounting. I imagined it unfurled, revealing the sweet, smiling countenance of Emmy Noether, said to be the most important woman in the history of mathematics.

Even a huge Sophie Germain fan like me would have to agree.

Virgil cleared his throat. "There was some other stuff. On the desk is a clear bottle of white powder, a crystally substance, the officer called it, labeled potassium chloride. The uniforms ask the janitor to come in and ID the bottle. Did he ever see it before, to his knowledge did it belong in this office, et cetera, et cetera. This is where I arrive with my partner, Archie — you've met him a couple of times, I think. We send the uniforms out . . ." Another pause to flip through pages. "The janitor says the bottle looks like it belongs down the hall in a chemistry laboratory, in a cabinet that's always locked."

"I know the cabinet you're talking about. A lot of people have a key," I said. Including Rachel.

"Your friend has a key," Virgil said, echoing my thought.

"But she's not the only one. Every chem and bio faculty member has a key, plus a couple of interns. You'd have to have a lot more than that before —"

My voice had risen again. Virgil put his hand out to stop me before I made a complete fool of myself. Perspiration that had formed on his forehead made its way down his face. Here was this very tired, very busy detective in my home, to accommodate me, as a courtesy to his best friend. He had no obligation whatsoever to be here or to share information.

"There is more," he said, mopping his brow.

"I'm sorry," I said, my voice back in control.

Virgil waved away the second apology I'd made in less than ten minutes. "An eyewitness saw Ms. Wheeler outside the door to Professor Appleton's office in the afternoon between one thirty and one forty-five, which looks to be close to the time of death, though we don't know that for sure yet. That was just a quickie guess by the ME. Could have been any time from about noon till the gentleman found him at four."

An eyewitness saw her? Probably Woody. I could take care of that little nothing of a clue. "Rachel went upstairs to take Keith some food from a party we were having on the first floor." I felt and heard a triumphant ring to my response. "We were celebrating Hal Bartholomew's doctorate. He teaches physics." That should clear things up.

Virgil scratched his head. "What kind of food was that?"

I described the paper plate with cake that

Rachel had assembled. "White frosting, blue icing. And a can of soda. I don't know which kind," I added.

Virgil flipped through his notebook. "I don't see a mention of food or a drink here anywhere in the office."

"There has to be food there. I saw her leave the lounge with it. It was a very nice gesture on her part. While everyone else was ragging on him, I might add."

"I'll check the photos when I get back."

"Wait. I remember Rachel said Keith didn't answer her knock. I'll bet she just left the plate outside his door. Would the photos show that?"

"If there was anything outside the door, yes, it would have been photographed."

Virgil shot me a sad, tired look. I was amazed he showed no anger or frustration, which, given my performance, I'd have completely understood.

"I'm really grateful to you for coming, Virgil," I said. "I'm getting concerned that you'll get no sleep at all tonight if you don't leave soon. I guess I lost track of the fact that you're doing me this big favor." I took a big breath. "I'm just worried about my friend."

"I understand, Sophie. I didn't come here for a party." He held up his nearly empty beer bottle and smiled, barely. "This was a good start, though."

"Can I get you another one? Or some coffee?" About time I showed my classy side.

"I'm good."

"I just want you to know I'd like to help Rachel Wheeler. She seems to think you're zeroing in on her. Maybe she's wrong?" I checked Virgil's face for signs of "Bingo, you're right; she's wrong." Nothing. "Or if she is at the top of your list because of something I don't know yet, maybe you could tell me and I could explain it for you."

I was out of breath as often happened when I rambled.

Virgil drained his beer then sucked his lips in tight. "We're withholding one thing. I'm going out on a limb here telling you. But what the heck, I don't think this is what's going to be the gotcha." I moved forward on my seat. "There were papers scattered over and around the victim's body and throughout the office. Pages and pages of yellow computer paper, eight and a half by eleven sheets, some with typed text, some with diagrams and pictures. They were crinkled up as if someone had thrown them around in anger."

I thought immediately of Rachel's thesis. The campus store sold reams of very inexpensive yellow paper that most students used for drafts of their reports that no teacher would see. Once they edited their papers and were ready to submit, they printed on a good white bond paper. I knew Rachel's thesis was still in the yellow paper stage, though she'd had a series of oral presentations on her data.

"Don't tell me," I whispered. I leaned over, put my face in my hands and partly over my ears, and pressed my body farther into the couch, but I could still hear Virgil as plain as day.

"The name at the tops of the pages was R. Wheeler and the pages were bleeding with red pencil corrections and nasty comments." Virgil shook his head slightly. "It doesn't look good for your friend."

I rubbed my eyes and breathed out loudly.

"Can I ask one more question, Virgil? If it's out of line, just tell me, but doesn't it look as though Rachel is being framed, that someone wants you to think Rachel killed her teacher? Everyone knows he's given her a hard time for years, and especially right now, about her thesis."

Virgil nodded. "I know what you're thinking. And you have a point. Who leaves the murder weapon and evidence of anger at the scene, practically shouting out 'me, me.'

But, with the janitor seeing her there, she's the best we have right now. And sometimes a smart guy will frame himself, so the police will say what you're saying. We're looking at all of this, believe me, Sophie."

He fell just short of saying, "We're not that dumb," and I admired his restraint.

I was out of ideas.

"Thanks again for coming by, Virgil. If there's anything I can do. I mean, I can vouch for Rachel." The offer sounded silly even to me but Virgil nodded politely.

"The best thing you can do is just sit back and let us do our job."

"Easy for you to say."

I was glad we could end with both of us smiling.

Almost.

"Archie will be in tomorrow," he said, gathering up his jacket and tie. He handed me Archibald McConnell's card. "Why don't you give him a call and you guys pick a good time."

I raised my eyebrows in a huge question mark.

"He needs to interview you. It wouldn't look good on the report if I did it."

I didn't know whether to be devastated or deliriously happy that Rachel wasn't the only suspect. I should have realized that sooner or later, the police would get to me on their list of people to interview.

"My, you'd think I was a suspect."

Virgil smiled, broadly this time, enough for the dimple on his chin to show at last. "I'm not at liberty to say."

We parted with a high five.

I'd just turned down my cool lavender sheets and placed a glass of iced herbal tea on my night table when the phone rang. I thought a new record had already been set for the greatest number of calls in one night.

I picked up and heard Rachel's wispy voice.

"I'm home now, but it was awful, Dr. Knowles. You'd think I was some big-time criminal. Our neighbors were waiting for me in front of my house, and I even saw some people standing watching on the curbs all along the way."

Probably an exaggeration on Rachel's part, but, on the other hand, in a town as small as Henley, there wasn't much to keep the citizenry entertained. A police drama was just what everyone needed on a hot Friday night.

I felt so bad for Rachel. I could barely understand her through her sobs.

"We need to talk," I told her. It came out

95

sounding not unlike the intro to a breakup.

I wanted desperately to talk to Rachel now that I had more facts — alleged facts — to work with. But not at this hour, not after this day.

"Yeah, for sure, Dr. Knowles. And without my mother and all my aunts and uncles around."

Where could we go? I realized that meeting on campus was not a good idea. Certainly not Rachel's home either. Here? Bruce would be by — too soon, I realized, looking at the clock. Ariana and her class would arrive at noon for at least a couple of hours. I'd have to call Ariana in the morning to let her know that I wouldn't be here, but she could still use my house. I hated to change the venue on her on such short notice.

The ideal spot for a private meeting would be a place at the edge of town, sparsely populated, with no crowded Starbucks in sight.

"Can you meet me around noon?"

"Uh-huh."

I had the feeling Rachel would have agreed to anything at that moment. "Can you get to the MAstar facility, out at the airfield?"

"Where Mr. Granville and Mrs. Bartholomew work? Sure."

I was reminded how long Rachel had been part of the Henley family; she knew more than just our class schedules. "Are you okay right now?" I asked her.

"Yeah, everyone's asleep, thank God. One of my aunts has this lawyer friend and he came by. He says it doesn't look good for me."

"He said that?"

"Not exactly, but I could tell that's what he's thinking."

"Let's start out positive about this, okay, Rachel?"

"I'll try, Dr. Knowles."

I couldn't bring myself to tell her that Detective Virgil Mitchell, Henley PD, said exactly what her aunt's lawyer friend had said.

6

I went to bed with a headache. My organic jade mist tea, a present from Ariana, smelled more like bitter almonds. The power of suggestion: Cyanide was more familiar to me than the poison Virgil mentioned in connection with Keith's murder. I'd read somewhere that cyanide had an almond smell, but that not everyone had the gene to detect the odor. Apparently I was one of those lucky ones who possessed the gene, and could smell cyanide even when there was none within miles.

I woke up with the same headache, but the aroma filling the room had changed to that of dark French roast. I sniffed again. Ah, cinnamon buns, too. The pleasant odors and the rattling sounds in my kitchen told me that Bruce had arrived. Or that Keith's killer had come to do me in, too, after serving me my favorite breakfast in bed. I turned over and put my pillow over my head. I was so beat I didn't care who was in my house.

Sniff. The aroma of coffee wouldn't quit. I lifted myself from my cocoon and shambled into the kitchen.

Bruce was ready with a steaming mug of coffee. "Here's a little something to get you started," he said, kissing my cheek. "It must have been a tough night for you."

"You could say that."

"Breakfast awaits in the main dining area." He took a little bow, waiter-like.

Maybe life was worth living after all. I accepted the mug, making a huge effort to smile in gratitude. In a couple of hours I wouldn't want to get near anything that sent a hot vapor bath to my face, but as a wake-up beverage, I'd take rich, hot coffee in any season.

I squinted. Why did Bruce look so much better than I did, even after he'd pulled his fifth all-nighter in a row? But then, I was a pushover for stubble. I ran my finger along his cheek and gave him a weak smile.

Bruce was a marvel, the way he got off a twelve-hour shift at nine in the morning, chipper and ready to start the day. He'd finally crash around two or three in the afternoon and be all set to leave for work again by eight in the evening. Then, during his seven days off, he'd snap back to a normal sleeping pattern. Granted he was often able to nap during the night on the cot in his MAstar trailer bedroom but there was that phone — the crew called it the Bat Phone — on the wall that could go off at any moment, a klaxon sound summoning them to an emergency. Flight nurse Gil Bartholomew, Hal's wife, compared the sound to that of a tack hammer working directly on her skull.

"I was hoping the smell would wake you up," Bruce said. "I hate to eat alone, especially in your kitchen." He took a step back and scrutinized my face. "Did you get any sleep at all, Soph?"

"Probably as much as you did."

He made a gesture meant to mimic a maitre d' toward the patio doors, next to which my old white farm table was set for two. More coffee, lightly scrambled eggs, juice, and cinnamon buns from a nearby bakery. My headache faded at the sight.

I'd met Bruce in Boston five years ago at the wedding of his cousin, who married a college friend of mine. We still didn't know for sure if Sean and Karina had put us at the same table on purpose, but it hardly mattered anymore. We'd moved from two hours of talk at the big round favor-laden table to two more hours at a late-night coffee shop.

I loved hearing about the odd jobs Bruce had worked — like flying helicopter tours over the Grand Canyon and transporting CEOs through the air to golf matches. He'd let me go on and on about how mathematics was a subject of study in its own right, and not simply a tool for science, as some of our upper floor Franklin Hall faculty thought.

Over the years I'd gotten to like Bruce's frequent movie references and he tolerated my birthday theories. At the time it was important to me that he didn't laugh when I told him he was destined to be a pilot since his birthday, June 4, was the anniversary of the demonstration of the first hot air balloon.

We were very well suited to each other and by now I'd forgotten life before Bruce.

This morning I was the one with the trauma story. Bruce had had a quiet, fogged-in night at MAstar. No patients needing transportation from one facility to another, and no accidents.

"None that we could get to, anyway," Bruce told me.

"I thought you had some new guidance system that let you fly lower than before."

"You do listen," he said, playing with my fingers for a moment. "The limit used to be a little more than eleven hundred feet, now it's three hundred sixty, but that's not zero, oh mathematician."

You'd think a mathematician would have a better concept of where three hundred and sixty feet up was located, but I had a hard time visualizing it, other than picturing a thirty-six-story building, which required a mental journey to Boston or Providence, Rhode Island. The tallest structure in Henley, Massachusetts was its combination courthouse and city hall, a whole six stories high.

I filled Bruce in on Virgil's visit and Rachel's second call. I was still smarting from how much evidence pointed to her, and still red-faced at how I'd kept shooting the messenger, Bruce's best friend.

"Did Virgil tell you how I was a basket case last night?" I asked.

Bruce bit into the center of his bun, the best part, where most of the gooey sugar was concentrated. I often stole that part from him. He shrugged his shoulders. The stall spoke volumes. I had to wait until he swallowed to hear his answer.

"Virge deals with a lot of people in critical situations; he's seen a lot of different responses, all legitimate."

I laughed, only slightly annoyed to be lumped in with "a lot of people." "Did you learn that in your 'How To Deal With Trauma Victims' class?"

He took another bite of pastry, hard to do when you're laughing. "Mmaypbe," he said.

"Seriously, Bruce, I don't know who could have killed Keith, but I know it wasn't Rachel Wheeler. I'm wracking my brain" — I shook my fork at him and a tiny bit of egg fell onto the table — "but not to *come up* with suspects. To eliminate them. The whole population of Franklin Hall could have done it, plus the entire membership of the faculty senate."

"Even you, huh?"

"Yes." I chose to ignore the attempt at derailment, but his comment did remind me that I had to call Virgil's partner to schedule an interview. "Did I tell you that Keith tried to change the bylaws for choosing a faculty member for the Aurelius Henley Distinguished Professor Award?"

"Uh-huh," Bruce said, but that didn't stop me.

"Do you think that's fair? Keith wants to change the requirements from 'twenty-five years of service' to 'twenty-five continuous years of service.' He only suggested it to eliminate Fran Emerson. My department head," I added, making it sound like a personal slight.

"She's been there almost thirty years but she took maternity leave twice," Bruce said.

I gave a vigorous nod and took a mouthful of perfect eggs, not dropping a morsel. "I could go on — not only a bunch of students, but even Dean Underwood has her beefs with Keith over a number of things." I paused. "*Had* her beefs. I'm telling you, Rachel's alleged motive, that Keith was giving her a hard time with her thesis — hardly even stands out in that crowd of suspects. Keith alienated almost everyone." I took another breath and evaluated my conclusion. "Sorry, that's a terrible thing to say about a dead colleague."

Bruce reached for my hand and let me wallow in guilt for a few moments. He knew me well.

"Maybe it's like *Murder on the Orient Express*," he said, holding his fork like a dagger. "You know, the movie where it ends up that everyone did it." I turned away as he mimicked stabbing motions with the fork.

"You're not helping." Not quite true. Both the awesome breakfast and the objectivity Bruce brought to the table helped a lot.

■ ■ ■ ■

After Bruce left, I had about an hour to get dressed, prepare the house for Ariana's beading group, call Archie at the police station, and get to the Henley Airfield where MAstar's base station was located and where Rachel would meet me at noon. The downside of sleeping in — the day flew by.

To make up for skipping the beading class, I set out my most prized snack, peanut butter-filled pretzels, for the more-loyal-than-me crafters and their instructor. I arranged a plate of number-shaped sugar cookies that a flunking commuter student had baked for me. The cookies were doing double duty as bribe offerings, it seemed. It hadn't worked for the student, who flunked anyway, but there was no law that said I couldn't give the treats another try. In a gesture toward good health, I poured out a bowl of baby carrots, and in a fit of overly cautious behavior, I tossed a bag of hickory-smoked almonds into the garbage, convinced that they had a bitter smell.

I wrote a note to Ariana telling her that my house and fridge were hers and, by the way, I'd just ordered a new book on how to make beaded napkin rings and would make her a sample set by Labor Day. Bribes, bribes, bribes. Promises, promises.

I stuffed a "best of" puzzle book in my tote and headed out to meet Rachel.

There were pluses and minuses to living in a town that was only twenty-five miles from Buzzards Bay, the north end of Cape Cod. One drawback was that there was no good route to avoid traffic on a Saturday morning in July. It was marginally better that I was heading away from the Cape, on highway 495, and not toward it. Henley Airfield was on the northwestern edge of town, the opposite direction from hot spots like Old Silver Beach in Falmouth and the quaint shops of Provincetown at the tip of the Cape.

Traveling in my direction were vacationers leaving the Cape, but with four lanes, the traffic was somewhat bearable. The common wisdom was that these drivers, having had to check out of their time-shares by eleven on Saturday, were the worst, since they were not happy to be heading back to their daily work lives. Having been cut off three times since leaving home, I believed it.

An ambulance sailed by me, sirens blaring. I'd trained myself to think positive thoughts about emergency vehicles on the road: help is on the way. Since Bruce, however, my first thought was: too slow; instead of driving you should have taken a helicopter.

As a mathematician, I tended to see everything in terms of logic diagrams and spreadsheets. I'd been mentally setting up a chart, even though it had been less than twenty-four hours since I'd learned of Keith's murder and Rachel's plight. I had nothing written yet, but I used the driving time to edit my lists anyway. I'd gone through possible suspects, alibis, motives, and access to the murder weapon. I'd started with everyone who attended the party, and added a few stray faculty members, plus the dean, all of whom I knew to have been at odds with Keith over one thing or another.

The mental lists were too long now, and I was having trouble driving and concentrating.

Screeeeech.

I jammed on my brakes, luckily not slamming into an SUV in front of me. Some states had a hands-free law — no cell phones for the driver without a Bluetooth. I needed a mind-free law — no thoughts of anything other than the rules of the road.

I needed to put off my diagramming task and switch to a different form of multi-tasking. Once I was on a back road to the airfield, I hit the Bluetooth device on the visor of my car and called Detective Archibald McConnell.

I wasn't looking forward to the call or the interview. My discomfort didn't make sense. Thinking rationally, I should be jumping at the chance to talk to the Henley PD. The more information I had from them, the better my chances of figuring out something that would clear Rachel unequivocally. So why was I resenting an interview with Archie? Ever since I realized that Virgil was not joking when he'd implied that I was a suspect like every other Franklin Hall resident, I'd felt uneasy.

Maybe just because, in general, cops were intimidating. I was a big fan of those whose daily jobs required putting themselves in potentially dangerous situations, just to protect and serve me and my loved ones. Bruce and the entire MAstar crew were in that number. Still, how many times had I been tooling along the turnpike at only one or two mph above the speed limit, and tapped my brakes when I saw a two-toned blue state trooper vehicle up ahead?

I could only imagine how much worse it

must be for the guilty.

My Bluetooth speaker came alive. "Henley PD. McConnell here."

I gripped the steering wheel. "Yes, this is Sophie Knowles. Virgil asked me to call you?" *But by the way,* my inflection said, *I can't imagine why.*

"Yeah, hi, Sophie. I think we met at some shindig or other. Sorry about your friend."

"Thanks. I think she'll be all right."

"Yeah, sorry about the victim, too."

Oh no! If I could have banged my head on the wheel without going off the road or activating my airbag, I would have. Before I could utter an apology for my insensitivity, Archie continued.

"What's a good time for you?"

"Some afternoon next week would work. Classes have been cancelled."

"Let's make it this afternoon, say, three o'clock?"

I gulped. "Okay."

Archie had managed to keep a pleasant cadence in his voice, appearing to ask if the time was convenient, while issuing a non-negotiable summons.

"Do you know where the station is?"

My first thought was to remind Archie that I'd been born and raised in Henley, a town that did not regularly move its government buildings. I recovered in time.

"Yes, but thanks for asking." Now I was brownnosing.

"Have a nice morning," he said.

I could hear a pompous smile in his voice. I didn't like it, but I couldn't blame him. I had a lot to learn about dealing with cops.

I loved being at the airfield on the outskirts of Henley. It wasn't at all like Logan in Boston, or Green International in Providence, or any major airport I'd ever been to. Henley Airport had a small control tower, only four runways, and acres of wide-open space. Rows of Cessnas and other two- to four-seaters sat parked next to hangars and on all sides of the trailers that comprised MAstar.

I got out of my car and relished the breeze, warm as it was, that swept through the landscape in all seasons. With the majestic wings of aircraft visible in every direction, I always felt I'd entered an adventurous world, as if I could simply stand beside one of the planes or under a wing and take off myself.

"Peter Pan," Bruce said every time I shared that feeling. "The nineteen fifty-three version with Bobby Driscoll's voice."

"You took the words right out of my

mouth."

During one visit, Bruce let me try on his night-vision goggles. I'd seen them used often as props on TV, but it was something else to have the heavy equipment on my face and see for myself how everything turned green. Bruce took me into a windowless office in the MAstar trailer. After only a second or two, the desk, chairs, and computers came into focus, albeit with an eerie glow.

One time was enough for me once I learned that a single pair of binocular goggles cost fifteen thousand dollars. It seemed that MAstar owned the latest and best in goggle technology, previously available only to the military.

Ariana had been with me that day. When Bruce explained how the system's optics took even the lowest available ambient light and multiplied it thousands of times, Ariana pretended to block her ears.

"I like to think they're magic, turning darkness into daylight," she'd said.

As a mathematician, I appreciated both the engineering and the mystical definitions. One of my favorite quotes was from John von Neumann: *In mathematics you don't understand things. You just get used to them.*

Night-vision goggles were a small reminder of how different Bruce's life was from mine. The polar opposite, in fact.

After college in Boston, I'd worked in software development while I did my graduate work in differential equations. By the time I was thirty years old, I had my doctorate in mathematics but hadn't traveled more than a few hundred miles from Henley. By then, Bruce, the same age as me, had done a stint as an Air Force pilot, flying helicopters over hostile deserts.

When I started teaching at Henley, Bruce was on his way to his medevac career, accumulating the necessary three thousand hours of flight time. He'd worked many commercial jobs, from carrying local broadcast photographers on a shoot, to flying oil workers to a rig in the Gulf of Mexico, to transporting the super-rich to galas and sporting events.

"The corporate world was my least favorite," he'd told me. "Mind-numbing — chauffeuring CEOs and celebs to the airport in their private helicopters. And toting a bunch of tuna watchers was no picnic, either."

"Back up. Celebrities? Anyone I know?" I'd asked.

"Oh, you know, the usual starlets on their way to a club or a concert."

"Rich, young, and beautiful?"

"Yeah, but I couldn't name one of them."

I'd been glad to hear it.

So, not all of Bruce's assignments had been life threatening or lifesaving in nature. And I did think I was making a contribution when I helped a student in such a way that she became a better member of society. When you added it all up, however, Bruce got the prize — providing a service that often meant the difference between life and death.

It felt good to have an in with the emergency services pool. I hoped I'd never need them. And if I continued to lead this very unexciting, no-risk life, I never would.

Rachel was waiting for me in the MAstar parking lot, outside a heavy-duty chain-link fence. We walked across the gravel lot and embraced. Or rather, Rachel threw her tiny self into my arms. When she stopped crying and had removed long, wet locks from her face, she asked, "Remember when I asked you to talk to Dr. Appleton for me?"

Strange question. Was I being criticized for not having had time to appeal to Keith on her behalf before he died?

"I do remember, and I was going to contact him right after the party," I said, a little on the defensive.

"No, no. I mean I wouldn't have asked you to do that, would I, if I were going to . . . to kill him?"

I patted her back. "No, you wouldn't have, Rachel."

Things were worse than I thought if that was her only defense.

With Bruce off duty these few hours, I'd called Gil Bartholomew and asked if she could let us into the MAstar trailer, secured behind the ten-foot fence.

"Oh, and I'd like to use your bedroom so Rachel and I can talk in private," I'd added.

She'd laughed. "No one's ever asked me that."

Gil was the only woman in the crew at MAstar's Henley Airport base, and therefore had her own bedroom. All the pilots were men, as were the other flight nurses. "Most of these nurses come from a military background," she'd explained, "and regular nursing in a hospital just doesn't have that edge. As much as they might deny it, they're looking for the thrill of the battlefield."

"And you?" I'd asked.

"Guilty," she'd said, with a smile. "When I got out of the reserves I took a job as an ER nurse, but even that didn't cut it. We flight nurses get a lot more training, especially in drugs, and we have a lot more autonomy."

"I'm not tempted," I'd said.

As requested, I called Gil now from my cell. She came out wearing her navy flight suit up to her waist, a sleeveless white T-shirt on top. Bruce called the outfits "extra large, fire-retardant onesies for EMS professionals." The jacket part of Gil's suit hung over her butt, its sleeves looking like the arms of a raggedy doll. Or a corpse, I thought, unexpectedly.

We climbed the rickety metal stairs, then entered the double-wide. Anyone's first visit to the trailer held many surprises. Rachel seemed to be examining the unfamiliar features as if she were being sentenced to live here.

The washer/dryer combo was situated right at the front door, where you might expect a comfortable chair and reading lamp, or at least an inviting rug. A toaster and other small appliances lined the counter next to the imposing laundry set, and the kitchen stretched out a whole ten feet back.

By trailer standards, this one wasn't all that bad. Sure, the brown paneled walls looked like they could use a good scrubbing, but the grime was hardly noticeable, with so many signs plastered all over —

schedules, maps, warnings about safety, flight preparation and protocol lists, even a kitchen duty sign-up sheet, the numbered lines on which were blank except for Gil's name. What a surprise.

The overlapping notices reminded me of the kiosk in the student center at Henley, which, of course, reminded me of the turned upside-down campus.

I glanced at the weather maps, which I always enjoyed perusing. I'd memorized the special coding to indicate flight — or not — conditions. Today's map showed some splotches of pink, which meant dense fog, but larger areas in green. Depending on where a call came from, this afternoon's victims and patients needing transport might not be stuck with snail's-pace ground level conveyances.

"REMEMBER THE KEYS" was the most prominent alert today, in large letters, tacked over the door we'd just walked through. Did helicopters have ignition keys? If so, did pilots really forget to take them out the door?

"Nice party yesterday," Gil said, bringing any small talk among us to a halt.

Except for the way it ended hung in the air, unspoken. Gil's face indicated that she wished she could take back the words. Our throat clearings and gulps were louder than whatever was clacking around in the dryer.

"Can I get a tour?" Rachel asked.

Gil gave Rachel a look that I couldn't interpret, but it was clear by her expression that being a docent wasn't on Gil's agenda. I sensed that Rachel wasn't that interested anyway, but simply putting off our conversation.

Gil moved quickly out of her unpleasant reaction to Rachel's request. "You bet," she said. She rubbed her hands together, scraping away her inadvertent reminder of the murder of someone close to us, and led the way down the hall.

It was sobering to realize how easily we returned to normal.

I was dismayed to note that my headache was back.

7

I'd visited the MAstar facility many times during my five years with Bruce and learned something new each time. First, that "star" was not a reference to flying up where the heavenly bodies were, but an acronym for "shock, trauma, air rescue." He'd taught me other acronyms, like LZ for "landing zone" and AGL for "above ground level." He'd had me lie down in the back of the aircraft to see how efficiently everything was laid out, each medical supply or instrument with its own slot. I was most impressed by a field EKG system that generated a report and transmitted it to the hospital before the patient arrived.

Today was different, the first time I was here without him. It felt strange to walk by the room he shared with another pilot, knowing he was now most likely napping in his own townhouse bed. I peeked in — once I knew his roommate was outside kicking the tires on the helicopter — and checked out the row of photos on Bruce's side of the dresser. I knew what to expect — small framed shots of the two of us on favorite outings, and a grade school picture of Melanie, his only niece, whom he adored. I felt a pang of missing him and couldn't wait until he was off for seven days, starting Monday morning.

With classes cancelled, that meant we were both off for a stretch and might be able to get out of town for a few days. The scorcher days were perfect for a trip to a sweet Hyannis beach.

It was a nice thought, until I recalled the reason summer school had been interrupted. My gaze fell on Rachel, walking slump-shouldered between Gil and me, her pink flip-flops slapping pitifully on the floor. Something told me not to get psyched for anything other than helping her until further notice. The Cape would have to wait.

We tiptoed past a bedroom with a closed door.

"Don't worry about making noise," Gil said. "You'd never be in this job if you needed a lot of privacy or the comforts of home. But it's the perfect career for a family person."

Rachel registered surprise. "I would have

thought just the opposite."

I knew better. The dynamic worked especially well when both parties had flexible schedules, as was true for Hal and Gil and for Bruce and me. Neither Bruce nor I was a Monday-to-Friday, nine-to-five kind of person, and neither were the Bartholomews, I suspected. It was the perfect combination: an EMS job offered long stretches of days off, and most college teachers, like Hal, had at least one day off a week during the regular semester, ostensibly to do research. Timmy Bartholomew, a kindergartener, was guaranteed to have one parent or the other free to drop him off or pick him up.

"Flight nurses work two twenty-four hour days in a week," Gil told Rachel.

"Like, forty-eight hours straight?"

"Not necessarily. I came on at four o'clock yesterday, and I'll be here until four this afternoon. But of course, we're not usually up and working all those hours. And then" — Gil spread her fingers, palms up — "I'll have four whole days off. Then back for twenty-four, and so on."

Rachel seemed to be considering this trade-off. At this point in her grad school life, even one day off without homework or lab work to think about would appeal to her.

Gil helped us settle in her room, pulling in an extra chair and carrying two glasses of iced tea on a tray. Were all flight nurses this agile?

I was pleased to see a copy of the puzzle I'd handed out at the party lying on top of a stack of puzzle books from my competition. I couldn't help sneaking a look to see how far along Gil had gotten. I ran my finger down the page. Not bad. Maybe Gil would be the one to validate this new entry of mine.

Gil caught me reviewing her work. "Don't you dare tell me how it ends," she said.

I zipped my lip. "Not a chance."

"Gotta go. Mi casa . . ." she said, closing the door behind her.

Gil didn't have to share this room, but the eight-by-ten space could have belonged to anyone in the crew. In fact, Bruce's room had more homey touches, with movie posters on one side (his) and NASCAR images on the other (his roommate's). Gil, on the other hand, had gone with the MAstar-issue dull blue bedspread, kept the walls free of decoration, and had just one photo, of herself with Hal and Timmy on Hal's graduation day.

I wondered if Gil had been ribbed by her colleagues about changing to a more feminine look, and so had changed back. As one of the few women in the graduate mathematics program, I'd had my own minor problems; I imagined Gil would have had even bigger ones. I remembered her mentioning how she chose her nickname.

"Most Gillians use 'Jill' or 'Lil,' " she'd said. "I use 'Gil' so when you're reading it, you might think it's a boy's name, a nickname for 'Gilbert'." She'd emphasized the hard G in Gil and laughed. "It gives me a little head start in getting an assignment. Then I show up and, voila, I'm a girl. But I do a good job, so it's not usually a problem from then on."

I understood perfectly.

Once Gil had left us, it was zero hour for Rachel and me.

Rachel sat on the edge of the bed, allowing me the luxury of the folding chair Gil had dragged in. An open window onto the airfield made the room seem less cramped and stuffy. I looked longingly at a twin engine, wishing I were airborne, or anywhere but here.

It was clear that Rachel wasn't going to start without some prodding. I could tell by the tears that started to well up in her eyes.

This was not my forte. Give me a student scared to death to take a math test or demonstrate how she evaluated a definite integral and I'll boost her confidence and have her ready well within her timeframe. I'd also had my share of successes in getting a girl back on her feet after being dumped by a cruel boy from another school. But a murder suspect looking to me for help — that was beyond the scope of my experience. I hoped I could get up to speed in a hurry.

I plunged in.

"Rachel, tell me what happened when you brought the plate of food to Dr. Appleton yesterday." Was it just yesterday?

Now her tears came in torrents, her sobs beating a quiet, steady rhythm. At least Gil's room was equipped with tissues. I handed her the box.

"You have to talk to me, Rachel."

I heard a thunderous clattering in response.

Clack. Clack. Clack. Clack. Clack. Clack.

The Bat Phone.

We covered our ears. I thought the pummeling sound would never stop.

Besides the assault from the Bat Phone, there was so much stomping and loud activity in the hallway that I was afraid to open the door.

I heard a man shout, "Four-vehicle crash on Route Three Southbound near the Sagamore."

Then, Gil's voice: "Code yellow, everyone."

I'd never been here when a call came. My heart raced as if I, too, had to suit up and rush out. I took a breath and told myself no one's life depended on me.

"Did she say code yellow?" Rachel asked. "I would have expected code red or code blue." She shuddered.

I was quick to share my insider knowledge with Rachel. "Code yellow reminds the crew to go at a sensible pace. Too fast and they might slip up; too slow and they'll blow their mission. Yellow means just right."

Seconds later, Gil crashed into her room. " 'Scuse me," she said.

She zipped her flight suit to the top of her very fit body, hooked a radio onto her belt, and grabbed her helmet from one corner and a backpack from another, in seamless, swift motions. Army Reserve training, I guessed, reinforced by all her jobs since. Rachel and I both went stiff, not moving a muscle, lest we interrupt the choreography. Gil dashed from the room as quickly as she'd entered, leaving the flimsy brown door to swing in its frame.

The clamor had shifted to the airfield where MAstar's helicopter was parked. Rachel and I turned to look out the window. A pilot — the PIC, pilot in command, as the in-group knew — was already in his seat. The tall, lanky guy next to the pilot in the front was one of two flight nurses that made up the group of three who responded to every call. Gil ran to the back of the aircraft and climbed in and they were up in a flash, maybe five minutes total from the call to liftoff.

I thought of Bruce. This was a regular part of his job, if not every day, then at least a few times a week. It's what he was here for. I hoped I'd be able to see him in action some time. As the helicopter became smaller and smaller in the air, I hoped most that wherever the MAstar crew was off to, they arrived in time to help.

I felt like saluting.

I turned to Rachel. "Well, that was exciting," I said.

And we both laughed.

With everyone gone on their mission, Rachel and I moved to the trailer living room, which sported dark brown leather-like chairs and a sofa, a combination television set and DVD player, and a wood-like coffee table. Magazines and DVDs were stacked neatly in a rack. No sign of a used glass or plate; no socks or towels flung around. The only stray item was a single remote control that was lined up with the edge of the coffee table. I wondered if the room was always this neat or if someone had picked up for our benefit this morning.

Knowing Bruce and the spit-polish code of order that seemed to prevail for military types, I guessed that even though the MA-star trailer was a sort of male bastion, these were males who'd had a heavy dose of neatness training.

We had a lot more space in this room, plus the dubious benefit of a barely working air conditioner. Rachel sniffed and cleared her throat. Her upright posture and firm expression indicated that she'd gotten over her crying jag and was ready to talk. Maybe the urgency of the flight mission had gotten to her and put things in perspective. She might be in trouble, but she was not sprawled on a highway or trapped in her car.

I sat waiting, a welcoming expression on my face.

"I lied, Dr. Knowles."

No, no, no. A chill overtook my body, and it didn't come from the low-end A/C unit.

Had I been that far off about my assistant? A woman I thought of as a friend? In an uncontrollable reflex, my eyes shot to the exit sign over the door. If not my rational self, some part of me seemed to think I was closeted in a trailer with a murderer.

Rachel didn't look like a killer, sitting there with her arms wrapped around herself, her straggly hair and faded jean shorts, frayed at the bottom, giving her a waiflike look. When she held a wad of tissues to her face and blew her nose loudly, it was almost comforting. Killers don't do that, I told myself uselessly.

I stared at a point over Rachel's shoulder where there was a map of the MAstar bases, eleven of them in all, spread across the state. I wondered if they were all on missions now and if any of their empty trailers were serving as confessionals. As for speaking, the best I could do was mimic a radio talk show host.

"I'm listening," I said.

"You're going to hate me."

"I won't hate you, Rachel." Unless . . . I bit my tongue.

"At the party, okay?"

I nodded. "Okay."

"I picked up a piece of the cake from the table and grabbed a can of soda to take to

Dr. Appleton, okay?"

"Okay."

"And I went upstairs, okay?" She paused to take care of her nose again. "When I said I knocked on Dr. Appleton's door and he didn't answer? That was the lie."

"Okay." I was getting into Rachel's rhythm. "So Dr. Appleton did answer the door?"

"No."

"You didn't knock?"

She shook her head. "No."

Bad question when the answer is ambiguous. I could see that I'd need to go into puzzle-solving mode to move this along. "The door was open."

"Yes."

Finally, getting somewhere. Possibly.

"You went in," I guessed.

Rachel nodded slowly and sucked in her breath; her eyes went wide. "You could see his legs, on the floor behind his desk. I put the food on the chair near his computer table and I tiptoed over to look in case I could help him get up or something, but I was scared because I knew he'd yell at me if he was busy down there."

"Busy on the floor?"

"Like, looking for something he dropped? Or going through the bottom drawer?"

I hadn't thought of those possibilities. "But he wasn't busy."

"No."

"What did you see, Rachel?"

She took a breath. "His shirt was torn open and you could see his undershirt. And his face was all red and his eyes" — Rachel closed her eyes as if her professor's body was in front of her at this moment in immodest attire, a lascivious look on his face — "I couldn't look. I didn't touch him, but I knew he was dead. I picked up the food and ran out. Then I put the plate and soda outside the door, to make it look as if I'd never gone in."

I let out a big sigh, feeling like I'd been at the scene myself and just got out in time before losing my lunch. I threw up my hands. "Why didn't you call the police, Rachel? Or at least let someone know? Anyone." I tried to keep my voice even.

"Everyone knows how bad things are going with my research, and you said yourself how I've been mouthing off lately. I was scared someone would think I did it."

I didn't feel it necessary to remind her that a very important someone did think she did it. And maybe wouldn't have, if she'd simply reported what she walked in on. She might have been just another suspect, instead of sticking out like a prime number.

"You have to tell the police. You have valuable information that they can use in a murder investigation. Don't you see how important this is?"

"It's not like I actually saw anything."

"You saw a dead body at a certain time and place yesterday. If nothing else, that helps establish a timeline."

"I guess."

"You guess?" I paused. The last thing Rachel needed was my anxiety-ridden response. I lowered my voice. "You have to promise me that you'll go to the police station. In fact, you can come with me this afternoon. I have an interview there myself."

I'd made it sound as though I'd initiated the meeting with Archie. Archie cop, me reporter.

Rachel pointed across the room to an old, round fan on a high stand. "It's roasting in here. Can we turn that on?"

"If it works." No promises from her about making a trip downtown, I noticed.

We shared the chore: moving the fan, finding a socket, adjusting the speed — all very legitimate distractions while Rachel stalled and stalled. I tried to think of another occasion when she'd put off a distasteful task. I couldn't. Not even when she worked on the biology floor.

"What else can you remember? What did the office look like?"

"Just his regular office stuff. But his desk was a mess and, you know, it's usually in perfect order."

"Did the police tell you what they found?"

"They didn't tell me much, except that Dr. Appleton had been poisoned, and that they were talking to everyone in the building. But I knew it was more than just routine with me because they asked me things like did I work more closely with Dr. Appleton than the undergraduates, and did I have a key to the chemical cabinet."

"What did you tell them?"

"I just said how Dr. Appleton was a strict teacher, but people respected him for it, and I was glad I had him for an adviser. I guess all that was another lie, but I wasn't going to make myself look worse."

"And the key to cabinet?

"I told them the truth but then when they asked me where it was, I couldn't find it. It's always on a separate key ring in my purse, the one you gave me, with the metal pi symbol on it? But I went to get it, and it wasn't there, Dr. Knowles. I lost it."

Or someone took it.

I didn't know too many legal terms, but premeditated was one that stood out. If someone went to the trouble of stealing Rachel's key ahead of time, then Keith's murder wasn't a random act, in the heat of an argument, but a well thought out frame-up of Rachel.

From outside, I heard the sound of a plane taking off. At least this time it was not an emergency mission, but one of the many small plane owners treating friends or relatives to a bird's-eye view of the beautiful New England landscape.

"Rachel, you said Dr. Appleton's desk was a mess. Did you see anything in particular that was . . . out of place? Papers strewn about? Anything like that?"

She frowned, thinking, then shook her head. "Not that I remember. I think his lamp was knocked over, but I'm not sure. I was only in there, like, a minute."

"So no yellow computer paper everywhere, for example?"

"You mean like what we use for drafts?"

"Maybe."

Rachel bit her lip. More thinking. "No, I think I'd remember that."

I tried to keep track of the inconsistencies without taking notes, which I was afraid would intimidate my witness. The crime scene people had not found the cake Rachel said she left outside the door, but they had found pages of Rachel's thesis on yellow paper, which Rachel had not seen.

A medium hard puzzle, I told myself, not impossible, once I have a little more information. And as long as I can trust Rachel to tell the truth from now on.

"Did you see anyone else in the corridor, when you arrived or when you left?"

"No, you know no one stays around on Friday afternoons except for a party."

"Did you see Woody, by any chance?"

Rachel twisted her lips in concentration, as she did when she was assembling a graphing lab for me. "I might have heard him. There was definitely some noise when I got there. It could have been Woody's cart rolling down the other wing."

I wondered why the police hadn't told Rachel that pages of her thesis had been crumpled up and thrown around the late Keith Appleton's office. I debated whether to tell her now. Virgil hadn't exactly sworn me to secrecy.

Another time, I decided. Rachel needed a breather from her intense confession.

And I had a cop to meet.

8

As I drove toward town, rolling around in my head was a big question: What obligation did I have to tell the police about Rachel's lie? It wasn't as if she'd confessed to murder, but the simple fact of withholding information from the police was a crime, wasn't it? If I didn't report Rachel, were we dealing with crime squared?

I wondered if I could trust Virgil with my question. I doubted it. Not after the ridiculous performance I'd given last night. I had to hope that Rachel herself, who'd declined my invitation to accompany me to the police station, would see the light and be completely forthcoming before she had to be grilled under a bare bulb.

The Henley skyline was coming into view, the golden dome of its city hall sparkling in the sun. The dome essentially *was* Henley's skyline, sitting atop its tallest building. Henley was a three-exit town these days, four if you counted the outlying one that led to and from the airfield. In the direction I was traveling, the next exit would take me to what was formerly an industrial area where all that was left were rows of abandoned factories, a few of which had been turned into warehouses. The following exit ramp ended up downtown, where the police station awaited me; the one after that, the last exit, practically flowed into the college campus.

My appointed time with Detective Archie loomed in my mind, but I had about an hour and forty-five minutes to spare. Thanks to my cheekiness, which put me in an apologetic mood, he now had an advantage, even more than his cop status gave him. I wondered what his birthday was. Knowing it always helped me get a handle on a person. Bruce claimed that knowing a person's favorite movie — if you could upload only one to your smartphone — told him everything he needed to know.

I'd done nothing to prepare for my two brushes with law enforcement this weekend. Big mistakes. I had to turn that around and I couldn't do it without trying to anticipate what Archie might ask and prepare an answer that spoke of complete cooperation.

Either that, or I needed more information

in my own arsenal.

Without further thought, I drove past the downtown exit and the police station and headed for the off-ramp that led to campus. I couldn't help myself. I had the gall to think that I might find something the police overlooked, maybe a scrap with scientific notation they weren't used to. To be honest, I also wanted to check on Franklin Hall. The only way I could explain that, if anyone asked, was that I was worried about the building and how it had survived this crushing blow. A silly reaction, as if the building itself had been affected by Keith's murder.

From a distance of a few hundred yards, nothing looked different. The administration building tower, taller than Franklin Hall's, was still intact; the surrounding brick buildings had the same aura of steam as yesterday from the heat wave that wouldn't quit. The various grottos with statues of our founders were standing in their proper places, as were the small fountain behind Admin and the blooming flowers around the library.

There was a significant lack of fun-loving students kicking up sprays of water.

I'd driven onto the campus from the south side, between Admin and the library. The walkways were empty, but that wasn't too strange for a Saturday afternoon, especially one that was a good beach day for those lucky enough to have houses or friends with houses on the Cape.

The lot closest to Franklin Hall had no cars. Evacuated, you might say. I didn't know what I expected, but the building I worked in stood there, same as always, red brick, one big solid figure shaped like an L with a slightly thicker short side. I saw no crime scene tape on the outside of the building, and no police presence. Had the facility I called home already been cleared by the police? All the better for them to be able to concentrate on interviewing people. Lucky for me.

I got out of my car and walked slowly up to the building. With every step I had to remind myself that there was no longer a dead body on the fourth floor. That didn't mean there was no one lurking on the first floor — my floor — however. I scanned the windows, not knowing which I preferred, signs of life or of emptiness. All that reflected back to me were the stark rays of the sun.

I climbed the stately steps under the clock tower, fumbling for my key to the large, heavy front door. I couldn't remember the last time I'd had to use it. I was almost never the first one to arrive. I preferred late morning classes and had the seniority to make the schedule work for me. When I did drop in on an occasional Saturday, I'd find at least a few people, students or faculty, cramming in the science library or grinding out what they hoped would be useful data in one of the labs at the last minute.

Not today. Inside, the building was as creepy as I thought it would be. The interior hallways were always relatively dark, and even more so now since Woody drew all the shades in the labs and classrooms in the summer. The contrast with the glaring sunlight outside blinded me for several seconds, the short fluorescent light in the display case at the entrance offering very little help. I wished I had Bruce's fifteen thousand dollar goggles.

I half expected to see Keith walking down the corridor toward me with his quick, purposeful stride, calling out a greeting then immediately engaging me in a discussion of a contentious issue. Faculty perks, student government representation on faculty committees, science requirements for humanities majors. Not even the choice of graduation speaker escaped his scrutiny. Of all the faculty, he'd be the one most likely to be here on a Saturday or Sunday. He'd be in a trademark striped shirt, long-sleeved in the winter, short-sleeved in the summer. His light brown hair would be neatly combed and his shoes polished. Never in a T-shirt as the rest of us would wear on an off day; never in jeans.

I regretted all the times I'd joined in making fun of his narrow wardrobe choices, and would have given anything to have him back.

Rachel's presence was here today also. She'd taken it upon herself to manage the glass-fronted display case, the first thing a visitor saw upon entering the building. It had gone for years with yellowed construction paper stapled to the back, broken push-pins holding a wildly out-of-date class schedule and various illegible notices, and an array of deceased insects on the ledge at the bottom.

Rachel had cleaned it all out and made a banner for the top of the case, an attractive photo presentation of the people and facilities of the four Franklin Hall departments. She'd stripped out the old construction paper and installed a clean corkboard. The former eyesore was now an inviting source of information that everyone checked on a regular basis.

This week she'd posted what looked like an oversized scrapbook page about a group of high school seniors who'd spent a week in a special program to prepare them for their first college math classes. She'd arranged photos, problem sheets, and contact information, along with souvenir ticket stubs from a performance they'd all attended. I studied Rachel's image in a photo of her in the student lounge with a crowd of teenagers around her. She was smiling broadly; it was clear they loved her.

I knew if she'd been able to, Rachel would already have put up photos from yesterday's party for the new Dr. Hal Bartholomew.

This was not the profile of a killer.

I had no desire to check in at my own office. I wanted to get in and get out of the building in a short time to minimize the chances of meeting danger, that is, coming upon a killer. Never mind that it made no sense that he'd still be hanging around. I had to admit also that I was a little creeped out at the possibility of finding an unwelcome something, or someone, on my own office floor.

I needed to get up to the fourth floor. My quandary: take the elevator or use the stairs? Ordinarily, unless I was carrying a heavy load of books and papers, I'd walk up, as a gesture toward fitness. Today I was lugging only a light fabric purse. But stairwells were notoriously scary, full of hollow sounds and creaking boards. I recalled a few dozen movies where nasty things happened through the door marked "STAIRS." Didn't fugitives enter and exit that way? Didn't hit men wait there?

Riding in the elevator wasn't that appealing either. Bruce, I knew would have reminded me of the elevator scene in *The Silence of the Lambs.* Brownouts were all too common during heat waves like the one we were suffering through. Even barring nefarious characters lurking about today, if there was a power outage, I'd have no hope of rescue.

In the interests of speed, and trusting technology more than the criminal element, real or imagined, I took the elevator. The ages old car rattled up past physics to the biology floor, where unpleasant odors seeped through the cracks, and then to chemistry. There was something to the old joke about how you could tell which floor you were on in Franklin Hall: If it smells, it's biology; if there's a glow, it's chemistry; if something's not working, it's physics. No one had come up with a good description of mathematics. That suited me just fine. I'd never tell.

The trip seemed endless. I pushed the

button for the fourth floor repeatedly. It was a wonder I didn't accidentally hit the red alarm knob. Finally, I stepped out in one piece and breathed a sigh of relief.

Keith's office was far down the hallway to the right, the last office in the crook of the L, overlooking the tennis courts. Every step I took toward that goal generated a loud echo. Every intake of breath seemed to bring a new, unpleasant smell to my nose.

I walked by familiar signs on the bulletin boards on both sides of the hallway.

My favorite had always been the cartoon-illustrated flyer listing "Six Major Dangers" in a chemistry lab. Burns, fires, spills, cuts, hazardous waste, and the one that stood out among all the rest today: poisons.

The vast number of warning signs seemed to be mocking me as I made my way toward Keith's office. "DON'T HEAT A STOPPERED FLASK," said one. "WEAR GLOVES WHEN CLEANING SPILLS," shouted another, and "KNOW PROPER DISPOSAL PROCEDURES," read another.

I would have bet that Keith was responsible for many of the signs and warnings. He was probably the most safety and security conscious faculty member in the building. A lot of good it had done him.

As I approached Keith's office, I could see that the crime scene tape had fallen from the doorframe, the last several feet of it lying in a heap to the side, daring me to go in. I reasoned that a dangling piece of tape simply meant that a policeman had been a little sloppy in removing the warning. He'd fully intended to let the world know the room was now open to the public. Like me.

For no good reason, I used the hem of my shirt to turn the knob. You might have thought I'd chosen my wardrobe in anticipation of breaking and entering. I was wearing a brown paisley top, which wouldn't show dust marks, over black cotton pants. The real reason for the conservative dress was to look serious for my interview at the police station, in case Archie's personality ran parallel to that of Henley's dean. The door opened easily and I stepped into Keith's office, as I had many times in the past.

But this was a different room, matching neither the way I'd always seen it, nor the description Virgil had given me of it as a crime scene.

Not a surprise: The office had been stripped of the main pieces of evidence — I saw no lethal bottle of potassium chloride and no yellow pages that were allegedly from Rachel's thesis. There was no white chalk line on the floor as I'd envisioned either. Today's law enforcement officers had new techniques, I supposed. I checked the trash for the party cake, in case no one thought to look there.

Only Keith's bookcases and the walls of his office looked as they did the last time I was here. Two walls were peppered with degrees, certificates, and photographs of Keith with distinguished scientists. Here and there were framed articles of his that had appeared in technical journals. I couldn't imagine doing that with my own articles, but that was Keith.

"If we don't promote ourselves, no one will," he'd said often.

Whatever works, I'd thought.

His newest award, the designation as Fellow for his distinguished participation in the Massachusetts Association of Chemists, hung front and center on the Keith A. Wall, or, alternately, the Apep Wall, as I'd heard the students call it. There wasn't a single family picture. There never had been.

I stood still, continuing my efforts to absorb the reality of Keith's death. I was ashamed that I'd come here partly out of curiosity, like rubberneckers unable to avert their eyes from an accident on the highway.

I wasn't proud of the other reason either, that I thought I was smarter than the police — hadn't I already proven otherwise, in several orders of magnitude? — and that I'd be able to see at a glance something they'd missed. Something that would exonerate Rachel, if not point directly to Keith's real killer.

Now that I was here, however, it behooved me to at least make myself useful. I looked around. Keith's bookcases were intact, as was an open magazine rack in which he always kept the latest technical journals. A black mesh organizer that held rubber bands and paper clips neatly separated had been left in its place at the corner of the desk.

A short side desk, where Keith had kept his laptop, stood empty.

I'd assumed the police would have confiscated Keith's computer. The last time I'd seen him in his office, a few days ago, he'd been updating his organic chemistry grade sheet and complaining about the poor quality of students in his class. No one above a C, he'd said. I'd thought of recommending a peer review of his teaching style. Now I was glad I hadn't.

I wished I could have had a look at his computer files. As I tugged at his desk drawers, I saw that the police hadn't completely emptied them, though they'd definitely been rummaging and probably had taken a significant bundle away. I pulled open the shallow middle drawer. Pens and pencils were arranged next to each other on a long built-in tray. The rest of the space held a familiar folder with Henley College letterhead and its blue-and-gold Henley seal, issued to every faculty member. Nothing else crowded the drawer.

My own middle drawer, on the other hand, had the same items, but tangled together and mixed with eraser shavings and cough drop wrappers.

I moved on to the top right drawer, which held full-size file folders. Here, also, were signs both of Keith's neatness and the slight disruption of order by the police. I imagined their going through every folder, taking only what seemed relevant, and wondered how they'd made their decisions so quickly.

I noted the labels on the manila folders and recognized committee names and issues actively being debated at faculty meetings. Keith was into every facet of life at Henley, from academic standards to fundraising to administrative policies and procedures. I was convinced that something in this office held the key to his murder, but I wouldn't have been able to explain why I thought the police might have passed over that all-important clue.

I wished I could settle myself in his leather chair, which belonged to him personally, and read through everything.

A rattling sound out in the hallway brought my rummaging to a halt and reminded me that getting comfortable here was not a good idea. Something or someone was bumping along the tile floor.

I took some calming breaths. No bad guy bent on malicious mischief would make that much noise. In fact, the sound was familiar, and one that Rachel had described, the sound of a large barrel on wheels, being driven by a janitor.

In a few seconds, Woody Conroy appeared in the doorway wearing his denim overalls and looking, as usual, well past retirement age. He'd been about to call it a career last year, but his wife of forty years died suddenly and he couldn't bear to be home alone all day. We were glad to keep him occupied.

"Afternoon, Dr. Knowles. Surprised to see you here today."

"Hi, Woody."

While I fumbled for something other than "I happened to be in the neighborhood,"

Woody went on with his own agenda.

"Isn't it awful what happened here?"

"It certainly is."

Woody shook his bald head and rocked on the heels of his thick work shoes. "Never in my life, and I'm an old man, did I see anything like that."

As I understood the crime, it was about as bloodless as you could get. But the impact of the scene, gory or not, would have been tremendous for whoever was unlucky enough to be the first to come upon it.

I wondered how soon I could interview this first-on-the-scene person without being thought too insensitive. I waded in.

"You must have been very upset, Woody. I'm sorry for Dr. Appleton and I'm sorry you had to see him that way."

"I hear things, you know, and I know a lot of people thought Dr. Appleton was mean or stuck up or just ornery. But he was always nice to me, always said thank you when he saw me taking out his trash."

What a surprise. "I'm glad to hear that."

Woody opened his denim shirt a bit and showed me a familiar Henley College logo T-shirt in blue and gold, the school colors. "He give me this for my birthday."

What? I who prided myself on knowing birthdays did not know our janitor's, and

Keith Appleton not only knew it but gave him a present? I could hardly stand it.

"How nice of him," I said. "When is your birthday, Woody?"

"May twentieth."

"Like Cher," I said.

"What's that, Dr. Knowles?"

"Never mind."

Woody took my comment as liberty for him to go on about the great Keith Appleton. "Well, there was also that time I was off a couple of weeks with pneumonia, he give me a little something to help out. Not that I asked, but he slips me a check one day and says how I probably could use a bit to tide me over while I got back on my feet."

Stunned, would have been putting it mildly. Keith the Good Samaritan? Keith the champion of the worker?

"He was kindhearted," I said, astonishing myself.

"No matter what anyone thinks, he was a man, you know, and no man deserves that." Woody pointed over my shoulder into Keith's office, where *that* had happened.

"You're absolutely right, Woody," I said, and meant it.

When Woody left, surprisingly not asking what I was doing in the deceased's office, I shook myself into focus. Information, clues, I told myself. You're here to work.

I went back to the desk and opened the second of the file drawers. This one had folders with names of students I recognized as Keith's chemistry majors. I flipped through and saw term paper after term paper. Again, I was overwhelmed with the desire to hide in a corner of the office and read every scrap of what the drawers contained. Now that I knew Woody was around, I felt more comfortable, as if an old man past retirement was all the protection I'd need against a murderer. I was glad neither Woody nor I would be here after sunset.

More noise in the hallway. Woody was back in the doorway, this time with a dolly piled high with empty cardboard boxes.

"This should be enough to start with, Dr. Knowles. Dean Underwood didn't tell me who she was sending over to clean out Dr. Appleton's office but I guess you're it."

No wonder Woody hadn't questioned my appearance at the crime scene. "Uh —" I stammered.

"Except I should tell you that I said to her, that'd be Dean Underwood, that, much as I like my job, there's just so much I'm willing to do. And goin' through the belongings of a person who'd just passed in that

150

awful way" — Woody paused and bowed his head, his skinny old hands resting on the handle of the dolly — "well, that wasn't one of them. So she said she'd send someone over to pack everything up, and then she wanted the boxes taken over there to her office."

I cleared my throat and forced an informed expression on my face. "Yes, well —"

"You sure got here fast, by the way."

"I was close by."

Woody gestured to the boxes behind him. "I brought these up from the cellar. Let me know if you need any more."

Could I pull this off? At least temporarily, why not? "That's super, Woody. I'll get started right away." Before my jig is up.

The old man dragged the empty boxes off the dolly, one or two at a time, and planted them in the doorway of Keith's office. I wondered if he'd ever go any farther. Given the small amount of time he had left to his career, probably not.

Woody pointed to the new addition to Keith's award wall.

"I come up here special to hang that new frame yesterday morning. Dr. Appleton wasn't in yet, but I wanted him to be surprised at how quick I did it. Now I don't

151

know if he even saw it more than a minute. I didn't spot his car out there until close to about noon, and I don't know when he" — Woody gulped, sending his Adam's apple on a trip along his throat — "you know . . . passed."

Noon. The same bracket Virgil had mentioned for the time of Keith's murder. Some time between noon and four o'clock when Woody found him behind his desk. How clever of the police to ask Woody that question. They were so thorough, maybe I was wasting my time.

On the other hand, here I was, standing between Keith's full file drawers, a dolly full of empty boxes, and a mandate from the dean to an anonymous person who might as well be me. I needed to get to it.

"I'm sure Dr. Appleton appreciated everything you did, Woody" — I pointed to the boxes — "and so do I." A gentle dismissal.

"Thanks, Dr. Knowles. Holler when you're ready to take them to your car. Probably best if you drive them over to the delivery door of Admin 'stead of pushing this dolly all across the campus."

"That's just what I'll do," I said, not mentioning the little detour I'd planned to my garage. I could bring the boxes back any time over the weekend, once I'd gone through everything. It's not like the dean needed anything inside them, or was hanging around waiting for the delivery.

Woody brushed dust off his bony hands. "I don't know who's going to want to use this office now."

I hadn't thought of that. And it occurred to me that Woody could be of even more use to me. I patted him on the hand. "I'll bet you remember every detail of the scene and will remember it for a long time." I cringed. I was such a hypocrite.

"You betcha I remember, Dr. Knowles. Everything tossed around like that" — Woody waved his arms around to indicate chaos — "all the papers, and the lamp, and the food and all."

"Food?" Did Woody say food? "Did you say food?" The word seemed to have a life of its own.

"Uh-huh, there was this pretty little paper plate with cake from the party downstairs, and a couple of cookies, and a can of cola" — he pointed to the chair tucked under the small desk — "right there."

I replayed my conversation with Virgil. No cake, no food, no drink he'd said. He'd flipped through his notes right there in my den and come up empty on edibles and potables. Rachel, on the other hand had claimed she left the cake outside the door. Now Woody was saying he saw the cake, but on a chair in the office. My head reeled.

"And you're sure, Woody — 'cause I know that scene must be so clear in your head."

"You betcha." Woody leaned over his barrel, his personal shield against the ill-fated office, and probably as close as he would venture for a while. "I got rid of it, you know, while I was waiting for the police to show up," he whispered.

I felt my heart beating up higher in my chest than it should have been. "You got rid of the food? Why did you do that, Woody?"

You destroyed evidence, I wanted to shout. But it was more evidence that worked against Rachel, who'd told the police she never entered the office, and who'd told me she'd — very confusing. So was I glad Woody tossed it, or not?

Why was this all so complicated? Why wasn't it like one of those simple yet fascinating puzzles where all you had to do was fill in a grid of letters, given a few clues like P is next to L, which is above Q but below G?

I looked at Woody. Apparently, although I hadn't shouted, the old man picked up on my distress. He clutched the rim of his barrel.

"I probably shouldn't have done it, but I thought Dr. Appleton would have wanted me to take that food away. First off, he always gave me things like that when anyone brought him something."

Another point for Keith, feeding the help.

"Did you eat the cake, then?" I asked without thinking.

Woody looked horrified. " 'Course not."

I chided myself: bad move, Sophie. "Of course you didn't, Woody. I'm just a little upset, like you. I'm not myself today."

"Oh, I know what you mean, Dr. Knowles. See, Dr. Appleton, he never allowed dirty plates or leftover food in his office. He wouldn't never leave cake or nothing just sitting around on a chair like that. Sometimes I'd see him right after he ate his lunch in there, carrying his bag of trash, and he'd toss it down the chute, and he'd say thanks to me even though he done it hisself. Like he knew I'm the one that takes it away in the end."

I could barely grasp this new Keith Appleton, who thanked people and gave them unsolicited presents.

Woody wiped away the beginning of a tear and went on. "I couldn't pick up all the stuff that was broke, but I figured I could at least take away that messy plate. It was the least I could do for him."

Woody set his chin with a determined, proud look, and I thought maybe he was the one person at Henley who genuinely liked Keith and whom Keith respected.

How could I blame him for trying to uphold his friend's reputation for neatness and order?

I had one more thing to clear up, once Woody was stable.

"I hear you saw Rachel Wheeler outside this door yesterday. Do you remember what time that was?"

"Yes, ma'am, Dr. Knowles. I know she's your friend and all and I didn't mean to get her in trouble or nothing, but I saw her while that party was going on. I figured I better tell the police everything."

Except for that little matter of disposing of evidence at a murder scene. "And you didn't see anyone else?"

Woody shook his head. "Just her. I come by the closet over there to pick up my rags for cleaning. Anyway, no way a sweet young kid like that did anything bad, and I'm sure everyone knows that."

I sincerely hoped so.

9

Alone again in Keith's office, I got back to my task. I piled what was left of his folders and binders into boxes. Each time I emptied a cabinet or a drawer of Keith's desk, I had the urge to mark the piece of furniture for salvage. I wondered what the administration would do with the office and furnishings. I hoped at least they'd redo the whole place before reassigning it, bad vibes and all, to some unsuspecting freshman teacher.

I worked quickly. By now I'd convinced myself that I really had been sent by the dean. I told myself that there might well be a voice mail from her on my cell, which I'd turned off before entering the building, or on my home phone, which I could access but chose not to.

"Dr. Knowles, please go to Dr. Appleton's office and take away everything but the office furniture," she might have said.

On the off chance that I wasn't the legitimate designee, I tossed material into the boxes without looking too closely, for the sake of speed. I counted on the fact that any sane faculty member — that would be the dean's actual designee — would wait until Monday to carry out an ad hoc task she'd assigned him.

All the drawers were unlocked but showed signs of having been manipulated by police tools. Another good reason for me to take them — the police had already declared them useless. It felt strange to fling grade books, lab logs, and even a little black address book into a box for later examination, not only because their owner was dead, but because Keith Appleton was undoubtedly the most private person I knew.

When he inhabited this office, he kept all his drawers locked. If you wanted a piece of paper from him, you had to wait until he unlocked a drawer or file cabinet, took out the document, then locked the drawer again. Now here it all was, available to anyone. To anyone foolish enough to be here on a Saturday afternoon.

When I finished, I decided not to call Woody for help loading the boxes into my car. Maybe he was taking quiet moments to grieve for his friend. Or maybe the real delegate from the dean had contacted him.

With the help of the metal dolly he'd left in the hallway, I could manage by myself.

I rolled my baggage back down the hall, noting the special building safety features Keith had added. Under the fire extinguisher was a metal box that I knew contained a fire blanket and first aid supplies. I remembered the Franklin faculty meeting when he'd made the proposal to outfit each floor with the kits.

Another time he'd come with a brochure from a company that made laboratory safety glasses out of recycled composition notebooks. We teased behind his back, asking each other what new thing Keith would come up with for the next meeting. We called him at various times, Green Keith and School Monitor Keith.

Now he was Deceased Keith. I felt the tension in my jaws increase with each step. I needed to stop the tape running in my head. Maybe whatever was in these boxes would hold the answer to the problem that kept me in this wrecked state.

I pulled my heavy load onto the elevator and pushed B for the basement, where there was a side door at ground level. Trying to get a loaded dolly down Franklin's white marble front steps would not be a pretty sight. I hurried along a dark hallway, past storage areas and the noisy generator room. The wheels of the red dolly rumbled by entirely too many dark and dusty nooks and crannies. I hated coming down here when the building was alive with classes; the eerie feeling and musty smell were even worse on a day like today, hot and scary and reeking of death.

I reached the exit at last, fully expecting to see Dean Underwood waiting as I opened the exterior door to Franklin's back pathway. I was ready with an answer. "Oh," I'd say, "I must have misunderstood Woody. I thought he said you told him that I was to clear Keith's office."

I moved the dolly in position, pushed the heavy door open, and dragged the load to the threshold.

No Dean Underwood with arms folded to greet me as I'd envisioned.

Instead there was a committee.

"Hey, Dr. Knowles," Pam Noonan said.

Liz Harrison and Casey Tremel stood on either side of her, blocking the path that led around the building to the parking lot. Pam and Liz wore denim cutoffs; Casey had gone for a spongy blue and brown trellis print that was popular in the seventies. They all had "aha" looks on their sweet young faces.

"Hey," I said.

I couldn't have been more disoriented if Virgil had been standing there with uniformed officers, holding out a set of handcuffs. I hadn't remembered to put my glasses on for the transition from the cavelike basement to the blazing sun. I squinted and thought I must have looked like a thief caught red-handed. Maybe because it was true.

"Need some help?" Liz asked.

"We've been dying to come over, but we knew the building was locked," Casey said, the clinking of her bracelets nearly drowning her out.

"Then we saw you go in." Back to Pam.

"We called you on your cell."

"We hoped you'd answer and let us in while you were in there."

"We've been watching for you to come out."

The trio, all junior chemistry majors, sounded like a Greek chorus, except that each girl took one line, in rotation.

I was acutely aware that the door to the Franklin Hall basement was open, being held in that position by the large dolly. Its chipped red paint seemed to glow where sunlight hit. The boxes it carried might have contained body parts for the anxiety I felt. *These are your students,* I told myself. *They have no power over you.* In fact, they were all in my applied statistics seminar this summer and I hadn't turned in their grades yet. Talk about power.

"You saw me all the way from the dorm? Aren't you in Paul Revere?" The residence hall that was farthest from Ben Franklin.

"We were sitting in the library," Pam said, pointing to the closest building, at the Henley Boulevard entrance to campus.

One wing of the Emily Dickinson Library jutted out past the entrance to Franklin. If the girls had been sitting there, they'd have a clear view of the parking lot and the south side of the math and sciences building.

"When we heard a car pull in, we all rushed to the window." From Casey.

"There's not much going on this weekend," Liz added.

"Except it's kind of cool to see what they're doing to accommodate the guys in the fall. Most of them will be in Revere because the bathrooms are bigger and they can, you know, fix them," Casey said.

Fascinating.

Pam pointed past me to the inside of Franklin Hall. "Can we go — ?"

"Not a chance," I said.

Message received, I noticed, as the girls dropped their shoulders and sighed.

Maybe it was all the texting we did these days that enabled this kind of shorthand communication even without the benefit of an electronic device.

"What's in the boxes?" Casey asked me, eyes on the dolly.

Not a chance I'd answer that question.

"Don't you think you're all being just a little bit disrespectful?" I asked. I stepped in front of the upright dolly and folded my arms. "One of your major teachers has been killed on this campus, in the building you practically live in every day. Hasn't that hit home to you? There's been a murder in Benjamin Franklin Hall and someone who cared about you and your education is dead. And until we find out who killed him, none of us is safe."

I'd accomplished my goal. All three girls looked sheepish and frightened. They shuffled their feet and looked over their shoulders. I had the sense that if it had been nighttime, they would have clutched each other, or joined hands and run.

"Do the cops have any idea who did it?" Pam asked, in a considerably more diffident tone than before my speech.

"No. And come to think of it, can you all account for where you were from noon to four yesterday?" Rachel had given me a smaller window for Keith's murder but I decided to stick to what the police were using.

Casey let out a little gasp. "I told you we should —" she began, addressing Pam.

Pam threw her arm out to Casey's chest, interrupting her friend. "Casey," she said, in a warning tone. "Like we told the police. We were at the party, like everybody else, then we went to the dorm."

"We didn't —" Liz began.

A look from Pam stopped her.

Very curious. "Have you all talked to the police?"

"They interviewed everyone last night," Pam said.

"Remember when we called and told you?" Casey asked me.

Pam gave her a look of approval, mixed with "but not another word."

I remembered the call last night, and now wished I'd taken advantage of the opportunity to quiz them, instead of virtually hanging up on them.

I wasn't prepared for the girls' behavior — suspicious, I thought, but given my state of mind, I could have been way off. As far as I knew Pam and Liz were doing all right academically, but Casey was on the edge of a passing grade in Keith's organic chemistry class. To everyone's surprise, he'd offered a makeup class this summer for the benefit of students like Casey. Their last shot.

I put the girls on my mental list of suspects, but only to add to the pool so Rachel wouldn't be alone. A few stuttering remarks weren't damning, but certainly called for a closer look. The idea of one or all them as killers seemed ludicrous at the moment, as they stood there, angelic and vulnerable in their crop tops and brightly painted toenails.

I needed a serious sit-down with them but not now. I couldn't afford to be late to meet Archie.

"We need to discuss the statistics seminar," I said. "I'll be working with each student individually to determine how to test and grade."

I was pretty proud of myself for coming up with that on the spot.

"Individually?" Pam asked.

"I think it's the best way since it will be almost impossible to get all twelve of you together. At least four I can think of have gone back to their homes."

"The three of us are in Paul Revere," Pam said. I made a note: The leader.

"Maybe we could all meet together in our dorm room," Liz said. I made a note: The follower.

Casey nodded vigorously. I made a note: The weak link.

I shook my head. "I don't think that would be appropriate. I'm sure Huey's will be closed tomorrow, but the library will be open." Huey, who ran the campus coffee shop, took every opportunity to close up and go sailing. Who could blame him? "Let's start at eleven with Pam. It shouldn't take more than twenty minutes to a half hour. Then Liz, then Casey. That sound okay?"

Pam, taller than her friends by a few inches, chewed her lip mercilessly while trying to maintain her position of leadership. Liz and Casey looked to Pam for guidance.

"Okay," Pam said, followed closely by nods from her subjects.

"Good," I said. "Now can you please let me through?"

The girls split up and stepped back onto the grass, leaving the path clear.

I pulled the dolly past them. Too bad I didn't have a recording device to plant on one of them. I'd have given anything to be in on their next conversation.

Three boxes that used to hold computer paper held what the police left behind. They just fit in the trunk of my car, once I

166

consolidated junk that I didn't need to be carting around in the first place. I considered what was I going to do with all that used to be Keith's. I had hopes for the address book — I pictured an alphabetical list, in Keith's own handwriting, with the heading "Likely suspects in the event of my murder." I shuddered at the way my mind worked.

At the very least the book might open the investigation to suspects other than the residents of Ben Franklin Hall, who were some of my favorite people, even the stubborn little chem majors I'd just scrambled with.

I drove off campus, past Maureen in the security booth. I waved good-bye to her as if it were any other Saturday when all that was in my trunk was the emergency first aid kit Bruce had prepared for me and a down jacket leftover from the long ago cold winter days. I finally let out my breath when I reached Henley Boulevard and merged into a steady flow of local traffic.

My Bluetooth was busy on the way to the police station. First, Ariana called to thank me for letting her use my place for her class.

"I'm afraid we ate you out of house and home," she said. "Let me bring dinner by tonight."

I was so wired from the day already, I hardly even remembered that there had been beaders in my home. While I was packing up and ultimately absconding with a murder victim's property, then entertaining three possible killers, notwithstanding the adorable outfits they wore, several Henley women had been sitting at my kitchen island making earrings and bracelets.

"Don't worry about it," I said to Ariana. "I can pick up something."

"I want to come. You've been avoiding me since all this happened."

"That was yesterday."

"See you around six. I have some new organics that are just what you need."

"Okay, thanks." There was no use arguing with Ariana once she went into her incense mode. I wouldn't have been surprised if she came ready to smudge my home and yard. "I have a meeting at three so I should definitely be home by six."

"Who are you meeting with?" she asked.

"Huh? Oh, sorry, gotta go." I clicked off with great relief. I'd rather tell Ariana after the fact about a successful session at police headquarters than risk potential confusion when she gave me advice on how to determine Archie's aura. Which she would certainly do. I wasn't sure I wanted to know

Archie's aura even if I had the skills to detect it. I did want to know his birthday, however.

Bruce was next. I told him how nice it was to see my photo on the dresser in his home away from home.

"How was it between Gil and Rachel?" he asked.

"What do you mean? Gil was very nice about showing us around and lending us her room, until the Bat Phone rang."

"I heard about that. Glad you could see the crew in action. We don't just watch movies, you know."

Not so fast. "What's this about Gil and Rachel?" I asked

"Nothing really."

I let out an exasperated sigh. "Bruce." I tried to sound like a stern mother. Or dean.

"Okay. It's just that Gil's always had a thing about Rachel and Hal."

This was news. "Rachel and Hal?"

"You know, whether they were an item."

Not only news, but shocking news. "I can't believe you never told me this."

"Thought you knew."

"Hal was Rachel's freshman adviser and they've always been close. Well, not close close. You mean there was talk?"

"Just talk. I'm sorry I brought it up. I

figured you knew but didn't want the talk to grow. I was impressed at your integrity, but now I see you didn't know."

Bruce laughed; I didn't.

"Where did you hear this talk?"

Bruce's long breath told me he was sorry he mentioned it. Too bad. Too late. "Gil brought it up once or twice, but not lately I don't think. Ernie told me she asked him for advice about it once. Ernie's the nurse that's on shift with her a lot. She asked him, should she confront her husband, that kind of thing. Then I think Sim got wind of it, too, and had a couple of talks with her."

Who would have thought? The MAstar trailer was gossip central, as bad as the Clara Barton, Nathaniel Hawthorne, and Paul Revere dorms.

"What other Henley gossip are you keeping from me?"

"Not a thing. What's new with you?" he asked, sounding eager to move on.

"I'm just leaving campus."

"I'd have thought the campus was still a crime scene."

"Nah."

"Where are you headed?"

"I'm going home, then I have a meeting with Virgil's partner."

"Archie? Watch out for him. He's single

170

and, you might say, hot. What's he want with you?"

"We're going to compare notes," I said, checking my rearview mirror for a state trooper on lie patrol.

"You're not getting into any trouble, are you?

"Pfft. Why would you think that?"

"Let's see. No reason. Except" — I heard a snap of his fingers — "oh, yeah, there was the time you put together a petition to get rid of the Chairman of the Board of Trustees —"

"He was breaking labor laws by posting jobs he'd already wired for his friends."

"I love how naïve you are about how things are done in the real world."

"Well, if that's reality, I'll take . . . math."

Bruce laughed but he wasn't finished with me. "And then there was the week you went to Washington to track down the fraud issue, and the proposals you submit every month to get credit for interns in spite of all the precedents against it, and —"

"I get it. But this time is different," I said, turning a corner. "I'm not sticking my neck out."

The sound of heavy cartons thunking around in my trunk flooded my ears.

■ ■ ■ ■

I'd decided not to leave my car with its special load parked in town, even though it would be in or near the police station lot. Actually, that was not a plus — I didn't want my special load anywhere near the police.

Thoughts of Rachel and Hal together swirled around my head. How could I have missed that? If there was anything to miss. One thing I was sure of, I'd now be focusing on how Rachel and Hal acted when I was in the same room with them.

I pulled into my driveway and hit the garage door opener. Attaching a garage had been one of the best home improvement ideas my mother and I had come up with. We appreciated it in all seasons. Today it served as a dumping ground for my boxes. I pushed aside shopping bags of clothing destined for a charity drive and unloaded the cartons onto a long workbench that the construction foreman had told me would come in handy whether or not I was a tinkerer. He'd been right.

I ran into my house and changed into a clean shirt, wanting no dust mites from a former crime scene falling off my torso in the middle of a police interview. I hadn't eaten since my candlelight breakfast with Bruce, so I spent ninety seconds putting together a peanut butter and rhubarb jam sandwich on whole wheat. I shoved the edge of the uncut sandwich between my teeth in a most ladylike manner, and ran out again to meet Archie.

Back in my car, I pressed the button on my opener and watched my garage door descend, locking in the boxes, inch by inch.

10

The miserably hot day that began with my interview with Rachel in a trailer was to continue with one in Henley's rundown old police building, in a part of town I seldom visited. My local travel was restricted to campus, MAstar now and then, and Ariana's shop.

The town budget hadn't allowed for an upgrade to the Henley PD parking lot, which was now full. Did all these vehicles belong to suspects in Keith's murder? I didn't recognize any of them as belonging to Franklin Hall faculty. Perhaps the criminal element I knew so little about was experiencing a surge in activity that caused an overflow in and around police headquarters.

I looked for easy street parking and found a spot mercifully under a tree three long blocks away, making me even happier that I'd left the valuable cartons at home.

The police station stood alone in a large area once occupied by a host of city buildings, including the library, performing arts auditorium, city hall, and the courthouse. One by one, the various components of civic life moved to a new building in a government center close to downtown. Chain-link fences marked off vacant lots that were their former turf. The police station was the last building standing.

By the time I walked the three sparsely shaded blocks, my clean shirt might as well have been dipped in water and wrung out. I entered through swinging doors that led to a shabby lobby, not at all like the cool, cavernous entryway to the new library, for example, or the inviting dome of the snazzy new city hall/courthouse combo.

Three narrow hallways radiated from the central desk that was staffed by a civilian volunteer, a thirtysomething woman whom, surprisingly, I recognized from a math anxiety class I'd given at an adult ed school. I made a note to mention this to Ariana, who thought I didn't know anyone in town.

I'd called the class "Getting Past Ten." I couldn't remember the volunteer's name, but I did remember that she'd been one of the quickest to catch on to arithmetic tricks I'd proposed. She'd taken the class to prepare for an administration of justice exam. I hoped it worked and that she had a more permanent job than the volunteer desk.

Terri Gable, I now saw from her name tag, brightened at my approach. A nice change. "Dr. Knowles. I've been meaning to email you. Those little tricks of yours have come in sooooo handy." Terri had turned *so* into a short tune, about eight bars long.

"I'm glad to hear it."

"Like multiplying by eleven in your head. Sooooo cool. Not that I have to do it that often, it just makes me more comfortable with numbers."

"That's music to my ears," I told her, sincerely. I didn't mention that my weekend was sorely in need of music.

"You're here to see Archie?"

My "yes" was weak. I would have preferred to stand there and do arithmetic for the rest of the afternoon with the chubby, curly-haired woman.

"I'll walk you down."

Terri waddled slightly in front of me, past several bustling offices. It seemed there was a lot of paperwork to law enforcement. Old model fax machines rolled out documents and keyboards clacked.

"Busy place," I said, to fill in a hole in our

conversation. My other option would have been to mention a new mathcast I'd seen on squaring two-digit numbers, but I didn't want to overdo the math connection.

Terri apologized in advance for the room I'd be waiting in. "It's really warm in there," she said. "I don't know why Archie told me to put you in Interview Two, when there are better ones available with more comfortable chairs and a working A/C and all."

I had some idea why.

Terri dropped me off in a dismal, stifling room with stagnant air. The furniture in Interview Two was worse than that in MA-star's trailers, by a factor of ten. I figured they were castoffs from the government departments that had left this part of town for the right side of the tracks.

Of the two gray metal chairs in the room, I chose the one with the least number of rips in its faux-cushioned seat. There was no clock in the room and since I tended not to wear a watch in the summer, the better to avoid a rash, I had no idea how many minutes ticked by. I alternated between letting my head hang freely from my neck onto my chest, to sitting up straight and stretching my neck backward. I paced for a while, but the room was so small the laps made me dizzy. No position was comfortable, but shifting my body around gave my muscles momentary relief.

I tried to use the time to organize my thoughts, but there was no controlling them in this hostile environment. Images of my three students, Pam, Liz, and Casey, wearing evil masks crowded my mind and alternated with videos of Keith Appleton falling off his chair repeatedly, clutching his throat and taking his last breath each time. In the mental video, Hal and Rachel were off in a corner while Gil searched for them, a hatchet in her hand. Who said mathematicians weren't creative?

I wished with all my heart that Pam had let her two friends — followers, I now saw — finish their sentences. Besides that, something else nagged at me. Something one of them said at the party? On the phone the night of Keith's murder? Probably something from the statistics seminar, like Casey's mixing up means and medians.

I shook my head to clear it. Bad move. A new headache set in.

I wondered how long Archie would leave me to sweat, literally.

The answer came when the door opened and Archie appeared. The large clock on the hallway wall behind him read five after four. I'd been ten minutes early, therefore,

I'd been captive for seventy-five sweltering, mind-numbing minutes.

"Sorry," Archie said as he entered Interview Two looking cool and crisp, and hardly sorry. He'd probably spent the time with a cold pack around his neck.

In spite of his name — which called to mind a bumbling, wrinkled old caricature of a detective — Archie looked like Hollywood's idea of the insightful young cop who one-ups his dumpy-looking colleagues and his boss and takes down the serial killer. His well-groomed, sharp look, the opposite of Virgil's, unnerved me.

"Can I get you some coffee?" he asked.

A hot drink. Just what I needed. I almost laughed.

I shook my head. "No, thanks."

"A soda?"

Another shake. "I'm good."

I kept my hands on my lap, careful not to touch anything. I pictured what Archie would do after I left, pulling out a handkerchief, picking up a soda can, and shipping it off for DNA analysis. Of course my fingerprints and DNA would be all over Keith's office anyway, but with legitimate reasons as well as the one bad one. Still, one couldn't be too careful.

Archie took the seat opposite me. Although he loosened his tie, he managed to sustain the in-charge male model look.

"So, Dr. Knowles."

"Sophie," I said, eager to put this experience on an informal, less stressful level.

"Sophie, then." If this was Archie, yielding, I'd hate to see his rigid side. "How well did you know Dr. Appleton?"

An easy one. I cleared my throat. "He was a colleague. We saw each other several times a week in Franklin Hall, plus there were faculty meetings, committees, the usual."

"Would you say you two were close?"

"No, not close," I answered, putting a spin on *close,* marking it as truly the wrong word.

"Would you say you were competitors, then?"

"No, not at all."

"Not even a little?"

"No," I insisted.

"I have in my notes that Dr. Appleton just won an award of some kind. Were you up for that award also?"

"You mean the Mass Association of Chemists naming him a Fellow? No, I don't belong to that group. It's not my field."

"What about Henley College awards? For good teaching, publishing, that kind of thing?"

"We've both had our share. We weren't

competing for them."

He scratched his head. "No offense, but it's kind of hard to believe."

"We're in completely different fields. Differential equations" — I pointed to my chest — "and protein purification." I cast my hand away from my body to indicate where Keith might be, were he still alive. I tried not to sound exasperated.

Archie appeared to be writing this explanation in his notebook, but I couldn't see the details. I wouldn't have been surprised if he were writing, "Beer, Chips, Beef Jerky." I was tempted to spell "protein purification" for him.

"One more time: You were on the same faculty. You were up for the same promotions, true?"

"That's not how it works. We don't have a pecking order like that." Not exactly, that is. I wasn't keen on reciting the bylaws' definitions for the various faculty rankings on a college campus, from adjuncts who taught one or two classes only, to instructors who were full-time but without significant credentials or seniority, all the way to full professors.

Archie flipped through pages of his notebook, back from where he started with me. "Weren't you both in the running for full professor, coming up this fall?"

"Well, sort of, but there's no law that says we can't both be appointed. As I said, we submit articles to different journals; we both have plenty of students signing up for our classes." I held my hands palms up, then quickly folded them on my lap again. There was no point in waving my DNA around in front of this man.

Neither did I want to share with this canny, knowledgeable detective that I'd set myself the goal of attaining full professorship for this year. I was on the young side of the demographic for the title, but I hoped my work supported it. Archie didn't need to know that Keith had two years in age on me and one in seniority.

I looked around the bare room, catching my reflection in a window on the side wall. Haggard would have been a good descriptor. Sagging eyelids, hair frizzed beyond belief, disheveled shirt. I wanted to leave and head for the nearest shower.

Where was Virgil? Where was Bruce, best friend to Virgil? Why was I stuck with this know-it-all young partner who was interrogating, not interviewing? I'd been expecting to answer questions about Rachel, or Pam, or Liz, or Casey, or Fran, or Lucy, or Hal. Even Dean Underwood. I thought I'd been sent here to help. Now I had to face the reality that Virgil had not been joking when he'd implied I was in the pool of murder suspects.

I was getting hotter and hotter and hoped I wouldn't pass out. I felt sure only guilty people passed out in situations like this.

Archie finished his flipping for the moment.

"Yeah, back to the promotions to full professor. There are perks with this, huh?"

"A small raise usually. We already have tenure. Mostly it's the status, I guess." I stopped. I should be answering with the smallest possible number of words. I'd read that somewhere. Or seen it on television.

"Usually you expect these announcements early in the fall term?"

Why was he harping on this? What made him think he knew anything about college faculty operations in the first place?

"That's right." Archie waited me out, and I added, "With four slots open in math and science, we were both very likely to get the promotion."

"When was the last time you saw Dr. Appleton?"

From left field, but not a problem. I thought back.

"Outside the dean's office on Thursday, I guess."

"You guess?"

"It was on Thursday."

"Was there a reason you were there, outside the dean's office?"

Uh-oh. "She'd sent for me."

"Because?"

I let out a heavy sigh. "Nothing that important. She wanted to talk to me about noisy parties . . . that is . . . seminars in our building."

"Had she received a complaint?"

"I think so, yes."

"Did she say who'd made the complaint?"

"No, she didn't."

"Did you have any guesses?"

"No." I'd crossed my fingers by now.

"And you saw Dr. Appleton where?"

I gritted my teeth. "Coming out of the dean's office."

"But you didn't assume he was the one who'd made the complaint about your noisy parties?"

"They weren't . . ." I paused and took a breath. "No."

"Because?"

"Well, she'd already sent for me long before he would have been in her office."

A victory, but a small, short one.

"You're close to your assistant, Ms. Wheeler?" Archie asked, a knowing look in his eyes.

"It's not like we go to movies together or anything, but yes, I consider her a friend."

"And yesterday, can you tell me what your interaction with Ms. Wheeler was?"

"I had a class in the morning that she had set up, and then she came at the end to take it down, before the party."

Archie checked his notes. "That would be the party for Dr. Bartholomew. And that was an actual party, not a seminar."

Smart aleck cop. "Yes."

"I'm curious. What's involved in setting up for a math class? Don't you usually just use a blackboard?"

I heard the hint of a jocular air, but no way was I letting down my guard. By now my lips were like chalk, dry enough to make a scratching sound on that blackboard he brought up.

"I'm in charge of a program to make students more comfortable with everyday math, giving them problem-solving skills especially. It's a hands-on way of teaching math. We use a lot of manipulatives."

"You mean blocks and balls, that kind of thing?"

I smiled and tried to strike a tone between

185

informative and condescending. "These days we use videos, online graphing calculators, interactive websites, *that* kind of thing."

"It's not the math I remember."

"It's not your father's math class," I said, with immediate regret.

He laughed. I sighed with relief.

"Thanks for coming in, Sophie. You can go now."

"I can?"

He nodded and gave me a genuine smile for the first time. "Thanks for your cooperation. Sorry to put you through this, but you know I had to."

Not really, but I knew I should count my blessings and split immediately. So, why didn't I?

"Do you have any leads in the case?" I asked, astonished that I hadn't dashed for the safety of my car already. I took one more stab at shifting police attention from Rachel. "I'd be happy to share with you what I've observed about Dr. Appleton's dealings with the students, the other faculty —"

"We'll let you know if we need you," Archie said, back to his serious cop tone.

I left without another word.

I replayed the entire interrogation over in my head a number of times on the way home. It seemed clear to me that Archie and/or Virgil had interviewed Dean Underwood before they got to me. I could think of no other way that Archie would have known to quiz me on promotions and on the summons to her office. I wondered what their approach to the dean had been, antagonistic or deferential. Was she an informant or a suspect? After all, if it weren't for Keith's support of the change to a coeducational institution, Dean Underwood might have been able to keep her ladies' academy fantasy.

In my mind, everyone was a suspect, except Rachel and me.

The clock on my dashboard, not the most accurate, read five twenty-five. I'd hoped to have enough time before Ariana arrived with herbs and lotions to get a decent start on Keith's files. I wasn't completely satisfied that the police had eliminated me from their list. I counted on something concrete to point to the actual murderer.

I turned into my driveway, pressing the garage door opener from a few yards away. The door rolled up and I headed in, between my treadmill and my workbench.

The treadmill was in its place, if forlorn for lack of use this summer.

The workbench was empty.

11

It took some time for me to fully accept that my garage had been burglarized and my plan for a big breakthrough had been thwarted.

My gardening tools were in place, hanging from a pegboard; my fire extinguisher and two wooden ladders, one long, one short, were in their usual spots against a wall. Small items on racks here and there seemed unmoved. Besides the boxes, the only things that appeared to be missing were the shopping bags with clothing and odds and ends I'd been collecting for the charity pickup. My guess was that the thief assumed the bags were part of my haul from the campus, if indeed that was what this was all about.

I stood there looking around uselessly until I realized the burglar could still be on my property, even inside my home.

I made a dash for my car, banged the door

locked with my elbow, and drove back out to the driveway. At least if he or she came out of my house, guns blazing, I'd have a little protection, and I might be able to screech away down the street.

Call the police, said my logical brain. And tell them what? my other brain asked. That I was a petty thief myself, having absconded with boxes of papers and office material that didn't belong to me, and now they'd been re-stolen? I supposed I could call the station, drag a couple of officers out here, and report that I was missing a few bags of used clothing and usable discards. I could list my old toaster oven, a pillow that was too frilly for my taste, and a stapler that I'd replaced with an electric version.

No, calling the police was out of the question. How inconvenient.

I started to formulate a Plan B.

There were three entrances to my garage — the first was through a door from my kitchen; the second was the electric roll-up door; and a third, side exit led to the narrow passageway outside where I kept my trash containers. The kitchen door, like the rest of my interior perimeter, was always alarmed when I left the house; the other two were not wired for security.

All I had to do now was open the kitchen

door a crack and listen for a beeping sound. Beeping would mean the alarm was still set and my house had not been entered illegally; no beeping would mean someone had intruded. Or might still be rattling around in there. If everything worked properly, in the event of an intrusion, the alarm company would have contacted me. But the system had never been tested in that way — both good news and bad.

I tapped my steering wheel, thinking.

I made my decision based on one, trusting the security system and its monitors, and two, the fact that I had neither heard nor seen, nor had I smelled, any sign of an intruder since I arrived.

I got out of the car, picked off a large rake from the pegboard, and headed for the alarmed but unlocked kitchen door. I turned the knob as silently as I could and pushed the door in, the long, potentially lethal rake at the ready in my other hand.

Beep. Beep. Beep. Beep.

I let out a breath. My home had not been violated. I entered the security code, the beeping stopped, and my heart rate returned to normal. I walked back out to the garage, to the side next to my treadmill, and examined the most likely point of entry, through the door between the garage and the side

190

alleyway. Sure enough, the push button on the knob was out, in the unlocked position. I imagined how easy it had been to pick the skimpy lock. Bruce had been after me forever to install a deadbolt and had offered to do it. Too bad I'd told him I'd take care of it.

Back to the problem of the missing boxes.

Maybe a gust of wind had blown through, knocking the boxes to the floor. Never mind that boxes were sturdy and heavy, and that there was no cross ventilation available. Even so, I looked under the workbench and behind the water heater. I walked around my garage like someone who couldn't remember where she'd put a large load of freight. Maybe I'd stuffed the cartons into the tiny area under the metal shelving that held seasonal decorations and archives from my teaching career, or behind the treadmill.

Of course, there was no sign of them.

I had to face facts. The boxes had been stolen. Re-stolen. Only Woody knew that I had taken them, and unless he'd been stalking me, he didn't know I'd taken them off campus. Even if he did know, I couldn't imagine the sweet old man making tracks to my house while I was at the police station and carting everything back.

Had Woody told someone? The dean came

to mind. But even if she'd already found out that her appointed messenger had been preempted, I couldn't picture her sending someone to break into my home to retrieve the material. She'd be more likely to have Courtney call me to her office at an inconvenient time so she could cluck her tongue at me in person.

The thought I'd been avoiding, that someone had been lurking, following my movements this afternoon, kept creeping back.

Each possibility was more unsettling than the next.

I sat on an old metal stool and leaned on the empty workbench, working hard to calm myself and think clearly. Why would anyone want files from a dead man's office? For the same reason I did, to look for clues to his murder. Or to remove something incriminating.

At the sound of a car entering my driveway, I started and nearly fell off the rickety stool. I'd never been so glad to see Ariana's happy face and animated wave as she exited her decades-old convertible.

"How come your car's out here?" she asked.

"I hope you brought your herbs and lotions," I said.

We sat in my den, sipping a special tea that Ariana promised would cleanse my body and my mind, as I told her the events of my day. Laying it all out for her helped me think more objectively.

I reviewed my meeting with Rachel and recalled how surprised I was to learn that she'd walked in on Keith after his death. It came to me again how horrible that must have been for her.

"Woody found the piece of cake and soda Rachel was taking up to Keith, sitting on a chair in his office. Why wouldn't Rachel tell me she left the cake there?" I asked Ariana. "She told me a bigger truth, that she lied to the police. Why wouldn't she tell me the whole truth? Why would she say she left the cake outside the door?" The rambling questions were for me more than for Ariana.

"Some people can tell the truth only in small pieces," she wisely observed. "I wish I could see samples of everyone's handwriting. I have a new book that shows how strong T-crossings and dark, dominant periods are indicative of someone about to explode in rage."

I checked to see if she were teasing. She wasn't.

I went through my harrowing interview with Archie and earned Ariana's sympathy and a few more of the small anise cookies she'd made.

When it came to my visit to campus, I fudged a bit.

"I borrowed the files from Keith's office," I said, as an explanation for why Keith's possessions had been in my garage in the first place. I wasn't sure why I decided on the spot not to admit to the ruse I'd used to acquire the material, unless it was to corroborate Ariana's theory that no one tells the whole truth all the time. I wondered if my skirting the facts would negate the effects of the herbal tea. "It's creepy that they're gone now."

"I wonder where in the universe they are?" Ariana mused.

"In the hands of the murderer is my best guest. My big problem is what to do when the dean finds out I took them and then lost them."

"I don't understand why you can't just outright tell the dean you want to help the police. What do you have to lose?"

I smiled. "Only my promotion to full professor."

"Is there a lot of money at stake if you don't get it?"

"A couple of thousand dollars at most. It's the principle."

"I knew that," Ariana said.

"Thanks."

"Not that I wouldn't miss you, but I wish there were some place better for you. I mean, I know you love Henley but there must be other colleges where they have math departments and cooperative deans. This is Massachusetts, right? The college state?"

"Yes, there are other colleges, but not necessarily other jobs. Most colleges are cutting back on full-time faculty and using adjuncts."

I explained the common practice of giving desperate, unemployed teachers the option of teaching for a flat rate per course. To put together a living, teachers would take on classes at several institutions. They ended up with a lot more work for a lot less pay.

"And no benefits, I bet," Ariana added.

"You got it."

"I'll never understand academia."

Sometimes I didn't either.

Ariana pushed herself off the easy chair and slapped the palms of her hands against each other.

"We need to cleanse your house and your garage."

Her thin caftan, in shades of red and blue to match her hair, seemed appropriate to her task. She went to her car and brought back her smudging kit, her ritual for purifying a person or a place. I watched as she opened all the windows and doors to allow the free flow of energy.

I often wished I had Ariana's faith in a smoldering bundle of herbs; I wished I could believe that the smoke from white sage would carry all the negative energy out of my environs. Instead, what came to mind was a lecture I heard at a conference, on the steady flow energy equation. It soothed me that I could picture the equation and fill in some numbers for the ambient conditions in my home.

Meanwhile, Ariana recited peace-giving words to the north, south, east, and west.

Might as well cover all bases, I always told myself when Ariana performed this ritual. It can't hurt.

I avoided my stove and oven in the summer months, eating directly from the refrigerator most nights. Ariana had no such fear of additional heat and set to work making dinner while I followed her instructions and took a bath with the rosewater salts she'd made in her own kitchen.

How bad a day is it that starts and ends with meals made and served by someone I loved in the comfort of my home? I smelled the stir-fry as soon as I entered the hallway. Peppers, broccoli, and soy brought my nose to life. Ariana's homemade bread baking in the oven added to the promise of a delicious meal.

"Tofu and rolls in ten," Ariana called out.

I used the time to listen to my voice mail on my landline, which I hadn't checked since I left home this morning. Twelve messages, mostly related to the incident that changed Henley's summer school schedule and scarred the campus forever.

Pam, Liz, and Casey assured me they'd be at the library tomorrow morning and wondered again if we could all meet together to save time. I thought not. Three other students in the statistics seminar wanted to know how I was planning to finish off the term. In spite of my bravado with the trio at Franklin Hall this afternoon, I hadn't given it a moment's thought. I'd return their calls when I had.

Sometimes I longed for the days when teachers had office hours that were defined by limits, and were not expected to be available twenty-four seven, at school and at home, in person and online, as if we were emergency workers. Now, all our phone numbers and email addresses were listed on the syllabi on the Henley College website, along with our social networking pages.

The next three calls had been hang-ups. I checked the caller log and saw that all were from the area code for Mansfield, Massachusetts, where the MAstar's flagship base was located. Bruce usually used his own cell phone to call or text me, but when he did use the facility phone, it was a Mansfield area code that came up, never with the same seven-digit number, from some central switchboard, I assumed.

It wasn't like Bruce to not leave even a simple "Hey, it's me," and certainly not three times. He'd try my cell before he'd try my landline three times. I replayed the messages and noted the time stamps. The first was at two thirty, when I was on my way to the police station after dropping the boxes off; the second was at three twenty, while I was waiting for my interview with Archie; the third came in at three forty, still waiting for Archie.

I texted Bruce: "U call?" and made a note to ask him about it after dinner if I didn't hear from him sooner.

Two calls were from Seth Phillips, our local reporter for the *Henley Forum*. I figured he'd been denied comments by the important people on campus and was down to mere associate professors.

Another student's message had come in, with an idea about how to finish the semester. She'd suggested, "Just have a big party and call the class over," followed by an "Oh, my God, that sounds totally awful after what happened. Sorry, sorry, sorry."

"And where were you on Friday afternoon between noon and four o'clock?" I asked my machine as each student reported in.

Ariana heard me speaking to the machine in a scolding tone. She smiled.

"Since when did you give up puzzles to take on a murder investigation?"

I picked up the nearest puzzle, a dodecahedral twisty puzzle made of plastic, one that Ariana herself had given me. I gave it two twists, resulting in further scrambling of the colors, just to make a point.

"Do I have time for one phone call before dinner? I want to get in touch with Keith's cousin in Chicago."

"Go for it," Ariana said.

I went into my office and checked my address book for Elteen Kirsch and found her number.

Elteen had the voice of a rather old woman, a little shaky and high-pitched. Was it physics that accounted for that? I'd have to ask Hal why voices went up an octave or two as we got older. Or maybe it was a nurse question for Gil, his loving but apparently jealous wife.

"I know who you are, Dr. Knowles," Elteen said. "It's so nice of you to call. Keith talked about you and considered you a very good friend."

I was used to this by now. I had no explanation for why Keith went around telling everyone what good friends we were but butted up against me at every turn on faculty committees. As recently as graduation last June, Keith became a one-man campaign against the speaker I'd proposed, a noted Harvard scholar in linguistics. Keith had serious disagreements with the man's political views. I'd argued that it was a coup for Henley to get him, that we weren't inviting him to talk about politics and, anyway, that shouldn't matter. This was America, wasn't it? In the end, after winning over the dean, Keith had prevailed and our substitute speaker was a retired botanist with no views whatsoever.

Elteen had been going on about her cousin. I came in at, "He was very good to us. I can't tell you how many times he bailed us out when Teddy got sick and couldn't work. And our Delia is going to a wonderful private high school thanks to her uncle Keith."

Here was a further glimpse into Keith Appleton's other life. The Keith who called me his friend, gave money to his relatives and to the school janitor. The kindly Uncle Keith.

"How generous of him."

"Oh, he was very generous. I feel so bad that he died so young. And right when he was finally starting to keep company with someone, too. A nice young woman, he said."

Excuse me? Did keeping company mean what I thought it did? Had Keith hooked up with someone? Bruce had claimed I was oblivious to things like that. But wouldn't I have known if Keith were dating? Or if Rachel and Hal had something going as Gil thought? Was I so buried in my job — make that jobs — that I didn't see what was going on around me? Well, too late now.

"Did you ever get to meet his friend?" I asked, trying to keep it gender neutral, just in case.

"Oh dear, no. You know he only met her this summer. Bonnie, wasn't it? Or Annie?"

Of course I knew. I was his best friend. I mumbled a name and changed the subject.

"Please let me know if there's anything I can do for you," I said.

"That's very kind of you."

I wondered if I dared try to use this condolence call to ask a question of a cousin who saw Keith only in the most favorable light. The "any known enemies" query died on my lips.

"We're all very blessed to have known him," I said, and left it at that.

I couldn't remember the last time I'd used the word "blessed." How strange that it should be Keith Appleton who inspired it.

Roasted peppers and balsamic vinegar notwithstanding, the tofu recipe didn't cut it for either of us tonight and Ariana and I ended up in my den with large bowls of mocha chip ice cream, cruising television channels until we gave up on finding anything decent. Nothing could make me laugh and no script was as dramatic as the one playing itself out in my life.

I watched Ariana clean her bowl with her long, thin index finger, which she then licked, a microcosmic symbol of what I loved about her. She had this endearing quality of being able to find the best in any culture. One minute she was burning incense, the next she was reading an international geopolitical thriller; she ate rice cakes one day and ordered fries with ketchup the next.

"Should I be worried about you?" Ariana asked.

"Nah. I mean, it's hard not to be upset about what happened to Keith. It's going to take time to get used to. He was a strong presence on campus." I almost said, "We were blessed to have him," but that moment had passed.

The notes to *Come Fly With Me* filled the room.

I looked over at my cell phone, charging on my end table. Bruce calling.

"I'm going to take this," I said.

Ariana got up and pointed to the clock on the kitchen wall, a room away. Twenty after twelve. "I should be going anyway."

We waved good-bye and blew kisses as I unplugged the charging cord and swished the phone on.

"You home?" Bruce asked.

"All fed and watered," I said. "Ariana, the cook and the queen of soothing gestures, is just leaving."

We spent a few minutes catching up on the day — Bruce had worked an evacuation drill and one real emergency call between nine and eleven thirty tonight, meaning hardly any turnaround or downtime.

"We worked with the Marines on the drill," he said. "Very cool. We could handle the truth."

"Huh?"

"Don't you remember in *A Few Good Men* where Jack Nicholson yells out at Tom Cruise, 'You can't handle the truth?' " Bruce's imitation of Nicholson left a lot to be desired.

"Oh, yeah. How could I forget?"

"One of my faves."

I was ready to ask him about the hang-ups. I tried to sound casual.

"Did you get my texts?" I asked.

"Yeah. But I couldn't tell what you meant. Did I call when?"

"Did you try to get me a couple of times today?"

"Not since I talked to you earlier. I slept till about five, then ran around doing errands, then the madhouse here. Why?"

If it wasn't Bruce, then who? Someone else at MAstar headquarters? Gil was the only other person I knew. If she wanted to track down Hal, she would have left a message. In any case, there were more telephones in the town of Mansfield than those at MAstar — one other number in my address book teased at the back of my head, but I couldn't remember — so I was fighting a losing battle trying to figure it out. I had to stop letting petty things get to me.

"Why?" Bruce repeated.

"Oh, nothing. I got a couple of calls with no message and just wondered."

"You sound funny. Everything okay there?"

My mouth was ready to form the word *break-in* but closed just in time, and opened on another note.

"Oh, yeah, just this thing with Keith and all."

"I should be there."

"Nah, you'd be in the way."

"So you say." I heard the familiar finger-snapping. "I almost forgot. How'd it go with Archie?"

"Nothing to it. I'll tell you all about it tomorrow. Right now, I'm going to bed, even if you can't."

"Love you."

"Love you."

"Lock up," he said.

Like never before, I thought.

12

I'd successfully avoided contacting my students until it was too late to return their calls. Technically, it was never too late to call a student in a college dormitory. Half the girls were up all night, the other half during the day, so there was always the chance that one of them would need her math teacher. As many calls involved personal distress, such as "He never calls me. What shall I do?" as homework, such as "Do you really expect us to do three problem sets every week?"

I wished now that my biggest problem was giving dating advice.

I patrolled my house twice, checking doors and windows. I hated shutting off all ventilation, but there was no other way to completely alarm my perimeter. I put in the alarm code, not simply out of habit tonight. I was tempted to test it to see if the human monitors two towns over were really paying attention. I wished I'd thought to take the rake in from the garage, but retrieving it now would mean undoing all the protections first and I couldn't bear to be un-alarmed even for that short time.

The unfamiliar feeling of vulnerability unsettled me. I crawled into bed, then crawled out and wedged a chair under the bedroom doorknob. I climbed under my crisp lavender sheet again, and climbed out again to make sure the door between the kitchen and the garage was locked, some-thing I never did unless I was leaving town for a few days.

Reading in bed was one of my favorite pastimes, but tonight I couldn't concentrate. I opened the drawer in my night table and took out a clipboard with a half-finished crossword. The puzzle was due to my editor in a few days and I hadn't looked at it at all yesterday or today.

The sad part: I'd been working on a chemistry-related crossword, with Keith's help. The overall shape of the puzzle was a beaker. Some clues were simple; for "tongs" the clue was "they come in a pair and hold hot things." I'd asked Keith if he'd contrib-ute a few difficult ones. Not too hard, though, since the puzzle was destined for a kids' word games book. He'd given me several, starting with "crucible," for which the clue was "porcelain container for reactions."

"These are perfect for middle-schoolers," I'd told Keith. "I didn't know you had experience with preteens."

He'd shrugged and said, "I used to be one."

I doubted it, but then I never would have guessed that Keith was seeing someone. Unless he'd made up a girl to keep his old cousin quiet. I wondered who she was, if she was real. I couldn't think of a Bonnie on the faculty. I counted three faculty members who could pass for Annie in one form or another — all of them were married, happily from all outward appearances.

Was Annie or Bonnie a student? I hoped not. Elteen had said she was young, but I couldn't take her literally. Keith might have referred to her as simply his own age. My very last thought was that the "girl" was not part of Henley College. I could hear Ariana saying, "I told you so" about my narrow view of the world.

I cast aside the puzzle that reminded me too much of Keith. Maybe some other year I'd be able to return to it. For now, I'd have to come up with a different theme. I'd already done one shaped like a helicopter with words and clues from aviation history, and I'd covered many other modes of transportation as well.

I attached a clean puzzle grid to the clipboard and tapped the blank squares. Usually I could count on a last-minute inspiration, but tonight I wasn't sure. Not even the lingering aroma of Ariana's tea concoction was enough to inspire me.

When the phone rang, my body twitched and the clipboard went one way and my pencil the other. At one thirty in the morning, I dreaded picking up the phone to hear a dial tone. Or worse, a threat. Or news of a second murder. The negative possibilities were endless.

I checked the caller ID. Rachel's cell phone number. I was almost happy to see it.

"Hi, Dr. Knowles. I know it's late and I shouldn't be calling. But I can't sleep in this bed."

"Where are you?" Please don't say jail.

"I'm home in my own room, but it feels weird not to be in the dorm."

"I forgot some of you were sent home."

"They closed my dorm. Everyone who couldn't get home is in Paul Revere with, like, maximum security. I don't want to be here with my mother still freaking out, but I don't know why anyone would want to stay at the dorm either."

I thought of three girls who were very happy to be there, close to what they perceived as "the action."

"I'm sure everything's secure on campus."

"Are you worried something will happen to you, Dr. Knowles? I mean what if some serial killer wants all the Franklin Hall teachers dead?"

Nice going, my friend. "I think you're overreacting, Rachel."

"Like, how can you overreact to murder?"

Good question. Until my garage was broken into, I hadn't seriously considered myself in any danger at home. Keith's murder had been no threat to me and had not invaded my personal space. At the front of my mind was what if the box thief didn't get what he wanted and was planning a middle-of-the-night return visit? Or even another middle-of-the-day visit. Hadn't Keith been killed between noon and just before two, when Rachel found him, in extremely sunny daylight hours, in his own office?

Until someone got to the bottom of this, no one was safe at any hour. I might as well do my share.

"Rachel, did you tell me you did *not* leave

the cake and soda in Dr. Appleton's office on Friday?"

"I did not. I put them on the floor, outside the door, so it would look like I knocked but the door was locked and I couldn't get in." Rachel sounded as though she were speaking to a child who didn't get it the first time she told me, and rightly so. "That was my big lie, remember, telling the police that I never got in?"

"Are you sure? You wouldn't lie to me now, would you?"

"No way! You're scaring me, Dr. Knowles. Why are you asking me this?"

"I'm just trying to review everything, Rachel. And I have one more question. It's about your draft thesis. Do you have a copy?"

"I have so many copies I can't count them."

I knew how that went. Draft after draft and hardly being able to tell which version was which. "How about the ones on those yellow sheets. Do you have more than one copy of those, too?"

"Like, a gazillion. I only use the white paper when I'm ready to show something to Dr. Appleton."

"So, Dr. Appleton would see only white copies?"

"Yeah, he hated those yellow sheets. 'If it's not worth more than cheap paper, something's wrong with it and I don't want to see it,' he'd say." Rachel had worked her voice into a reasonable facsimile of a male's.

"Does anyone else have copies?"

"Yeah, we all pass them around to whoever will review them. Not you, because you always say all you know is math, though I know that's not true. But Dr. Bartholomew would read early versions, and Dr. Emerson, just for, you know format and stuff."

Fran, my own department chair, read yellow research papers. That meant I couldn't hide behind the cloak of mathematics any longer.

"So, lots of people had copies —"

"Oh, my God. Dr. Knowles," Rachel interrupted. "You asked me before if I saw any yellow sheets in Dr. Appleton's office. Was my thesis in there with him? Like on him or something? Oh, my God, is that it?"

"Calm down, Rachel."

"Oh, my God."

I wished there were something I could do about her fever pitch, but we were miles apart.

"Rachel, I'm working on this. I didn't mean to upset you. I just want to be sure I have all the facts straight."

"But I didn't see any yellow pages when I was in there. I swear."

"Then there's nothing for you to worry about."

That last statement nearly choked me. Unless Rachel had hired a real detective and wasn't counting on me, worry should be her middle name.

Shriek. Bark. Shriek. Bark. Shriek. Bark.

Not quite the Bat Phone, but the deafening noise woke me up.

After all of four hours sleep, the loudest noise ever in my home brought me straight up in bed. The most raucous party in Ben Franklin Hall couldn't compare on the decibel level.

I had no idea what to do. Punch in the alarm code? Anyone who knew me could figure out the code: 0-1-1-2-3-5, the first six numbers of the Fibonacci sequence. The keypad was near my headboard. I held my fingers over it, about to hit the zero and the rest of the series that would stop the roar. But wouldn't that defeat the purpose of having the alarm monitored? I should let it keep blaring and wait for the call from SoMass Alarm Company. I should stay in my bedroom until the cavalry arrived.

Shriek. Bark. Shriek. Bark. Shriek. Bark.

Again and again, while I was too numb to act.

Then, six beeps, and nothing.

Until Bruce smashed through my bedroom door, knocking over the chair. Hadn't I been brilliant adding that extra level of security?

Rrring. Rrring

Now the phone.

"SoMass Alarm. What's your password, please?"

"Fibonacci."

"Everything all right there?"

I looked at Bruce who was by my side and breathing heavily. He was wearing his blue MAstar cap and looking me over, not in a sexy way, but checking for blood or bruises, I knew.

"Sorry, false alarm. Everything's fine." I wondered briefly if security monitoring fees were like insurance rates, which rose every time you needed a service.

"Okeydokey."

Who said that anymore? Clearly the SoMass guy did.

"What's going on, Soph?" Bruce asked, his breathing almost back to normal.

"I set the alarm. You're always telling me I should be doing that."

"I never expect you to obey me. I almost

had a heart attack."

"Aren't you supposed to be used to this? Alarms and all?"

"Not in your house. Not when I'm coming to make breakfast. What gives?"

I looked at my bedside clock. Seven-thirty. "What are you doing here so early?"

"I had this weird feeling after we talked. Bodie always comes in early anyway, so I asked him to cover and took off." He removed his cap and wiped his brow with the back of his hand. "Then I open the door and get this blast worse than the Bat Phone. I don't know the code by heart, so I have to dig it out of my wallet." He pulled me to him and held tight. "I didn't know what I'd find in here."

"I'm so glad you're here, Bruce," I whispered.

"I know you. You sounded worried about something." He released me and pointed to the chair, on its back, one leg twisted out of shape. "Guess I was right. Are you going to tell me about it?"

I nodded. "How about over breakfast?"

One shower later, I walked in on Bruce cleaning up a carton of broken eggs and spilled OJ in the kitchen. It seemed that he had lost control of the groceries at the first

Shriek. Bark. I couldn't help be amused — now that I was safe and sound with my honey — that my hero emergency worker, Air Force vet, crisis-trained medevac pilot boyfriend had been thrown by a suburban burglar alarm. Not that I would mention it to him again. He'd explained it very well — it was different when it was personal.

While he was cooking, I coaxed him into telling me about his drill partnering with the Marines.

"Like I said on the phone, it was very cool, even for Air Force guys like me and Bodie. I really wish they'd make more USAF movies, though. It's always the army or the Marines that are the stars, like *Platoon* and *Full Metal Jacket*."

"There's the guy in *Little Miss Sunshine*," I volunteered.

"The whacko guy who won't talk until he gets into the Air Force Academy? Thanks a lot. Anyway, in real life there's this training site down the Cape for mountain warfare and they do mock evacuations every quarter. This time we were asked to join forces, which makes sense. In a real evacuation, it would take every agency in the area to pull together."

Bruce had begun the omelets, a Sunday morning tradition. He shook a spatula at me. "You're reaching now. I should have known you were stalling when you encouraged the movie talk."

In reality, I hated to hear about Bruce's flights. A few years ago in the Southwest a medical helicopter crashed during a training mission. The entire crew had been killed. I'd just met Bruce and spent many sleepless nights worrying after that. Now sometimes I took for granted that Bruce was no more at risk up in the air than I was tooling along the highway.

"When's breakfast?" I asked, pushing happy thoughts in front of depressing ones.

"In two minutes breakfast will be served and it will be your turn for a full report."

"Okay."

Fair was fair.

I waited until Bruce had tasted his three-cheese and mushroom omelet, made with stale eggs, and pronounced it perfect. He took a sip of dark roast that I'd brewed from freshly ground beans a few minutes earlier, and looked at home and relaxed in my sun-filled kitchen.

I told him the story of Woody and the red metal dolly.

"You took what? From where?" Bruce leaned across the table, wide-eyed.

"I think the dean wanted me to," I said.

He suppressed a grin. "Yeah, sure. I'm surprised she's not on the doorstep right now thanking you for your service, presenting you with an award."

An award. Why did that sound familiar? Something clicked, something about Keith's wall of awards, but I couldn't quite finish the thought.

"Hello?" Bruce said, waving his arms to get my attention. "What were you thinking when you cleaned out the office of a murdered man and carted his stuff home?"

"That I could help. My two police interviews didn't go well. I made a fool of myself with Virgil and I don't know what happened with Archie, except that he was this close" — I indicated a very small gap between my thumb and index finger — "to accusing me of murdering Keith, and I got no new information from him."

"Why do you need information about a murder case? You're not a cop; you're a math teacher."

"Associate professor of mathematics at a renowned college," I said. Going for distraction through humor, since I hadn't even gotten to the empty workbench yet.

"Where is all the stuff, anyway?"

Uh-oh.

■ ■ ■ ■

"Someone broke into your house —"

"My garage."

"— and you didn't think to call the cops?"

"Nothing was taken except those boxes and some usable discards. What was I going to tell the police?"

"I see your point. You had stolen goods in your possession."

"I wouldn't say stolen exactly."

I hated being grilled by Bruce. His crisp white T-shirt seemed to blind me as he threw questions and accusations at me. The fact that he had my own well-being in mind should have mattered more than it did.

Bruce had left his seat by now. I looked at his omelet and imagined I could see its molecules turn to a cold gel on his plate as he paced around the table. My own omelet was untouched.

"Sophie, I want you to promise me you'll cool it on this . . . this investigating."

"What investigating? I've barely talked to anyone but Rachel and the police."

"Who saw you take Appleton's things?"

"Just Woody knows about it, I think. A few of the girls saw the boxes but they had no way of knowing what was in them. And I suppose anyone could have been looking out a window and seen me, but I could have been cleaning out my own office for all anyone would guess. It was broad daylight, but it's not as if the boxes had Keith's name written on them."

Bruce sat back down and pushed food around his plate. His thick, dark eyebrows were pinched in concentration. He took a long pull of his juice. From his look and his body language, if I didn't know it was OJ, I'd have sworn he was swigging down a stiff drink.

"That's it," he said, setting the glass on the table with a purposeful thud. "I'm moving in until this is over."

"How romantic."

Bruce smiled. "You know what I mean."

"I do, thanks."

"Do you want me to cut out of my shift tonight?"

Bruce had one more shift, from nine tonight to nine tomorrow morning, and then he'd be off for seven days. I could certainly keep myself safe for twenty-four hours.

"No, I'll be fine. Just call me often."

"Deal."

I looked at my breakfast. Even the apple slices had gone brown.

We clicked mugs and picked from the plate of scones, the only still appetizing part of the menu.

13

It came to me that I'd imposed a deadline on myself when I called for meetings with Pam, Liz, and Casey. Though my real reason for wanting to talk to them had to do with what Bruce might erroneously have called "investigating," I needed to have a proposal for an acceptable ending to the summer statistics class by eleven o'clock this morning.

Bruce moved into the living room and picked up the Sunday newspaper, a break from our routine. He usually left for his home across town right after breakfast, did errands or puttered in his workshop for a while, and then took a short or long nap, depending on how busy he'd been all night. Since last night had been extra stressful, I'd expected him to be on his way to a Big Sleep. Like the movie, he'd have said.

I kissed his scruffy cheek as I walked by his chair.

"Gotta go prep for my student conference," I said. I was glad he couldn't see my face, which would have outed the half-truth.

I sat in the comfy leather chair in my office. The only window looked out on a large maple that was as old as the Henley hills. I swiveled toward my west-facing side yard, shadowy now before noon. There was no reason that a tree should remind me of Keith, but everything seemed to have that effect on me this weekend. I thought of the kind words both Woody and Elteen had for him, neither one of them obliged, as the dean was, for example, to sing his praises. There was no question, he'd been a large and powerful presence on campus and the hole he left would be obvious only when the fall semester began without him.

I turned from the window. Work beckoned.

I picked up my copy of the text, an intro to the practical uses of statistics. I wanted to have a list of potential topics to suggest to an uncreative student. I made a quick list: health and nutrition data, such as cholesterol levels; designing samples for studies of all kinds; testing the significance of survey results.

All fascinating to me.

I opened the "Applied Statistics" folder on my hard drive, and clicked on the file,

"Roster." The names of twelve students, all of whom were science majors entering junior year in the fall, popped up on a spreadsheet. The three who yesterday had achieved special status as persons of interest in a murder investigation were chemistry majors taking an extra math class as an elective.

I added a comments column where I could write notes on each student according to her current grade and how I saw her finishing the class.

I made some quick decisions. For the students getting an A so far, I'd ask for a short paper, due in two weeks, on a topic of their choice. Three students, including Pam, fell into this category. I jotted down some useful references and more detailed topic ideas to get them started. I hoped one of them would work on kinetic theory, since there were such beautiful equations involved. For the six B students — Liz was in this group — I'd ask for a longer paper. For Casey and two other students with C or lower, I'd require a paper plus an oral exam with me some time in the next two weeks.

I'd present this plan to the students by individual emails, except for the Big Three who would hear it in person soon. All was negotiable, to a point.

As I rushed off to my bedroom to get dressed for my consultations, I noticed Bruce, legs over the arms of the easy chair, working the crossword puzzle in the newspaper. Another great deviation from the norm.

I walked over to him. "What's this?" I asked.

He shrugged his shoulders. "It's sort of relaxing."

No "I told you so" left my lips.

No question, the world had shifted since the death of Keith Appleton.

Briefcase in hand, I went to tell Bruce I was leaving. The living room chair was empty except for a neatly put back together newspaper. Curious. No see-you-later kiss or "Hi, honey, I'm leaving."

It all became clear when I entered the garage, with its door already rolled up. Bruce was belted into my smokestone Fusion.

I dumped my briefcase in the back and climbed into the driver's seat, turning to face my passenger. "I didn't realize you were actually moving in *now.* Into my car, too?"

"I've always wanted to see that new library on campus. It's a good day for a tour."

"You should be home sleeping. Weren't

you up all night? And besides, I don't need a babysitter." And three more reasons I couldn't quite think of why Bruce should not be accompanying me to the library.

"I can nap in the library."

"I thought you wanted a tour of it."

"That, too."

"I have to go over class work with three different students, separately." Never mind the "what's your alibi for Friday afternoon" part. "It could take a couple of hours and there's nothing for you to do there. The library isn't exactly conducive to napping."

"I can read."

"They don't subscribe to *Air & Space* magazine."

"Why not?"

Sensing a losing battle and running out of time to argue, I grunted at my droopy-eyed boyfriend and started the car.

I parked in the vicinity of my usual spot near the tennis courts, avoiding the exact slot that was the site of yesterday's box-loading episode. Bruce had his briefcase with him also. As a cover? Or was he sneaking in more word puzzles? Maybe I could enlist him to help me with my crossword deadline.

We entered the main reading room of the

library, nicely appointed with a decent shade of beige carpeting and floor to ceiling windows looking out onto the imposing academic buildings and brilliant green lawns. Most of the chairs were big enough for a family of four — or for one student, a backpack, and a laptop.

Bruce took a seat in the corner with the best view of the campus. I wondered if he was using his USAF surveillance training, or just liked looking at the landscape. I noticed he'd brought his own copies of *Air & Space* and a couple of other flying periodicals. His puzzle phase might be over already.

My three students were waiting at the other end of the room, where there were groupings of chairs and small tables, suitable for study dates. I tried to think of this morning's meetings as a series of three study dates.

After brief greetings, Pam got us started. "We were thinking we could all go in together," she said. "It would save you time."

I laughed. "What are you? Trial lawyers in disguise?"

"It's just that we're nervous," Liz said.

"She means about our grades," Pam said, with her now famous reproachful glance at her friends.

"Me, too," Casey said, by way of nothing.

I was not in the mood for more arguing. My breakfast of coffee and a few crumbs of scone, meager as it was, did not sit well.

I looked each one in the eyes. "Here's the plan. I'm going to take you one by one in that corner" — I pointed to the farthest set of table and chairs — "and the other two will wait here. Is that clear?"

"Okay, then," Pam said. "Go ahead, Casey. You'll be fine."

What? She never quit. Didn't they all know I had a cushy side job that honed my skills as a strategist every day? Last year I had a perfect score on the Mensa quiz-a-day site. I could certainly outmaneuver three nineteen- or twenty-year-olds.

Pam was the leader here, and she recognized that Casey was the weak link. She wanted to play cleanup. I knew what I had to do — start with Pam and let the weak link stew for a little longer. I mentally rubbed my hands together: Then she'd be mine.

I looked at the three girls, lined up abreast, waiting for my next words. Had they deliberately all worn something pink today, to look soft and innocent? Pam had pink sandals with enough plastic daisies to look like she was standing in her own private flower patch; Liz and Casey, both blondes, wore pink tank tops in different shades and different placements of lacy trim. With my pale green sundress and dark hair, I felt I was in a stand-up life-size chess game where pink had three times more pieces than green.

I'd had these students in class every semester since they began at Henley. I'd taught them two semesters of calculus and special topics that fit them as chemistry majors. They were the types to hang around teachers, often volunteering as party cleanup crew, so I knew them better than I did most of my students. Was I seriously thinking that one or all of them was involved in a monstrous deed?

Don't be fooled by the pastels, I told myself.

"First, Dr. Knowles, I want you to know that Liz and Casey and me, we're one hundred percent eager to cooperate," Pam started out. She sat up straight, primly, hands folded on the table, in the chair opposite mine. It might have been a job interview, with Pam as the one doing the hiring.

I pulled out my roster and slid the sheet onto the table between us. "Let's start with your status in the applied statistics class," I said, smiling. A pleasant countenance, but not an overly happy face, was my goal. Me teacher, you student.

Pam's shoulders slumped, her long light brown hair falling across her cheeks. It didn't take much for poor posture to take over with the backpacker crowd. "I think . . . I hope I'm doing good."

"You're doing very well," I said. "You have an A so far. As you know, the administration has asked us all to make arrangements for ending the summer courses without holding any more formal classes."

Pam nodded, definitely more deferential, following my lead. "Uh-huh."

I explained my plan to Pam — that if she would submit a five-page paper, instead of the two-page reference report listed on the original syllabus, on a mutually acceptable topic, the exam would be waived. She did, after all, now have a week free of classes. Was that agreeable to her?

"Totally," she said, waving her hands to dismiss all doubt. "I'm thinking of switching my major to biostatistics and I already have a start on a paper."

This was news. My gut feeling said that students would be going in the other direction after Friday. I figured that those who were on the fence and afraid of the Entirely Too Demanding, Legendary Dr. Appleton would now be flocking to chemistry, not away from it.

"You're switching to the new interdisciplinary major?"

Here was another area where Keith and Dean Underwood were in agreement.

"I don't like hyphenated names for classes, let alone major fields of study," she'd said.

"Interdisciplinary is another word for watered down," he'd said.

Keith and the dean had been outvoted by the new, hyphenated, watered down generation.

Pam nodded vigorously. "I'm going to talk to my adviser this week. I have enough bio credits to make the switch, and I love that there's more math in the new program."

The way to my heart.

"Have you already come up with a topic that fits your new direction?"

"I started my report on it and I can easily expand the table of contents and flesh it out. Eventually I want to work on a human genome project, so I'd like to do a paper on statistical genetics."

Impressive. I looked ahead a few years and saw Pam one day running a research institute or managing data analysis at a pharmaceutical company.

"Okay, then. Have it to me two weeks

from tomorrow."

"Done," she said, and placed her hands to lift herself from her seat and be off.

"No obligation, of course, but if you have another minute, I'd like to go over a different matter with you."

Pam let out a heavy sigh. "Sure."

Where was the one hundred percent eager to cooperate attitude?

I lowered my voice though the reading room was nearly empty. "Remember yesterday when I asked your whereabouts on Friday afternoon, say, between noon and four o'clock?"

Pam rolled her eyes, involuntarily I was certain, and nodded. "Mmm hmm."

"We never did finish that conversation."

"We were at the party for Dr. Bartholomew, like everybody else, then we went to the dorm."

"I'm asking where you were, not your friends."

"Okay. *I* was at the party for Dr. Bartholomew, like everybody else, then *I* went to the dorm."

Cute. "I thought there was some hesitation yesterday, or some details you'd left out. Inadvertently."

"No, that's about it. Remember the three of us helped you clean up after the party?

Then we all left together around two?"

"The four of us didn't exactly walk out arm in arm," I said, with a chuckle.

"We may have gone to the restroom," Pam said. "Me, that is." Her tone said she intended to stick to her story and she was pretty much done with answering any more questions about it. While she didn't ask for a lawyer, I sensed the idea had crossed her mind.

I foresaw the whole morning going this way, with Pam, Liz, and Casey alibiing each other.

On the tip of my tongue were a couple of niggling phrases that didn't fit what Pam claimed. Without forceps to drag the words out in the open, I was at a stalemate.

I had no option but to send Pam off with a request to ask Liz to come into my den.

"We were at the party for Dr. Bartholomew, like everybody else, then we went to the dorm," Liz said. Was that an echo? I deemed it useless to ask her to repeat the line using only herself as subject.

We'd already covered her topic for a significant paper to wrap up the applied statistics class. Liz had turned in her seat and was now in the "ready, set" stance, waiting for "go."

"Liz, I'm sure you know that sometimes even a very small omission can mean a great deal in a murder investigation."

"Are you investigating Dr. Appleton's murder?"

I didn't expect that blow. Pam must have stayed up all night prepping her girls.

"No, of course not," I said, "but like every other teacher and student at Henley I'm concerned that his killer be found quickly, so we can all feel safe."

Liz flinched. It was a cheesy shot to throw in the safety angle, but I was losing.

"Aren't the police supposed to take care of that?" she asked, with a shaky voice.

I felt only a little guilty scaring her, but I knew I should quit.

I was officially exhausted from the deviousness of my pursuit and more glad than ever that I hadn't gone into any aspect of law enforcement. I was ready to admit defeat. "You're right, Liz. And you have no obligation to tell me anything."

"So we're through?"

Liz had regained her composure and came off as unflappable.

"We're through. Why don't you just get started on that paper? And please tell Casey I'll need a few minutes before I go over her work with her."

Liz shot out of our little corner.

How did detectives like Virgil and Archie do it? I couldn't even break down cute little soon-to-be coeds. How difficult must it be to work with hardened criminals?

I stood up to stretch and guzzle a few ounces from my water bottle. I decided to treat myself and pay a visit to Bruce whom I'd left at the front of the library. I figured he'd been alone long enough and might need a little human interaction and a peck on the cheek.

Not necessary.

I approached the area and saw my boyfriend engaged in animated conversation with two women. Coeds? No, older than that.

The group of three, with their backs to me, made for an unusual tableau on a Sunday morning in the college library: Bruce Granville, medevac pilot; Gil Bartholomew, flight nurse; and Phyllis Underwood, academic dean.

Bruce and Gil had met the dean at holiday gatherings and celebrations, but hadn't exchanged more than a few polite words with her.

Now the two emergency workers appeared to have found a willing audience for their exciting tales. I held back and tuned into the conversation.

From Gil: "Then there was the time we simulated a bus crash with thirty people on their way to a casino."

From Dean Underwood: "Does someone think that could really happen?"

From Bruce: "Anything can happen."

Oops, the dean never wanted to hear something like that. But I hadn't been asked to edit.

From Gil: "The idea is to practice our drills, get to know each other and how we operate, you know, just in case."

From Bruce, who had read the dean correctly: "On the outside chance."

From Gil: "We brought in twelve fire departments, three law enforcement agencies, an emergency communications agency" — she ticked off the list I'd heard more than once from Bruce — "the state office of emergency services, and the coroner's office."

From Bruce: "Plus hospitals and an air ambulance."

From Dean Underwood: "My."

Gil was the first to spot me. She waved me to a seat next to her. "Hey, Sophie, look who's all here."

I'd noticed. "Hey, Gil. Bruce." I cleared

my throat and all but bowed. "Dean Under-wood."

Bruce stood and took my arm, leading me to a seat. I was sure the dean would be impressed by his old-fashioned chivalry, and the way I seemed to accept it. I also knew that's what Bruce had in mind.

"Hal has something to pick up or leave off or whatever in Franklin Hall, and Timmy's with his grandmother," Gil said, "so I thought I'd ride over and then get a lunch date out of it."

"You're off today?"

"Not supposed to be, but the schedule got crazy this week, with all hands on deck for the big drill and people switching here and there. Happens a lot."

"The nurses have it a lot easier," Bruce said.

Gil gave him a mock frown and pulled something from her purse. She handed me a sheet of paper. My word puzzle, com-pleted. The one everyone else at the party had complained about and declared impos-sible.

"Terrific. You did it." All it took was one positive response to cheer me, and Gil was often the one who gave it to me.

"It took me a little longer than usual, but I like that kind of challenge."

Suddenly the dean stood, and everyone stood with her.

"Well, I must get to the reason I came by in the first place," she said. She held up a stack of books and pointed to the returns desk.

I wouldn't have thought the dean would be subject to the same circulation policy as the rest of us, but, hey, what did I know?

"Dean Underwood," Bruce said, nodding. I was proud of my guy's good manners.

I was ready to return to my interview corner, but the dean beckoned me to her side with one of her crooked fingers. "Sophie," she said.

I gulped. Hearing the dean address me by my first name was, ironically, like hearing my mother use my full name, as in "Sophie Saint Germain Knowles," followed by, "Stop that this instant."

Bruce and Gil seemed be involved in a conversation of their own now. I heard phrases like rotor downwash, high payload, and something about a new litter, which I took to be not about puppies or kittens.

"Yes?" I croaked at the dean.

Out of the corner of my eye I saw Pam, Liz, and Casey approaching. All I needed was for one of them to ask if I was through with my questioning them as part of a murder investigation.

"I'll see you in my office immediately," the dean said.

On a Sunday? Wait a minute. The dean might be able to make or break me career-wise, but she wasn't in charge of my weekends.

I swung my arm in the direction of the students who now stood a discreet distance away, thankfully, as if they were in line for an ATM. "I'm holding my student conferences this morning, to plan out the end of my summer classes. As President Aldridge requested."

I'd learned a long time ago how rank-conscious the dean was. Name-dropping was always a good bet for gaining the upper hand.

She pushed back the sleeve of her pale linen jacket, her idea of casual Sunday attire, and looked at her watch. Could it be that she had a life? I doubted it. I'd often thought that the reason she and Keith got along so well was that he didn't have one either. They were each other's nonlife.

"Very well, then. I'll see you in my office right after President Aldridge's all-faculty meeting in the morning."

"President Aldridge also called for each department to hold a meeting after the all-hands assembly." I was almost huffy this time.

The dean let out a long, annoyed breath. "Of course you'll follow that directive. But, for now" — in a most unusual gesture, she took hold of my elbow and ushered me to a spot in the stacks, farther from the students — "you are to return to me the boxes of material you took from Dr. Appleton's office immediately."

"What are you —"

The dean's "don't you dare deny it" look cut me off. She stomped off in her sensible pumps.

"See you then," I said to her back, then flapped away in my sandals.

14

I'd had no time to dwell on the boxes except to think about hiring a PI to locate them for me. My phone rang as I was on my way to my temporary conference table at the back of the library. I clicked my phone on and used hand signals to tell Casey to meet me there in five minutes.

When did my life become so complicated? On Friday, when Keith Appleton was murdered, I remembered.

Bruce was calling me from the other end of the library. I'd seen Gil leave the building and Bruce wander off to the periodical rack, maybe to slip in copies of *Rotor* magazine as a recruiting device.

"I heard the dean call you 'Sophie.' That couldn't have been good," my perceptive boyfriend said.

I growled. "She wants the boxes back."

"Good luck with that."

"Bruce!" The volume was low but the tone

was a shout.

"Kidding. Want me to help? I can call Virge."

"You can't call Virge."

"Because you're a thief? You know I love a good heist movie. *The Score, The Thomas Crown Affair* —"

"Bruce!"

"Go take care of your students. Let me see what I can do, okay? Do you need your car for an hour or so?"

"Where are you going?"

"Don't know yet."

"You can take my car, but you can't call Virge," I repeated. "And I didn't do a heist."

I had one more chance with the Triad. Casey was the Queen of Bling, with a different set of shiny, tinkling baubles every day. While I couldn't even stand to wear a watch on hot days, Casey decorated her wrists, ears, neck, toes, fingers and patches of bare skin with jewels and decals no matter what the weather.

It was tough to search out her small face with today's distraction, a matching beaded set of earrings, necklace, and bracelet, in shades of red and purple. I was tempted to ask if she'd made them herself, and if so, had she bought the beads at Ariana's shop, but that would have compounded the distraction.

I decided to try a new tactic with the third interview of the day, not counting the dean's with me, and start with the elephant in the room.

"Casey, I felt you had more to say yesterday, when we were chatting outside Franklin Hall. Is there something you want to tell me?"

"We were at the party for Dr. Bartholomew, like everybody else, then we went to the dorm," she said.

Not again. I sent a soft, compassionate breath her way. "Casey, I know Pam can be a little intimidating —"

"I don't have anything more to say, Dr. Knowles. Can we just get to my grade for the class? Please?"

Casey's "please" was a drawn out plea. That and her eyes, on the verge of tears, got to me. Time to move on. I knew these girls were hiding something, but when push came to shove, I couldn't beat up on this child.

Casey was not doing well in applied statistics. To keep her scholarship she needed at least a B in each class. In my class she was hovering around C, plus one day, minus the next. I told her the kind of research paper she'd have to do to bring her grade up, and that she'd need to take an exam.

In my experience, there were two kinds of test takers, those who preferred oral exams and those who dreaded them. I gave Casey her choice.

"Oh, my God, I love orals," Casey said. "I get all clutched up when I have to write and I can't explain myself because the questions are too . . . too . . ."

"Too specific?"

She nodded. "Like Dr. Appleton's. Like, with true/false it's do or die" — she clamped her hand over her mouth — "I didn't mean it that way."

I patted her other hand, the one with six inches of thin multicolor spangles. "I know you didn't mean it. You had that extended organic chem class with Dr. Appleton this summer, right?"

"I like that. 'Extended.' Actually it was makeup, since we did so badly this spring."

"Do you know yet how that will be wrapped up?"

"Uh-huh, that new teacher, Ms. Bronson, is taking over now as far as working out our grades."

"I'm glad it's taken care of. What grade do you have going in?"

A simple query, to show my interest, not meant to be a trick question. I was past trying to dupe the girls into giving me information I could use to clear Rachel. And I'd decided some time ago that getting to the truth of who killed Keith Appleton was more important even than a single student. I needed to follow the evidence and the logic of the murder, no matter where it led.

I was taken aback to watch Casey stumbling over my simple question and looking as rattled as if she had one million dollars riding on her answer. She ran both hands through her unruly curls. "Uh . . . an A," she mumbled.

That was a surprise. But why mumble an A when it might be the first one you've had in a long time? Maybe I'd heard wrong.

"Did you say an A?"

"I have an A going in," she said, not much more clearly.

"Good for you. I thought you were struggling with that class."

"I, uh, was, but I, uh, pulled it up."

I looked across the table at Casey. She hadn't been this flustered even yesterday while she was lying to me. She fidgeted in her chair, looked up to the ceiling and down to the table, glanced back over her shoulder toward the lobby, and then repeated the sequence. My guess was that she wished she could beam Pam and Liz over here to bail her out. Pam and Liz, on their part, were inching closer to us as it became increasingly obvious, even from a distance, that Casey was in distress.

Casey's behavior threw me back to being in Keith's office a few days before his death.

Keith is working on his laptop, updating his organic chemistry grade sheet. He's in a hurry to finish up and print out the sheet to take to his class. "Look at this." He spins his computer in my direction and shows me the screen. "Not one student even close to a B," he says. I look. Sure enough, no grade above a C and most below it. I know he wants me to commiserate about the pathetic abilities of Henley chemistry majors. I don't comment. He turns the laptop back and pecks away at his keyboard. He shakes his head. "Dumb sophomores," he says. "Dumb juniors. Dumb every student at this dumb college."

Now a picture started to take shape, and it wasn't pretty. I saw Casey and her friends poisoning Keith — the details weren't clear — and changing their grades on his laptop. I tried to chase away the picture. Of all the motives I could think of, this was one of the weakest. I imagined every college in cities and towns across the country losing a few teachers every year if this practice became popular.

Something was missing in my theory. I played with the murderous picture in my head, running a blackboard eraser back and forth across it but it wouldn't disappear.

Out of the blue, Woody Conroy with his barrel of mops and brooms, invaded the scene that was taking over my vision. I heard Woody mention how he'd hung Keith's Fellow award that morning. Pam entered the picture and I heard her tell me how she and her friends hadn't seen Keith all day on Friday. Then Casey's or Liz's voice joined in, talking about the Fellow award on the wall.

Someone was lying. Either Woody put that award up the day before, or the girls had been in Keith's office the morning he was murdered. How else could they have seen the award on the wall?

I left the scene, with the imaginary Woody and Pam and Liz and Casey arguing about who was telling the truth. My chips were on Woody.

My mind reentered the interrogation corner of the Emily Dickinson Library.

"Casey, did you change your grade?"

Casey lifted her head from the cushion of

her arms on the table. Her blond hair was wet from tears that had started when the subject of organic chemistry came up. Her face was streaked with poorly applied eye makeup. She opened her mouth but no words came out.

Pam and Liz had reached us by now. Liz began stroking Casey's back. Pam's arms were folded across her flat chest.

"We can explain," Pam said.

"I'm all ears."

"Let's go somewhere else," Liz said. "This whole place is creeping me out." She wrapped her arms across her thin body as if she were freezing. Or at a crime scene.

"I can't stand this campus one more minute either," Casey said, in a low scream, pointing toward Franklin Hall. She'd pulled herself together enough to stand up. "Can we go to, like, a coffee shop downtown?"

"I have my car," Pam said, before I could respond. She looked at me. "Unless you're afraid to ride with us?"

"Of course not," I said.

How foolish was this? Was I now the same obstacle to Casey's college funding that Keith had been? I refused to believe these young women would harm me.

Still, I hoped Bruce wouldn't travel too far out of range of my cell.

■ ■ ■ ■

We sat at a round table in Back to the Grind, only a few blocks from campus, an easy walk in better weather. The place wasn't air-conditioned, but a large fan kept the room bearable. The ride over had been silent except for the sounds of an old AC/DC album in Pam's CD player.

Now with various levels of caffeine drinks in front of us, it was still silent. Until Casey started to tear up again.

Pam put her hand on Casey's arm and the waterworks stopped. "We just wanted to help Casey out," Pam said.

"So you two were happy with your Cs and Ds?" I asked, addressing Pam and Liz.

"We just thought, while we were there, you know, we might as well up ours a notch, too," Liz said.

I rolled my eyes, shook my head, and otherwise showed my extreme disapproval.

"Oh, come on. How many students does Dr. Appleton really flunk in the long run?" Pam asked in an updated version of "pshaw." "Not that many when it comes to final grades. He likes to scare us is all. I'd have come out fine one way or the other."

"I knew I could make it up," Liz said.

"Honestly, a C or D here or there isn't going to ruin my life. But Casey would have had to leave school."

"And that was worth your teacher's life?"

The girls turned to me, eyes all wide, mouths open.

I heard the beginnings of sentences.

"Oh, no . . ."

"We didn't really . . ."

"How could you think . . . ?"

Their protests were intermingled; I couldn't tell who was saying what.

Pam and Liz each held one of Casey's hands. All were in tears when the next round began.

"He was already dead."

"I wanted to just leave." This, I was sure, was from Casey.

"We went there to help Casey try to negotiate."

"We started to knock, but the door just pushed open."

"I didn't want to go through with it." Casey again.

"I've been a wreck." And again.

"It was a stupid thing to do, but he was dead. And there was his computer screen —"

"With all our grades."

Eventually, the girls started from the

beginning, when they'd headed up to the fourth floor around two thirty on Friday. They took turns describing the crime scene, with their professor on the floor behind his desk. It was like hearing Rachel all over again and I realized they didn't match the profile of a killer any more than Rachel did. Assuming I'd know one when I saw one.

"We really are disgusted with ourselves," Liz said.

"You should be," I said. "But I'm glad you're telling the truth now."

"What should we do?" Pam asked, surprising me. I'd have expected her to exact a promise from me to not breathe a word.

"You should go to the police," I said, all virtuous.

"Aren't you working with the cops?" Liz asked.

Uh-oh. Virtue was about to fly out the open window next to our table.

"Yes, I am," I said, mentally reserving the fact that the cops didn't know it. "And I have a couple of questions if you don't mind —"

"Oh, my God. Can we help?" Casey said, while Liz and Pam gave me an "anything you like" look.

I took a notebook out of my purse, as befitted one helping out the Henley PD.

251

"Let's start with your arriving at Dr. Appleton's office, about two thirty you said?"

"Uh-huh. After the party. His car was still on campus, so we knew he was in and we thought if we all went up together we might be able to make him see reason."

An intimidating group, but I doubted Keith would have been fazed by three of his students. I envisioned his standing up behind his desk and flicking them out the door.

"You all stayed to help me clean up, so it was after that?"

"We wanted to make sure you were gone," Casey said.

Pam shot her a look. The old Pam was back. "We didn't want anyone interrupting us," she said.

I got it.

"About Dr. Appleton's office. I know it won't be pleasant, but if you can go back in your minds and tell me if you saw anything out of the ordinary?"

The girls closed their eyes, séance style, and at that moment I felt they were putty in my hands. I wasn't proud of the rush I got. Was this how Archie felt when I was cowering before him yesterday afternoon? If I didn't get my promotion, was I too old to sign up for the police academy? Questions for another time.

"It was a mess," Pam said. "And, you know, Dr. Appleton always kept everything in order."

"A real neat freak," Liz said.

"Was there any food around?"

The girls looked at each other and nodded.

"There was a paper plate with cake outside the door," Pam said. "I think I saw Rachel make up a plate for him."

"And a can of soda," Liz said. "Some kind of cola, I think."

"We were going to pick it up and take it in, but we decided not to move it, in case that's where he wanted it," Casey said.

"You know, like, maybe he was trashing it," Liz added.

I tried to process this factoid and insert it into my mental timeline. Rachel took the cake upstairs and left it outside Keith's door at about one forty-five. The girls saw it there at two thirty, but Woody saw it on the chair in Keith's office at four. And, of course, the police didn't see it all because Woody tossed it to protect Keith's reputation as a neat freak.

I was already juggling all the visitors to Keith's post-murder office. The killer was there before Rachel and the girls arrived, but someone else was there between the girls' visit and Woody's discovery. It had to have been the killer coming back to plant evidence against Rachel. Would a killer risk two trips? I wondered if all crime scenes were as busy as this one.

It was clear that I was going to need to create a real, physical timeline. I wished I'd brought my laptop to the library, but there'd be time once I got to my home office.

"I know things were broken and on the floor, but was there any extra paper? I'm wondering about that yellow paper you all use for your drafts."

"Dr. Appleton wouldn't look at the yellow drafts," Pam said.

"Never," Casey said.

So I'd heard. "And no one had, say, just dumped some there?"

"Not that I saw."

"Nope."

"Nuh-uh."

I made a note. For Rachel and the girls, it was yes on the cake at the door; no on the yellow pages. For the police, I recalled, it had been no on the cake and yes on the yellow pages. Something kept bugging me about the yellow pages, but I couldn't put my finger on it.

If I could just separate all this from the horrible fact of Keith Appleton's murder, it would be a fun puzzle.

15

The old problem of withholding information from the police reared its head again. I now had information from Rachel, Pam, Liz, and Casey that would be useful to Virgil and Archie in establishing a timeline. I also had that clue from Keith's cousin that he was seeing someone. I assumed the police could track her down even without a name and probably had done so already. Wasn't that the first thing they did, look to the spouse or significant other?

I wished they'd told me if they found a girlfriend in Keith's life. More than that, I wished I had an official role in the investigation, but how realistic was that? Both Virgil and Archie had made it clear that I was useless at best, a hindrance at worst.

I'd encouraged all four girls to go to the police with the truth about their tramping on the crime scene. Maybe that was it, as far as my responsibility as a citizen. Should

I waste time reporting to the police and nagging the girls, or wouldn't it be better if I could just figure everything out first and hand everyone the solution? That process worked well with my puzzle editor. Why not with the Henley PD?

Yeah, right.

My interview with the girls had been so satisfactory, I almost forgot about the boxes and the dean. Pam had given me a ride home. As we'd approached my driveway and I'd dug out my spare remote control for the garage door, I'd had the fantasy wish that the boxes might have reappeared.

No such luck.

At three in the afternoon on Sunday, alone in my house, I had approximately nineteen hours before the president's meeting, followed immediately by my meeting with the dean, at which time I needed to have either the boxes or a good story.

I checked my messages. There was nothing that shed light on my current state. Even a ransom note would have been welcome. I imagined: "Give me an A in applied statistics and I'll return the boxes."

"Deal," I'd have said.

A message from Ariana reminded me about the next beading class where we would make "fun, fantastical, magical luggage tags." Ariana liked to note that her December 5 birthday was the same as Walt Disney's. I pointed out that the same day in the same year was also the birthday of Heisenberg, the quantum physicist who came up with the uncertainty principle.

I wished I could fit something fun or magical anywhere on my to-do list.

I left a text message for Bruce. "Where R U? Where's my car? I need U."

Clear enough, I thought.

In my office, the piles of work, all with imminent deadlines, sat waiting. I owed the dean three syllabi for the new term, one each for linear algebra, real analysis, and differential equations. I needed to contact the nine other summer students about their grades. I had a crossword with gaping holes where clues should be. And that wordplay puzzle, the butt of jokes at Friday's party, that only Gil had been able to solve.

Instead of tackling the piles, I downloaded a simple timeline program that allowed the user to enter hours of the day and events into a table. The software then spit out a linear version of the input.

Maybe if I organized the information I had about the crime scene, something would pop up that had arrows pointing to Keith's killer.

I entered everything I knew about who was in Franklin Hall in the afternoon, including students other than the four who were most involved with the party. As much as possible I wrote down names and when I thought they'd arrived and left. I included faculty members who were at the party — the department chairs, Fran, Judith, and Robert; the new girl, Lucy; Hal, and even Gil. I widened my scope a little more by including a couple of faculty senate members with whom Keith had had serious conflicts. I omitted only myself and Woody.

I couldn't help think of the woman Keith was seeing, according to his cousin. I wished I could find her. But with only a first name, two possible first names at that, it didn't make sense to pursue that line.

With some hesitation I added Dean Underwood's name to the list. She and Keith were simpatico most of the time, but admitting male students to Henley was no small issue and Keith had been instrumental in gathering enough support to override the dean's vote.

I had no doubt why Keith had been such an advocate of coeducation, but he'd confirmed my guess one day when he said at a faculty meeting, "Let's face it. A women's college will never have the same status as a men's college or a coed institution."

Having been around academia — make that, having been around, period — I couldn't argue with him.

I recalled a group of us females standing in front of a notice on an easel outside a meeting room at a math conference in Hartford.

"Panel Today on the Role of Women in Mathematics."

"Where's the one on the role of men?" a female colleague had asked, through gritted teeth.

"Maybe we can take on the role of the multiplication sign," another woman had said. She'd won begrudging laughs from the men in the vicinity.

I'd done my best as a teacher to change attitudes and create opportunities for my female students. But that wasn't the most pressing issue on my agenda this Sunday afternoon.

I had a puzzle to solve.

I printed out my timeline on legal size paper and tacked it up on my bulletin board. I recognized the inadequacy of focusing only on the people who were in Franklin Hall or on campus that day. Someone from the town of Henley or anywhere else could have made it onto the property and into the building.

Security on the college property was very casual. You pulled up to the checkpoint at the southwest entrance, off Henley Boulevard. If Maureen or Bill or any of the other guards didn't recognize you as a staff member or a student with a special permit, you had to give a reason for wanting to enter. You could say, "I'm here for the history seminar," or "I'm with the band," and the bar would be raised for you.

As for walking onto the campus, no one monitored the walkways or pedestrian entrances. And the buildings had no extra security except at night when the doors were locked. I'd often thought the security posts were there simply to be sure the parking lots wouldn't be overrun.

Once in a while when a crime occurred on campus the school newspaper would run a story about poor security for the dorms, but all it took was the onset of exam week and everyone would forget the disturbance.

The murder of a faculty member was more than a disturbance, however, and I hoped Keith's death would inspire a good look at campus safety overall.

I needed to do my part.

I studied my timeline and made some embellishments. I used a red marker to

261

indicate the probable time of Keith's death, bracketing the hours from noon to one forty-five. Only Rachel and I knew that the deed had been done by one forty-five when Rachel showed up with the cake. If, as Woody thought, Keith didn't arrive much before noon, then he'd been correct in assuming that Keith hadn't had a lot of time to admire his new Fellow award.

I hadn't even given Bruce the details of Rachel's confession of sorts when I reported on my meeting with her at MAstar. And though I wished it with all my heart, I doubted that Rachel had offered up her story to the police.

Virgil said the medical examiner had placed the time of death between noon, based on Woody's having seen Keith's car at that time, and four, when Woody found him.

I was getting increasingly uncomfortable knowing more than the police did, thanks to Rachel's reluctance to tell them the whole truth. The Big Three's two thirty visit to Keith's office didn't shed any new light on the time of death, but it did give us information on the cake and the yellow sheets that were allegedly Rachel's thesis.

If I really wanted a good night's sleep, I should go to the police.

Now, a conscientious voice inside my head said.

You don't have a car, said my bad girl voice, looking for any excuse.

Give yourself one more chance to put it all together, said my puzzle voice.

Two to one. I'd give myself that chance, at least until the dean cornered me tomorrow.

I sat at the counter in my kitchen with a reheated omelet. Not recommended.

I had to come up with a strategy. I could query the Ben Franklin faculty. And ask them what? If they'd followed the cake trail by any chance? If they'd followed the journey of the boxes by any chance?

For once I was looking forward to a faculty meeting. I'd had an email from Fran that all the departments of Franklin Hall would meet separately after the president's address, as she'd requested.

When I was stuck like this, puzzling always helped me. I finished the crossword puzzle I'd been working on that was formerly in the shape of a beaker. I'd turned the grid into the shape of a teapot and now I sent it electronically via my laptop to my editor in Kansas City. It felt good to complete a task, if a relatively unimportant one. I liked it when my life was easy to figure out.

The sound of a motor caught my attention. Either Bruce or the box thief had opened my garage door. I almost wished it were the box thief, come to apologize and explain himself.

It could happen.

Not this time, but Bruce's "Hey" was very welcome. I had to admit it felt a little creepy in my house today, knowing someone had intruded at least as far as my garage when I was out. The sooner I got to the bottom of the ill wind that had swept through Henley, the sooner I'd feel safe and grounded again.

"Have you slept at all today?" I asked my boyfriend.

Bruce shook his head. "I'll get some tonight. There won't be anything big at work, not two nights in a row. I'll bet the most we'll have to do is an IFT. A half hour and we're back."

I knew about interfacility transfers. When a patient needed equipment or care not available in the hospital he was in, MAstar could be called in to transport him to another. The Bat Phone summoned them for that mission also, I'd learned.

"You're saying you can't have two busy nights in a row at work. Is that a rule?"

"It's statistics. Know anything about them?"

Cute. "I think you should at least try to nap."

"Before or after I tell you what I learned from Virge?"

I jumped off the stool and grabbed Bruce's arms. "Come here, you."

Surprise, surprise, the Henley PD had been working on the same case I was, and they had their own ways of getting information. Without stealing material from crime scenes or browbeating young coeds. It might turn out that while I was busy doing the above, eliminating a lot of pesky paperwork, the Henley PD had actually culled facts to work with. Another approach to a murder investigation.

I had no problem buttering up my hungry boyfriend/coconspirator to get the most out of him. I cooked up a fresh soufflé and served it to him with cinnamon toast.

"You're enjoying this, aren't you? Keeping me dangling like this," I said, taking a seat across from him.

I loved Bruce's disheveled off-duty look, when the dark hair on either side of his widow's peak formed unruly arcs, the ends of which touched his eyebrows. It was what people called the "Dark Irish look," though you'd have to go back a couple of generations to find Bruce's Galway Bay roots.

"You're the one who told me not to call Virge."

I poured coffee for both of us. "I know I said that, but that was stupid," I admitted.

"Mmm hmm," he mumbled through a mouthful of toast. He knew better than to agree completely with a statement like that.

"I'm waiting," I said. I'd set my laptop in front of me on the kitchen table, across from Bruce and his breakfast/lunch/dinner combination, poor guy. I was ready to take notes. I tapped my fingers on the keyboard.

"I always get the greatest stories from Virge. Like, this teenager on a bicycle tried to rob four people along Henley Boulevard one day last week. First, he tried to hold up a couple and when they told him they had no money, he just rode away. Then he stops a jogger, and that guy didn't carry his wallet, so the kid tries an old lady, and, well, I forget the rest, but I guess this was all within one block, so all the victims jumped on him and held him down while one called the police."

"What a kick," I said, with no kick in my voice.

"Okay, I've had my fun. Not that Virge

told me anything top secret, but he was willing to share for whatever reason. Everyone down there wants this to be put to bed quickly, believe me. The commissioner's phone is ringing off the hook."

"Are you saying that he thinks I could help?"

"Not in so many words. But I think it would be a good idea if you went down and talked to them."

"You mean tell them about the boxes and all. Didn't you tell him today?"

"I don't even know what the 'all' is, by the way," Bruce said. I wasn't shocked that Bruce was aware that I'd been holding back from him. He'd had a lot of experience with my moods, tone of voice, and signs of tension. "And no, I didn't tell him about the boxes. That's for you to do."

"I don't see the boxes as all that important anyway," I said. "The crime scene people had already been through Keith's office and taken whatever they wanted. Eventually Woody or some other faculty member would have cleaned out the rest of the stuff. Why not me?"

"I'll buy that," he said.

"I hope the dean does tomorrow."

"It's not as if you're withholding evidence."

"I might be."

Bruce put his fork down. His heavy eyebrows moved closer together.

"Hit me with it."

What kind of psychology training were medevac personnel given that Bruce was able to turn things around and I ended up spilling everything first?

I told Bruce about the parade of people who walked through the crime scene and even messed with it, as Woody did.

"Soph," was all he said.

"I know, I know. I'll go by tomorrow right after I see the dean, I promise. Now it's definitely your turn."

"Well, I'm glad to report that the cops are on target. They're putting the murder at sometime after one o'clock, which fits with Rachel's finding him already dead at quarter to two."

Whew. The police figured it out on their own. I felt marginally better. All I needed to do was give them the curious timelines for the cake and the yellow sheets.

"Are the results in on the poison? Can they tell what it was that killed him?"

"Potassium chloride."

"Like the label on the bottle on Keith's desk."

"Uh-huh. I actually saw the crime scene

photo of the bottle. It was transparent, with a white label, and it was in solid form, a granular white powder. But it's very soluble in water. I guess it's common in a chem lab. We probably even have some in the supply trailer."

I thought of Rachel's missing key to the cabinet in the main chemistry lab. "So someone used Rachel's key to get it out of the cabinet, melted it in water, and put it in a syringe?"

"I don't think melted is the right word."

I shrugged it off. "Close enough. Where did all that happen? I mean, do you just go to the sink and mix it all in a glass?"

"I haven't a clue. Virge says there was no such evidence in the Franklin Hall chem lab. No glass, so to speak, as in your scenario, or stirrer. They think the actual mixing was done off-site."

"Then why would the killer put the bottle on the desk? Isn't it obvious it was just a plant, to point to Rachel?"

"I don't think Virge has a theory on that. Wherever it was prepared, apparently Keith was given an injection of an unnaturally high concentration, about the same as they use for the death penalty."

"He'd have to be unconscious, don't you think? Otherwise he'd fight off the attacker."

"Or else it was a surprise. Someone he knew got close and . . ." I shuddered. Bruce put his fingers on the side of his neck. "The injection site was right here. The heart just stops."

"The heart, or Keith's heart?"

Bruce took my hand across the table. "Sorry, Sophie. They're saying it was very quick, anyway, that he didn't suffer for a long time. Some comfort, huh? I know it's tough on you, even though you weren't best friends."

"Some people think we were." I told Bruce about the many nice words for Keith that came from his cousin and Woody, how generous he was behind our backs.

"Who would have guessed?"

"Not me," I said.

I hadn't given much thought to the biological details of Keith's death. While I'd certainly heard of potassium chloride in connection with fertilizer, it wasn't in my skill set to remember much of chemistry and chemical formulas. Way too complicated. Besides, chemistry was dangerous. One little atom off and a substance went from harmless to lethal. There was sodium chloride, which was simply salt, and potassium, which I believed was in bananas, but potassium chloride was something that could kill.

I found it amazing that an ingredient commonly kept in a college chemistry laboratory, where students and teachers walked around every day, could be lethal. I knew it in theory, I supposed, a century ago when I took general college chemistry, but this made it in-your-face real.

Bruce had said Keith had been injected. "Did they find the needle?"

"No, nothing like that. They're still doing fingerprint matching from the furniture, et cetera, but they doubt there will be any that can't be accounted for from the people who regularly came and went in his office."

"It sounds like the police are kind of stuck."

"Well, they don't have much more."

"How fragile we are," I said, by way of nothing.

Bruce led me to the den where we sat on the couch for a long time, leaning against each other. I assumed Bruce's thoughts were, like mine, about the tiny line between life and death, sometimes an atom or a pinprick away.

16

"Did you ever figure out what all those hang-ups were on your answering machine yesterday?" Bruce asked when we were ready to resume our lives.

"Haven't given it any more thought."

"Did you say there was no caller ID?"

"No name came up, but it was a Mansfield area code. A lot of faculty live there." I stopped a second. "Come to think of it, that's where Fran Emerson lives. I'd forgotten. I don't know why she wouldn't have left a message, but I'll check with her tomorrow. I'll see her at two meetings."

"Did you try using the reverse directory online?"

"I made one pass. For a few bucks I could have taken it another step but it's not a big deal."

"I don't like it, especially the timing, probably right before the break-in, to make sure you weren't home."

"But that's good, right? That means they weren't out to harm me; they wanted the boxes is all."

"I still don't like it."

I smiled. "You're just trying to make a case for staying here."

"Do I need a case?"

Thus ended our briefing for the time being.

I was strangely unafraid of being alone on Sunday night after Bruce left for work. Maybe because I had a pseudo plan, meaning the will but no actual appointment, to tell all to the police on Monday. I knew I'd feel hugely relieved once I talked to Virgil. I hoped it was Archie's day off.

It also helped that Bruce called or texted every hour before midnight and wanted me to do the same every hour after that if I was awake.

"No way. I want you to get some sleep," I told him. "Let's just have a code. If your phone rings and no one's there, it's me, and I need help."

"Not funny."

I worked for a while on what I called the Unpopular Puzzle but couldn't seem to simplify it and still keep it interesting. Maybe I'd ask its only fan, Gil Bartholomew, if she had any ideas.

At some time during my fitful sleep, I found myself being pelted with frosted cake wrapped in yellow sheets of paper. The sheets were overwritten with crosswords that had no order or design. A nightmare.

No one liked faculty meetings. Whenever you were at a meeting of any committee, it was time away from your students, your research, your class preparation. And so few meetings were actually productive except when you walked away with yet another chore you'd "volunteered" for. I noticed more and more hands on laps these days, as texting and surfing the 'net became the best tactic for surviving the surfeit of meetings.

All-hands meetings were a little different in that you seldom came away with more work to do. Today, roughly one hundred of us, full- and part-time faculty plus another twenty or so staff members, spread ourselves out in the auditorium on the first floor of the administration building. The auditorium was pretty cool and comfortable. The room held rows of blue leather–covered seats, all on one level, enough for five hundred people, with a stage at the front end. It was the original assembly place for the college when the total enrollment was little more than four hundred young ladies of the early to mid part of the twentieth century.

The story went that all students were required to gather here one day a week while the academic dean read to them from one of the discourses in John Henry Newman's *The Idea of a University.* Each student had an assigned seat and attendance was taken. There would follow a short lecture on a topic from Newman's book. No Q and A, no discussion, no voicing of opinions. And, need we mention, no talking before, during, or immediately after the hour. I pictured the girls filing silently to their next class, like a line of nuns on the way to chapel.

Those were the days when the faculty ruled the school. I thought of a stickie Fran had on the edge of her computer: "When it gets to be your turn, the rules change."

I would have bet that students back then didn't question the choice of textbook, whereas on a routine basis I heard, "Why did you pick this book, Dr. Knowles? There aren't enough graphics," or "The quizzes are too close together. We need more time to study." Neither would early twentieth century students have dared to negotiate grades.

It would have been a paradise for the

dean. I wondered how I'd have fit in.

I took a seat near the back of the auditorium, not caring to be chatty with any of my colleagues today. They'd situated themselves mostly by department, in groups of two and three, which was about the only way you could interact in rows of seats that were bolted together straight across.

I saw Hal and Lucy in front of me to my right. Lucy looked despondent. It couldn't have been easy for her to learn that her brand new boss was murdered in the middle of the day while she was partying. Lucy had pulled back her shiny black hair today and held it with a pale blue scrunchie to match her spaghetti-strap dress. The effect was to make her look even younger than the late twenties I guessed she was.

We all waved, but solemnly.

It was nearly ten o'clock, almost time for President Aldridge to convene the meeting. I had no good story for the dean, post-assembly, and no idea where the boxes were.

Fran Emerson, in flowing, pale green, gauzy fabric, slipped into the seat next to me.

"They should excuse department chairs from attending these meetings," she said.

"Really, all mathematicians."

"I'm sure Aldridge is going to announce a

memorial service for Keith. Do you know when the real funeral is?"

"Me? No. Probably he'll be sent to his family in Chicago." I'd forgotten again how I was the one in the know as far as the deceased was concerned. "Oh, by the way, did you try to get me on the phone a couple of times on Saturday afternoon?"

Frown lines, a pause, then "Let's see. Saturday? No, it was soccer day. Why?"

"Just wondering."

"How do they do that?"

"Do what?"

"Send dead bodies across the country."

Another misconception: the girlfriend of an emergency worker was in the know when it came to transporting the dead.

"I have no idea."

Whiiiiiiiiiine. Whiiiiiiiiiiine. Whiiiiiiiiiine.

The microphone whined its way through feedback, getting our attention more than a bell would have.

President Aldridge, a fiftysomething woman with a physique like Fran's, tall and imposing, stepped to the microphone at the center of the stage, between the American flag and the flag of the Commonwealth of Massachusetts. She wore a dark suit with a loose jacket, and managed to make it look classy rather than stodgy.

277

Behind her the college vice presidents and deans sat in a row. I couldn't see Dean Underwood's expression from this distance, but her posture was the stiffest on the stage. Heavy blue drapes hung behind them all.

The assembly began.

"Thank you all for coming on such short notice. I'm sure you know why I asked you to gather here this morning." A pregnant pause. "Henley College has lost one of its most distinguished professors. We are all the more shocked at his violent death."

There was no mention of Apep, Keith's nickname, after the god of darkness, the destroyer of dreams.

The room was hushed, the audience attentive, although any one of us could have given the sincere if uninspired speech — a wish that the perpetrator be brought to justice and heartfelt condolences to Dr. Appleton's family. The president treaded lightly on the security issue, warning us all to be extra cautious on campus though certainly nothing like this had ever happened in Henley College's history and we had no reason to think it would ever happen again. She was working on a brand new security program for the campus, most of which would be in place by the time school reopened for fall classes. She closed with a reminder that we should continue to co-operate fully with the Henley police department.

That last I assumed was directed at me.

As for the new security program, that was probably directed at parents, alums, and the press as much as anyone. I hadn't thought what a PR nightmare this must be for the administration.

As for our teacherly duties, we were to work with our students to a mutually satisfying conclusion to the summer session. The staff was working on a memorial to be held in this very hall as soon as arrangements could be made.

We stood for a moment of silence, during which I wondered how exactly they did send a body across the country. Maybe Bruce would know.

Ten minutes later, after a hot, sweaty trudge across campus, the Henley College math and science faculties reconvened in Franklin Hall. Although all of us had keys to the front door, we waited on the wide landing at the top of the steps for the last person to arrive, then entered the building as a group, practically shoulder to shoulder. It wasn't hard to guess why.

The hallway was dark and hostile. We were

greeted by the indeterminate sounds of an empty building, followed by buzzing fluorescents when we flicked on the lights. We walked past classrooms and laboratories and right past my office; I still hadn't entered it since Friday afternoon. Afraid of what I'd find behind my desk? I couldn't explain it.

Strangely, no one spoke until we reached the lounge on the first floor where the two sides of the L met.

We were minus only a couple of instructors who were too far away on vacation to make it back, and the physics department chair who was still doing research on the other side of the Atlantic.

The Franklin Hall lounge, where we last met for a party, was more like a funeral parlor today. Where a few days ago the long table against the wall had held cake, frosted cookies, drinks, and colorful celebration napkins, today the gold lamè cloth had been replaced by a stark white paper covering. On it were iced tea, lemonade, and simple shortbread cookies. It was what my Catholic friends told me Lent was all about. I assumed Robert Michaels, Keith's chairman, had made arrangements for this spread. In a normal time, it would have been Rachel's chore.

As clear as day, I pictured Rachel slipping

a piece of Hal's cake onto a small paper plate. The next image was of Rachel bending over Keith's body, realizing he wasn't reaching for something that had fallen behind his desk. In my mind I saw her place the cake on the floor outside the door, but then the cake flew back on its own, landing on the chair in the office, and then flying out again, hovering over Woody's barrel in the hallway, ultimately descending into the trash.

While I was mentally drawing the trajectory of the cake and starting to plot the course of the yellow sheets of paper, the meeting came to order in a weird kind of way.

The three department heads sat on the only couch, at one end of the room: Fran Emerson, head of mathematics; Judith Donohue, head of biology; and Robert Michaels, head of chemistry, who looked the most despondent of all.

Robert, mid-thirties, I guessed, with a thick shock of reddish hair, was serving his first term as department chair. He spoke first. "It's unreal, isn't it?" he asked. "One minute you're at your desk, and the next . . ." His voice trailed away.

Murmurs and short exchanges rippled through the room in answer. I noticed Lucy

Bronson keeping to herself and thought again how difficult it must be for her, with only five weeks under her belt at Henley. If I remembered correctly, she'd come from a small school in Maine and, therefore, had little of the support needed at a time like this. I made a note to reach out to her, if only to invite her to a beading class.

Robert pulled a greeting card from his briefcase. "I'm going to send this around the room now for everyone to sign, and I'd like to arrange for flowers to be sent to Keith's family also. Since we don't have a secretary for the summer, Sophie, can you do that? And can you see to it that the family gets the card?"

"Of course," said I, the official liaison with Keith Appleton's family.

Fran shot me a look that said, "I knew you were his best friend."

The department chairs took turns going over which classes remained to be brought to an orderly end. I'd neglected to mention to Fran that I'd jumped the gun with three of my students, combining the conference on grades with an interrogation. One that had yielded interesting results, by the way. I didn't feel guilty in any way for not waiting to follow department procedure. All that mattered in my book was that each student finish the summer term and that my grades be in by the deadline.

Another announcement from Robert brought sighs of relief: due to the unfortunate circumstances of last Friday, to give everyone a chance to recover sufficiently from the shock of a death in Franklin Hall, an extension had been granted by the dean: grades did not have to be posted until the end of August.

The business over, people started getting up from the chairs and heading for the buffet table. The mood remained subdued.

"Can everyone wait just a minute?" I asked. "I think we should talk about the investigation into Keith's murder."

Heads turned in my direction, toward the back. Eyebrows went up, hands reaching for cookies stopped midair, but I was the most surprised person in the room.

I hadn't exactly planned it, though in the back of my mind this sort of meeting was the ideal forum to make progress on the investigation. Ariana would have said my subconscious mind knew all along that I would do this, this way. Bruce would have asked what had brought on such rashness. I didn't want to dwell on what I knew the dean would think.

"What are you saying?" Robert asked,

incredulously. "That we do our own investigating?"

"We're teachers, not cops," Hal said.

"How would we go about it?" Judith asked.

"I don't have a plan," I admitted, addressing Judith, who might be an ally. "But it seems to me we should do more than sit around and wait for the police, who at the moment have nothing solid."

"There's a rumor going around that Ms. Wheeler is their key suspect," Robert said.

"That's just what it is. A rumor," I said. "Who here really believes that Rachel Wheeler, who gives over and above what her job requires to make sure classes and labs in this building run smoothly, who believes she's a killer?"

"How would we know? I don't know any killers," Hal said.

Why was Hal resisting? Maybe there was truth to the rumor that he and Rachel had crossed the teacher/student line. Or were still crossing it. What if Keith found out and threatened to tell Gil her fears were well-founded? Taking on Gil would have been a formidable task for Hal. Easier to eliminate Keith.

I hated the way I was thinking. It was the product of a frustrated mind the logical powers of which had hit the wall.

"I don't see the harm," Judith said, stirring sugar into a glass of lemonade that was already too sweet for my lemon zinger taste. "Why don't we just brainstorm for a while? Who knows? We might come up with something."

Bless you, Judith.

"I suppose it wouldn't hurt," Fran said.

"It'll be useless," Robert said.

"We're the ones who knew Keith best," I said. "Surely we can spare a few minutes to think about whether we saw anything unusual in the days before he died. Someone in the building who didn't belong, maybe, or someone doing something out of character."

"We've been through this with the police," Robert said.

"This is different. We're his friends," Judith said, joining the ranks of one, me, who made up his cadre of friends.

Besides the young woman he was seeing, of course. I still couldn't get my head around that. Keith on a date. With a woman. With someone he thought enough about to mention her to Elteen. I hadn't abandoned the possibility that he'd made the woman up out of whole cloth so that Elteen wouldn't keep trying to set him up with a nice girl in Chicago. When did I become so cynical?

"We could start with who would have a really strong reason to want Keith dead."

"You're kidding," Robert said. "You mean like that he kept me from getting full health care benefits because I took a lighter load the term my daughter was born?"

"That was an administrative decision," I said. "Keith was only one vote on the faculty senate."

"The deciding vote," Robert said.

I'd forgotten that. It was harder to justify Keith's vote in this case as beneficial to the college, unless it was to prevent faculty from sloughing off just because they had families. If so, I'd have to call it cold.

I looked at Fran, who was biting her lip. Probably dying to mention the change in bylaws that would have denied her the award she deserved for distinguished service.

"Let's face it," Hal said. "We'd have a hard time thinking of someone who didn't have a gripe against him."

How well I knew.

A loud noise interrupted us. The sound of Lucy's chair as she pushed it back across the tile and dashed out of the room. I didn't get a look at her face as she uttered a raspy

" 'Scuse me, please," but I doubted she was smiling.

Thanks to support from Judith, my faculty friends indulged me in telling me how they'd spent the day on Friday. Of course not for an alibi, I told them, just to see if something useful surfaced.

Nothing did.

"Too bad Lucy left," Fran said.

"She's new. She's probably whacked out by all this," Judith said.

I snapped to. Or she's the girlfriend, I thought. Bonnie, Annie, Lucy might all sound the same to elderly ears. And Lucy's last name was Bronson. Both Bs, two syllables. Close enough.

Lucy could be the name of Keith's girlfriend.

Or his killer.

17

I passed on joining the Ben Franklin faculty for lunch downtown. I felt I'd gotten all the information I could out of the group — that is, none — and I'd put off my meeting with the dean long enough. If I wanted to have lunch with anyone other than Bruce, it was Lucy Bronson. I made a note to make that happen.

Like a good employee, I headed for the boss's office. After one stop and one phone call, that is.

The stop: I'd brought with me the manila envelope with the journal article I'd finished on Friday night before things fell apart. I stepped into the business office, two doors down from the assembly hall, said hello to Joey behind the desk, and slipped the envelope containing my twenty-first peer-reviewed research paper into the outgoing mail slot. Now I could say truthfully that I had more than twenty publications on my resume, should it come up. I wouldn't mention the hundreds of puzzles and brainteasers.

The phone call: I settled on a bench along the path between Franklin Hall and Dickinson Library. The heat from the concrete quickly penetrated my thin cotton dress and I shifted around to put more fabric between me and the cooking seat. I pulled out my cell and punched in Elteen's number in Chicago, where it was mid-morning. I wasn't proud of what I was about to do, but extraordinary circumstances, etc., as Winston Churchill, or someone of that ilk, once said.

"Well, hello again," Elteen said when she learned who was calling.

"I'm sorry to bother you," I said. "But I wonder if you could help with a little task."

"Anything I can do, surely," she said.

"It's about the young woman Keith was seeing. Lucy, wasn't it?"

"Oh, yes, yes, I couldn't think of her name, but yes, Lucy Brownson, something like that. What about her?"

"Aha" nearly slipped from my lips.

"Would it be all right if I gave her your address in case she wants to send a card to express her sympathy?" I looked up to the searing sun and hoped its rays wouldn't turn into lightning bolts, set to chastise a sinner.

"Oh surely. Do you have my address?"

"I do have it, but I didn't want to give it out without consulting you."

After a few more utterances from Elteen about how very sweet and thoughtful I was, I was nearly in tears and finally hung up the phone and hung my head in shame.

"She should be back any minute," Courtney said as I approached her desk. We both knew who "she" was. Courtney's long, red hair was pulled back tight off her face, her short skirt dangerously close to the dean's limit. She had a tall glass of lemon zinger iced tea ready for me. "Just in case," she said.

I thanked her and gave her a hug.

"Oh, one little thing, Courtney. Lucy Bronson had to leave the meeting early and I'd like to get in touch with her. My faculty directory is in my office in Franklin." I swung my arm in the direction of the faraway building, such a tough journey on a day like this. "Can you give me her numbers?"

"You know, she's so new, I don't think she's in the directory yet anyway." I knew that. "But I'm sure I have it here."

"Thanks for being the only cooperative person on campus at the moment," I said.

Courtney gave me a knowing smile as she handed me a pink stickie. She probably thought I was referring only to her boss.

I took up my post on the waiting bench. Any more of these summonses and I'd expect a plaque with my name on it nailed to the back. At least this seat wasn't giving me a third-degree burn. I was itching to talk to Lucy and annoyed that the dean was taking my time.

I dug in my briefcase for a small metal puzzle with interlocking rings. The idea was to unlock them, freeing them completely from each other.

In a way I felt sorry for Dean Phyllis Underwood. In a couple of months her long-held fantasy of Henley College was to end as young men poured onto the campus, requiring separate restrooms and careful monitoring in the dormitories.

Dean Underwood's last-ditch effort before the recruiting for men began had been to warn the board of trustees that all alumnae funding would come to a halt if the admissions policy were changed.

"They won't send money, and they certainly won't continue to send their daughters," she'd prophesied.

Now that I thought of it, it had been Keith Appleton who'd come up with statistics to prove otherwise, based on similar situations across the country. My privately held response to the dean's argument was simply, what daughter obeyed her mother anymore?

The last time I sat outside the dean's office was also the last time I saw Keith Appleton. I wondered if Benjamin Franklin Hall birthday parties would ever be the same. Would we maintain hushed tones in his honor? Eschew cake and soda? I shivered as I thought of the turn all our lives had taken.

Today the dean approached her office from the outside, presumably having had things to do between the president's assembly and our meeting.

She addressed me immediately, even before we were behind her office door. "I suppose you think that was a very smart move, Sophie, but let me tell you it was not."

Courtney busied herself at her computer, seeming to make more noise than necessary as she hit the keys and slapped papers on her desk. I wouldn't have been surprised if she broke out into a high-pitched *la la la la la la la.* At one point she gave me a sympathetic look.

I took a sip of tea. It felt good on my

parched lips and throat. "Dean Underwood, I'm sorry I misunderstood. I thought you'd be happy someone took care of packing up Dr. Appleton's office."

The dean, more perceptive than I was used to giving her credit for, was not impressed. I'd had a whole day to come up with a better cover. Too bad I hadn't done so. "Don't insult me, Sophie."

"Really, it's just one more task you don't have to worry about."

The dean shook her head in a "tsk-tsk" manner. "And then returning them like that. Did you think that would be the end of it?"

Returning them? I didn't know what she was talking about and was about to say as much.

By now we were in her office. She closed the door behind us and I saw a brown cardboard mirage in the corner between two antique bookcases. Three cartons, two on the floor, one piled on top. My boxes? Rather, Keith's boxes? The boxes had been returned? The box thief stole them to give to the dean? I blinked my eyes a few times, and thought of pinching myself.

"I hoped it would be, Dean Underwood. The end of it, I mean," I said. When in doubt, fake it.

"You've gotten poor Mr. Conroy very

upset and he doesn't deserve that."

"No, he doesn't."

"He thinks it's his fault that you went off with those cartons and didn't take them immediately to my office."

"It wasn't at all his fault."

"And then, when he found them outside today at the basement entrance to Benjamin Franklin Hall . . . well, he was completely confused. He called Courtney, quite distraught."

"Poor Woody. I'll bet his head was spinning." Like mine. "Who was supposed to collect the contents of Dr. Appleton's office, anyway?" I asked. No harm trying.

"Dr. Knowles." I thought it was a good sign that she was back to our normal mode of address, though the tone was an exasperated one, as if I had such nerve asking a question like that.

"I'm sorry. I meant no harm."

"I'm not dumb, Dr. Knowles, whatever you and your liberal friends think behind my back. I know that your assistant, Rachel Wheeler, is the main suspect in Dr. Appleton's murder. And I know how important it is to you to clear her name. That's very noble. But investigating a murder is not your job. And it is certainly not seemly in a faculty member of Henley College."

Is it seemly to be murdered on campus? I wanted to ask, but didn't. The dean's face was red enough already. The campus couldn't handle another medical emergency.

Why did the dean want the boxes anyway? What was the big deal that she didn't get them right away? She could have assigned that task to Courtney or her assistant. She could have had them shipped, unexamined, to Chicago since the police were not interested in their contents. Was there something special the dean was looking for among Keith's possessions? His little black book? I thought about asking for her alibi on Friday afternoon. Another time.

"I apologize for any inconvenience. I didn't realize the boxes were that important to you."

"I insist you refrain from further investigation, Dr. Knowles."

"With all due respect, Dean Underwood" — a phrase she might appreciate — "whatever I've done has been on my own time." Like my puzzle work and my beading, I added silently.

"You're a full-time faculty member, and one who is interested in doing the kind of research that will qualify you for a promotion. I find it hard to believe that you have time for a frivolous romp into police work."

"My classes, my faculty participation, and my research are all going smoothly. There has been no interruption in my duties here," I said. I might as well have used the term "superwoman" and been done with it.

"I don't think you're fully grasping the importance of what I'm saying."

"It's very important to me to assist the police in discovering who committed the horrible crime on our campus. I would think it would be important to the administration as well." That should get to her. "I plan to help my assistant in whatever way I can. And again, it's all on my own time." That is, none of your business.

"Is it worth your own promotion?"

I raised my eyebrows. I wished she hadn't asked that question. It sounded strangely like blackmail. "What are you saying?"

"I think you know exactly what I'm saying."

With that, Dean Underwood took her seat behind her desk and didn't give me another look. It was one of her famous nonverbal dismissals.

The dean's message was clear: Behave yourself or stay at the associate professor level for the rest of your career. And just try to get a teaching job anywhere else. The long arm of academia.

The brief meeting threw me off balance, seeing the boxes reappear and hearing a threat against a promotion and a title I wanted and deserved. But what occupied my mind as I walked down the stairs and out the door of the administration building was, what had the thief done with my usable discards for the charity pickup?

My first choice for a lunch partner was Lucy Bronson, but she wasn't answering any of her numbers. Not wanting to overdo it and frighten her away, I left only one cryptic message on her cell. I hoped we could chat.

Maybe a normal lunch would be better anyway. This morning at nine was the start of Bruce's seven days off. I usually gave him a little breathing room at the start of the week, but nothing had gone as usual lately.

I called my boyfriend and invited him on a date.

"Unless you're completely exhausted," I added.

He flexed his muscles. "Not me," he said. "And anyway, I'm moving in until this situation is resolved, remember?"

I took that as a date.

The small sandwich shop next to campus,

about halfway between Bruce's place and mine, was too crowded for the kind of private murder and mayhem talk I had in mind, so we switched our order to takeout and Bruce and I drove separately back to my house.

Working backward on my day so far, I gave him the rundown on my meeting with Dean Underwood as well as the saga of the boxes.

"She's blackmailing you," Bruce said, setting up my kitchen counter with plastic boxes. Pasta salad, carrot salad, and turkey sandwiches from the shop competed for space on the marble-topped island with my own veggie chips and supplementary condiments.

"I hoped you'd see it that way."

"That doesn't mean I don't agree with her."

Two negative words, like multiplying two negative numbers, gave a positive. Too bad. I'd counted on Bruce's support as I continued to work out the scenario for Keith's murder.

"You know I can't drop this," I told Bruce.

He sighed loudly, close to a whistle.

"Can she do that? Can she actually kill your chances for full professor?"

"She's the dean."

"Can't you appeal or something?"

"It's her word against mine. She can always make up something that sounds like a good reason to deny me."

"Such as?"

I shrugged, thinking of the legion of cases where deans like mine have wielded power against a teacher they didn't like. One hour at the bar at an academic conference will give you a plethora of stories. I started a litany of examples.

"I don't participate enough in college life."

"You're always there."

"Again, her word against mine. I don't have enough publications."

"You have a packed resume. How many publications are enough?"

"There's no magic number. What I'd have to do is show that so-and-so got promoted last year or whenever with fewer publications and less committee work, blah, blah, blah. But do I want to spend my time on that kind of research?"

"You'd do it for someone else."

"Maybe. But in the end it's subjective anyway."

"I don't understand academia."

"Get in line with Ariana."

"Why do you even stay?"

"Because I love teaching and I love the

interaction with the students. And the good outweighs the bad. Not all the administration is like this particular dean. Our vice presidents are terrific, and so is President Aldridge, with a real commitment to education. And, cue the violins, I feel like I can make a difference."

"I thought you'd say that."

"Not like you with life and death on the line. Working with emergencies all the time."

"That's my life. Emergencies interspersed with the popcorn maker."

"I still think you should learn CPR, however," I told him.

He screwed up his nose. "Not me. I don't like touching patients."

We took a few minutes to rehash a conversation we had early in our relationship. I'd been amazed that medevac pilots stayed in the helicopter at the accident scene while the nurses tended the patients. The pilots had no medical training beyond the first aid class I'd had as camp counselor one summer.

"Hello-o-o," Bruce had sung out. "I'm busy in there. I'm checking our position; the fuel; the GPS, figuring out the best hospital to target, depending on what the nurses tell me; determining what the highest obstacle is between us and the facility, figuring in the power lines, the telephone poles; calculating the weight of the crew plus patients."

"Okay, you're off the hook," I'd said.

But I still thought a class in CPR wouldn't hurt.

Bruce had finished his lunch.

"Are you going to eat that?" he asked, pointing to my half sandwich and mounds of salads.

Without waiting for an answer, he reached over and scooped up my half sandwich. It had happened before, especially when I'd been doing all the talking during a meal.

Though I didn't need it to make my case, I offered another horror story.

"An associate professor I met at a conference in Pittsburgh told me his dean went after his students in order to make a case against tenure. He claimed that not enough of this guy's math majors got into good graduate schools. Underwood could do that to me."

"Is it true?"

"I don't know. I don't think so, but there again I'd have to spend a lot of time appealing the decision with data."

"I thought you loved statistics."

"Yeah, well."

"So what's your bottom line?" Bruce

asked me.

"Meaning?"

"Is it worth it to lose your promotion over the investigation?"

Leave it to Bruce to ask tough questions. I surprised myself by how quickly I knew the answer. "I'm not going to stop trying to help."

"No matter what it means to your career?"

"No matter what."

"That's my girl," Bruce said.

I was glad to hear it, but my head hurt. "Let's talk about something else."

"Have you gone in to see Virgil yet?"

"Something else else."

18

Probably because Bruce was ready for a nap, I was able to finagle my way out of making the call to the Henley PD immediately and into getting him to talk about his own dealings with them yesterday.

We'd moved to the den and I sat on the couch with his head on my lap. I used my most soothing voice while I rubbed his head.

"Did you think of anything else from your meeting with Virgil?" I asked. Manipulating girlfriend.

"I told you everything, about the poison and all. I know the police have questioned everyone from the president to the grounds-keepers. Even delivery people and trash collectors who were around that week. The chief is pretty shook up. This kind of thing doesn't happen every day."

"It's the same on the campus. I wouldn't want to be working in counseling or admissions right now," I said. "Can you imagine how frantic the parents are? Of the incoming freshmen especially. I wouldn't be surprised if there were already some withdrawals. The sooner we get to the bottom of this, the better. I'm going to try to meet Lucy Bronson, the new girl in chemistry, later . . ."

No sense continuing. Bruce was fast asleep. I wondered how much of my rambling he'd heard. I slipped off the couch and put a pillow under his head to replace my lap. On a cooler day I might have tucked him in with one of my afghans, but the heat had let up only slightly and my west-facing den was warm from the afternoon sun.

I checked my cell in case I'd missed a call back from Lucy. Nothing.

I considered calling the police station to be sure Virgil was there. I hoped it was Archie's day off. In the end, I decided to take my chances. I didn't want to go on record as having preferred one cop over another.

I remembered hearing about a forty-eight-hour rule — that most murder cases are solved within forty-eight hours or not at all. It was already more than seventy-two hours since Keith had been murdered. What hope was there?

I had to give it a shot and talk to the PD,

no matter how delinquent I'd been up to now.

My timeline was complete and printed out. I stuffed it in my briefcase.

There was nothing left to do but turn myself in. I left a note for Bruce and took off.

I was the only guest on the bench in the waiting area of the police building, a common posture for me this week, sitting in wait for a superior of one brand or another to chide me. Hanging around the lobby was much better than sitting in Interview Two, however, where I'd stewed before my meeting with Archie on Saturday.

I'd attached a small, round MAstar pin to my knit top. I'd picked up the pin and a cap and other logo items at a visit to the facility. My thought was that the whole emergency services thing might resonate with the cops in the building and provide good karma.

Uniformed officers, young and old, male and female, passed by me, chatting, carrying clipboards and folders, talking on cell phones. A few were behind the high counter making and taking calls. Every now and then one of them smiled at me or asked me if I'd been taken care of.

I checked out the oversized bulletin board across from me. I smiled at several cartoons and one-liners, my favorite being "If someone with multiple personalities threatens to kill himself, should it be reported as a hostage situation?"

My attention was caught by the word *STATISTICS* at the top of a series of bar charts. Lo and behold, tacked to the board was a graphic profile of Henley, Massachusetts, compliments of Bristol County.

I'd finished extracting the metal loops of the twister puzzle while waiting for Dean Underwood this morning and didn't have another handy. Lacking anything to read, I walked to the corkboard and took a look at my hometown from a different perspective. Laid out on several sheets of legal-size paper was the Henley data on gender (exactly half male and half female, what were the chances?); race (ninety-two percent Caucasian); and age. I was dismayed that on my upcoming forty-fifth birthday, I'd jump to the next bracket, comprising eighteen percent of Henley's population. Henley had a median income slightly higher than that of the state. Good to know.

Crime statistics were on the sheet also. Only seven police incidents labeled property crimes were noted for last year. If I reported all the times the boxes from Keith's office had been stolen, the total would go up by two or three for this year. I had no clue whether the person who took the cartons from my garage was the same one who carted them to the basement of Franklin Hall. Maybe the thief who robbed the thief (me) was also robbed. I felt a wordplay puzzle coming on.

As for violent crime, there hadn't been a murder or manslaughter in the last eight years, which was as far back as the chart went. I was sure the numbers were very different for Boston, forty miles to the north. Leave it to Keith Appleton to give our town a memorable, one of a kind statistic.

I'd been waiting almost an hour, amusing myself with other trivia on the statistics chart. Motor vehicle theft was down fifty percent from ten years ago; the month with the most number of crimes was July for three years running; the total population was up six point nine percent from last year. I flipped through data about climate and the educational level of the Henley population.

"Fascinating, huh?"

The loud voice startled me, though I saw that he hadn't intended it. I hoped I didn't look as crestfallen as I felt when I turned to face Archie McConnell.

He, on the other hand, was smiling. It was the smile of victory.

"I like numbers," I said.

"You would."

He ushered me into a large office with room for three desks and several extra chairs. A lot of coming and going and paper shuffling throughout the area, but no one was seated.

Archie took his place behind a desk with his name on it and indicated the chair I should take. We both knew that I was about to concede defeat. My role as unofficial police consultant had come to an end.

Archie was nicer to me than last time, leading me to believe I was no longer a viable suspect in his mind. He nodded politely as I announced that I had information from some of my students and from the janitor at the college. I hated to drag Woody into the morass of those who lied to the police, but I felt that once I explained his motivation, he'd be forgiven quickly and not held accountable.

"It's about the cake and soda," I said. "I know why you didn't find any at the scene."

I spread out the timeline, which included what I knew of my students' visits, without naming them. To my chagrin, Archie had had no call from anyone at Henley since his initial interrogation. I wondered about the legitimacy of marking the three applied statistics students down a grade for their cowardice. I was most disappointed in Rachel, over whom I had no grading power. Not that I would ever do such a thing.

I oriented the timeline so Archie could read it. I'd marked the events of the day and laid them out in a straight horizontal line. "I've been over this a million times," I said, breaking my rule never to exaggerate with numbers. "This is what I have."

Ten A.M., Woody hangs Keith's award on his office wall.
Eleven forty-five A.M., Woody sees Keith's car in the lot.
Twelve fifteen P.M., Franklin Hall party begins.
One forty-five P.M., Rachel finds Keith dead, sees no yellow sheets, leaves cake and soda outside door.
Two thirty P.M., Three girls arrive, see Keith dead, see cake and soda outside, no yellow sheets.
Four P.M., Woody arrives, calls police, removes cake and soda from office, sees yellow sheets.

Four ten P.M., Police arrive, see no cake or soda, but do see yellow sheets.

I indicated the place on the line between two thirty when the cake and soda were still outside the office, and four P.M., when the police found yellow pages, allegedly of Rachel's thesis.

"Here's where the killer came back," I said. "To incriminate Rachel, he went back and planted the cake inside the office and threw pages from Rachel's thesis around, except Woody messed things up by trashing the cake. It's the only thing that makes sense."

Archie stroked his chin while his head bobbed comically.

"The killer came back and messed with his own crime scene," Archie said. "Busy guy."

Archie picked up my timeline and held it close to his face, studying it. "So you're saying the killer was essentially hanging around the crime scene waiting to plant evidence. I'm assuming you think he also planted the chemicals from the cabinet so it would point to Rachel, who had a key." I nodded. "Why didn't he just drop everything at once? Why risk going back?"

"Well, there was no cake and soda until

310

Rachel took it upstairs. That gave the killer the idea. And then I guess throwing the marked-up yellow pages in was just an afterthought. Overkill. So to speak."

"So the killer was at the party and saw Rachel head up to deliver the cake and soda and decided to take advantage of the situation. The overkill. Where'd he get the yellow pages?"

I felt my face flush. My eyes suddenly itched. All along, I'd suspected the killer was one of the attendees at the Franklin Hall party, but that had been theory. Now the fact seemed to emerge from the timeline and the logic of the movements on Friday afternoon. The killer saw Rachel leave the room with the cake and soda. The killer had access to draft pages of Rachel's thesis. I saw draft sheets in the trash around Franklin all the time, though something was different about those sheets compared to the way Virgil had described the ones at the crime scene. I wished I could remember his exact words. No matter, the point was that the killer could have picked them out of the trash any day of the week, if he was part of the Franklin family.

I didn't like my theory so much anymore.

Apparently Archie did.

"Nice work," he said, "which we could

have —"

"If I or the girls had come to you immediately, you'd have come up with this."

"I could charge you all with obstruction," he said. I drew in my breath. "But I don't see the point." I let out my breath. "I'm assuming Rachel Wheeler told you she entered the office and found the victim, then exited and put the food outside the door."

I nodded, grudgingly.

"I notice you haven't given me the names of the three students who went to the office at two thirty."

"I can't tell you my sources."

"What? Are you a reporter now?"

More like a priest, I thought. "Do I need a lawyer?"

"Come on, Dr. Knowles. This is not one of your math puzzles. This is a murder investigation."

He was right. When he shoved a pad of paper and a pen in front of me, I acquiesced and wrote "Pamela Noonan," "Elizabeth Harrison," and "Casey Tremel."

"You did give us the janitor without a problem."

I hoped Archie didn't mean that poor Woody was about to be accosted by the Henley PD.

"It was hard to explain how the cake went

missing in the end without involving him. But he was only —"

Ding. Ding. Ding. Pause. *Ding. Ding. Ding.*

A low-level alarm went off on Archie's watch. He checked the time and got up abruptly. "Excuse me one minute."

It was more like fifteen minutes. I saw many no smoking signs in the room, but no warning against using electronic devices, so I took out my phone to check my email. There were messages from my applied statistics students as well as companies trying to sell me shoes and posters, but nothing from Lucy. I was curious to know if she'd admit to dating Keith, and, if so, whether that put her higher or lower on the list of suspects.

Maybe I should have shared that info with Archie, too. Nah, I wouldn't want to spoil my reputation as The Great Withholder.

I chose one of the games my phone offered to keep me amused. I decided on an easy one: moving three boxes of graduated sizes from one pile to another in the smallest number of moves. The restriction was that only one box at a time could be moved, and you could move a box only on top of a larger one. This was a very smart game in that if you tried to move a bigger box onto a smaller box, a nasty beep sounded. After a few seconds the game reminded me of the movements of the boxes that held Keith's office effects. I quit the game.

I went online again, clicked around, and found a neat game to foster algebraic reasoning. I bookmarked it for use in a math workshop. When things got back to normal.

The algebra game put me in a good mood by the time Archie returned with a cup of coffee in a mug that had seen better, cleaner days. Strange to take coffee at the sound of a wristwatch alarm, but to each his own. Maybe he was on medication that required a concomitant dose of caffeine.

"I'd have gotten you a cup, too, but I don't recommend it. Can I get you a soda?" Archie asked.

"I'm good," I said.

"So where were we?"

"I'm very concerned that it's too late to solve this murder. It's been more than forty-eight hours."

"I know you hear that all the time, but it isn't a hard and fast rule. For big cities it might be true since those guys are dealing with at least a murder a day. They can't afford to let fresh ones go, so a case is considered on its way to cold much sooner than here."

The idea of a homicide as "fresh" brought back the taste of the spicy pasta salad I'd had for lunch. I rubbed my nose, smelling a ripe body.

"What's next?" I asked.

Archie laughed. "What? Are you part of the squad now?"

I shrugged. "You have civilian volunteers, don't you?"

"Yeah, to make the fund-raising calls and fill in as crossing guards. Interested?"

I was beginning to like Archie. "I'll pass."

"I thought so."

"So, what *is* next?"

Archie looked past me, over my shoulder. I turned to see what had attracted his attention. Virgil and Rachel had entered from the back and were headed for a desk and chair set across the room. That couldn't be good.

Archie stood and I followed. He led me out of the room in the opposite direction while I strained my neck to get a glimpse of the expressions on Virgil's and Rachel's faces. Too far away. I consoled myself with the observation that Rachel was not in handcuffs or prison garb.

It amazed me how little it took to give me comfort these last few days.

"We'll call you if we need anything else

from you," Archie said, all business now, nearly pushing me over the threshold, back into the waiting area.

I guessed he wanted to join the conversation — I hoped not another interrogation — with Rachel.

Walking past the bench I'd waited on and past the busy telephone desk, it dawned on me. Archie didn't have a prescribed, alarm-triggered need for meds or coffee. He'd come out here to tell his cronies to pick up Rachel Wheeler. How dumb was I? I felt betrayed, for no good reason, since deep in my heart I knew Archie was just doing his job. Why else would he want everyone's names? I was lucky he hadn't charged me.

I couldn't see why Archie couldn't at least have been honest with me. So what if I hadn't been completely forthcoming with him right away. Sworn officers of the law should be held to a higher standard. It was low and tacky to fake a timer alarm on your watch.

I made a note to see if I could pull that same trick with my watch, should an occasion warrant it.

On the whole, I was back to not liking Archie.

19

I drove toward home, defeated. I felt I should have been smarter, quicker, more persistent in my role in Henley's first murder investigation in at least a decade, and three floors above my own campus office to boot. Ask me to construct a crossword puzzle or a brainteaser and I was on the job. I managed to meet a rigid schedule of producing original puzzles and mindbenders for several publications. But when it came to something really important, like helping a friend out of deep trouble, I was a failure, plain and simple.

I wondered where Rachel could have been that they found her so quickly. On the threshold of coming in to the station herself, I hoped. And the other girls? I'd thought all along they weren't taking their actions seriously enough, but did I really want them grilled by Archie? I wouldn't have been surprised if I'd been well within my rights to have kept all the names to myself. Something to check, if I thought I'd ever again need to know.

The image of Rachel, slump-shouldered, walking in front of Virgil came back to me. The fact that I'd brought it on with my oh-so-spectacular timeline made everything worse. I called myself every name I could think of from ratfink to snitch to stoolie to the good old-fashioned tattletale, and variations thereof.

I wished I were one of those special television characters who could sneak into a building, plant a bug, and listen in on all conversations from an unmarked, well-equipped van. Or better still, that I'd been able to find a clue, a giant clue, that would have led us to the true killer.

Rachel's freedom was out of my hands. I hoped her aunt's lawyer would do better by her than I had.

Letting go of the idea that I could help left me free for what I should be doing. I had a mountain of work to do at home, what with reading student papers from last week, scheduling my summer students, and creating next month's puzzles for my editor, but Bruce hadn't called and I knew he would as soon as he woke up.

I selected number one in my CD player,

Tim McGraw, and hummed along. *Just be still . . .*

I needed another comfort destination, other than my home. As luck would have it, Ariana's shop was only a few blocks away. I made a quick right and headed for A Hill of Beads.

I found Ariana starting to close up. I thought she was quitting early until I realized it was after five o'clock. The day flew by when you screwed it up.

My friend took one look at me and said, "Sweetie, what happened?"

Either Ariana had the special powers I'd always suspected, or I looked much worse than I felt. Visiting the heavenly-smelling shop was the best choice I could have made. I entered the world of beads and charms and faceted stones, none of which had done me wrong, and vice versa. I helped Ariana put away stray beads that customers looked at but didn't return to their proper trays. I breathed in the calming aroma of incense as I opened cartons of new products and ran off flyers for upcoming demonstrations and classes, including one on handwriting analysis. I wondered if she'd planned to teach it herself or bring in an expert. I supposed there were such people.

After I sprayed all the counters and wiped

them down, I dragged the vacuum cleaner from behind the heavy beaded curtain that hid the kitchen and workshop area.

"You don't have to do that," Ariana said.

"Yes, I do."

I pushed and pulled a very old Hoover, feeling the tension transfer from my arms and legs to the long handle of the vacuum cleaner. Now and then I heard a disturbing click that was a bead on its way into the dust bag, but I knew from other closing time visits that a certain loss of inventory by this route was normal. When I was finished, the mauve area rug in the middle of the store bore satisfying tracks from the Hoover's wheels. I wound the cord around the back of the vacuum and tucked it in at the top.

I swapped the vacuum cleaner for a soft, damp mop and attacked the slick linoleum that covered the rest of the sales floor and extended to the back room.

All flooring in A Hill of Beads was now spic and span. A job well done. Almost as pleasing as ironing.

"What else needs cleaning?" I asked.

It was great to be in control of something, if only housework.

When I'd spent enough physical energy to

feel relaxed, we retreated to the back of the store. A tea and conversation corner was a must with Ariana and I was very comfortable here in my favorite overstuffed chair.

Ariana assumed a yoga position, pulled a beading case onto her lap, and went to work. Not work for her, I knew, but a pacifying activity. She knew enough not to foist anything on me, however. Beading was still a distant second to puzzling as far as being a stress-free activity for me. Ariana claimed it was because I took too mathematical an approach to the craft. What was wrong with that?

"Lose the symmetry," Ariana had told me by way of advice after an early class. She'd laid out one of my newly crafted bracelets. "Look at this," she'd clucked. "One large blue, three small white, three tiny gold; one large blue, three small white, three tiny gold. All the way around. It's like an equation."

"Your point?" I'd asked.

I knew what Ariana meant, but I had no confidence in anything other than a strictly ordered pattern.

Add to that, I felt I'd never be really good at beading, no matter how much my friend encouraged and coached me. As small-boned as I was, my fingers seemed to be as big as those of a college wrestling champion when I tried to fold back the end of a fine-gauge wire and insert it into a tiny bead.

Eventually I'd master the art of tucking wires into small places and attaching fasteners in an unobtrusive way, but my talent for design was sadly lacking. My beaded necklaces looked like something from the nearest day care center, produced by a kid who knew his colors and was just learning to count.

Ariana had been commissioned to make jewelry for an entire wedding party — necklaces, earrings, and bracelets for the bride, maid of honor, four bridesmaids, and a flower girl.

"I finally convinced them not to have matching sets," she told me, working magic fingers with a magnificent set of colors. She'd assembled pale turquoise, coral, onyx, pearls, and clear crystal beads. "It's kind of a flapper theme the bride has going, so we're doing a choker and a long strand of button pearls for her, two strands of pearls each for the attendants, and drop earrings for all, I think. I haven't decided on what the flower girl should have. Maybe just a bracelet with a single pearl choker.

I was mesmerized as my friend took beads that didn't look to me that they went together at all and wove them into a design where they seemed to have been made for each other.

"Why did the dean want the boxes so badly?" I asked Ariana, out of the blue.

"She's looking for something that might make her look bad."

"Or a proposal she doesn't want seeing the light of day."

"Or she killed your Dr. Appleton," Ariana said, jabbing a tiny wire into the opening of a coral bead.

I shook my head. "I don't think so. I don't think she has it in her. And she doesn't know a thing about poisons. Or any science, or any scientist, living or dead. She'd have stabbed him or shot him."

"Nice," Ariana said.

"Maybe she was just peeved at me on principle. She'd wanted someone else, I still don't know who, to pick up the boxes and I barged in and took them. That would be enough to upset her world."

Ariana closed up her beading box and took a three-ring binder from the small table next to her.

"I should look at her handwriting," she said, cruising through pages in the binder.

"Still on that kick?"

"I'm going to get certified to teach a class in the fall."

"I saw the flyer."

"Don't sound so skeptical."

"Me?" I asked, all innocent.

"Do you have any samples of the dean's handwriting?"

"Probably somewhere."

"I could look at them."

She held up the binder and fanned the pages at me, but I couldn't read the writing by the dim light of the blue and green lava lamp. "These are my notes. I've already picked up more tips from this lecture I heard last week. Did you know you can tell a lot about a person even from the pressure of the pen on the paper?"

"What if you're using a pen that doesn't write dark, or is running out of ink?"

Ariana ignored me as she usually did when I brought a rational explanation into a conversation.

"A slant to the right means emotionally outgoing and to the left means you're re-strained."

"What if the person is left-handed? Bruce is a lefty and his writing is slanted way to the left. I wouldn't call him restrained. Would you?"

"If the person writes very small it means a great ability to concentrate on small details."

I'd long admired my friend's ability to

slide right past a question or a comment and continue with her own agenda. I couldn't do it. Maybe it was an occupational hazard from my years of working with proofs and logic, where the requirement was to have each statement follow from the one before, without skipping a single step, even a simple one.

"Do tell," I said. She would anyway.

"You should see a sample of Albert Einstein's handwriting. It's tiny, tiny, but very, very accurate as far as the shape of the letters. Charles Darwin's, on the other hand, is all over the place, with a very wavy baseline and wide spacing between the words."

I couldn't resist. "Well, Einstein could have had a limited amount of paper and Darwin might have been on the ocean on his 'Beagle' when he was writing."

"You're no fun."

"I hope you don't still have the letters I wrote to you while we were in college," I said.

My friend gave me a wicked smile. "I marked them up with a red pencil. I put notes in the margin —"

Ariana might as well have hit me with her red binder. Why did it take me this long to see it?

"That's it!"

I slammed the palms of my hand together, creating one loud clap. "That's what I've been trying to figure out. It's been bothering me forever, but I didn't know why. Now I do: if they were really Rachel's yellow pages that were strewn around the crime scene, they wouldn't have red pencil marks."

"Should I be following this?" Ariana asked.

"Keith never looked at students' yellow sheets. All the girls have told me that. He simply would not read drafts. They were beneath him. So there was no way Rachel would have given him a copy on the yellow paper, therefore, no way he would have read it, and therefore, no way he would have marked it up in red." I opened my palms to signal how clearly each step followed from the one before. The conclusion wasn't quite up to snuff mathematically, but it was obvious to me. "The yellow pages were marked up and planted by the killer."

"This is good, right?"

I hugged my friend. "This is very, very good. I need to call the cops."

Ariana was elated that she'd given me the key to deciphering a major piece of evidence at the Franklin Hall crime scene. She cleared her desk for me — no small task since neither neatness nor doing paperwork received a lot of her attention on a regular basis. She put piles of folders on top of other piles of folders and left me alone with my cell, a pad of paper, and a pen. I intended to take my handwritten notes immediately out of her presence as soon as I was finished.

I mentally rolled up the imaginary sleeves of my sleeveless knit top. Not a problem; I'd taught a whole course in imaginary numbers last year.

I called Virgil. He, and not Archie, answered on the second ring. So far, so good.

"I don't want to disturb you if you're still talking to Rachel," I said.

Virgil chuckled. "Your friend is doing fine. We just needed to get a few more things straight."

"She's still there?" I wondered if anyone but a lawyer or blood relative was entitled to that information.

"She'll be here for a while."

"Like, all night?" I heard my voice rise and my language lapse into studentese.

"Hard to say."

"Did you pick up — ?"

"Invite in for questioning, you mean?"

"Did you invite the other three girls I mentioned, too?"

"Not yet."

"Did you arrest Rachel?"

"Not yet."

I gulped, unable to ask about Woody. Surely there was an age limit for this kind of thing. "Do you have new evidence?" I asked, holding my breath.

"Other than Ms. Wheeler's and three other students of yours lying to the police? No."

"This is my fault," I said, not meaning to.

"They're the ones who lied to us, Sophie. That's the crime. You did your part, encouraging them to come forward. And then coming in yourself was a nice, cooperative gesture."

"So I couldn't have been charged if I hadn't come in?"

"Nope. More's the pity. Anything you heard from Rachel or the other girls was essentially hearsay. You had no way of knowing if they were telling you the truth. It's not as if you witnessed a crime."

"Archie led me to believe —"

"That's Archie. And, for better or worse, police are allowed to lie to suspects or persons of interest or . . . just about anyone as long as they're not under oath."

It didn't seem fair.

"Well, I have something that I think will

convince you that Rachel is innocent."

"That's exciting. You've got my attention."

I didn't want to disappoint him. "It's not a hair or a fiber or anything."

"You'd be surprised how seldom a hair or a fiber cracks the case."

"Not like what we see on CSI?"

A loud guffaw. "Like where you take a piece of carpet thread from a body and a few minutes later you have the name of the only manufacturer who makes that particular color rug and they give you a list of the four stores in New England that they sell it to, which you then put into your computer and presto a mug shot pops up?"

I'd clearly hit a sore spot. "Yeah, like that. Not the way it is, huh?" My goal now was to strike sympathetic notes no matter what Virgil said.

"Remember I served ten years in Boston, so I've seen my share of homicide crime scenes. Let me tell you, it's sheer brute force ninety-nine percent of the time. Interviewing, walking around meeting people who knew the deceased, talking to everyone in as much of an area as you can cover. A lot of times it's what's *not* at the crime scene that will solve your case for you."

"Hard work will do it every time," I said.

"And even if you have something as

simple as fingerprints, do you know how long it takes to get that processed? Forever. There's no money, no staff. And DNA? Don't get me started."

Too late. "Most people don't understand how underfunded and overworked our police departments are."

"You got that right. So what's this theory you have?"

My turn at last. I laid out my logic to Virgil, explaining the Rules of the Yellow Sheets, according to the scientist residents of Franklin Hall. Then I summed it all up.

"Ergo, the killer wrote the nasty comments and sprinkled the pages around, so there'd be one more thing that pointed to Rachel."

A long pause followed. I pictured Virgil, in all his bulk, scratching his head above his widow's peak, thinking, not about to commit without a lot of thought.

I blinked first. "What do you think, Virgil?"

"Worth looking at."

Yes! "Can I look at the sheets of paper?" Might as well keep on this roll.

"You can look at the photos of the sheets of paper."

Good enough. "When?"

"Tell you what. Let us take a look on this

end." I wanted to rush in and offer Ariana Volens, my own handwriting expert, but I resisted. "Maybe I'll swing by tonight and see my man Bruce, too, if you think he'll be there."

I was elated. "Bruce will be at my house. He's sort of camping there until all this is sorted out."

"It's a good thing, because you certainly can't count on the Henley PD to keep you safe."

I hoped that was a chuckle I heard in Virgil's voice.

I knew it was premature, but I couldn't help rejoicing. All we — I was back, aligned with the police — had to do was determine whose handwriting was on the pages of Rachel's thesis, probably rescued from the trash, and we'd have the identity of the killer.

Giddiness set in.

I briefed Ariana on Virgil's response and thanked her over and over for jarring my brain into gear. I felt bad that I had to quash her idea that she come along to look at the handwriting and do her own analysis. I didn't want to overwhelm Virgil. I promised I'd scan the photos and take copies to her if Virgil permitted.

I left a message on Bruce's cell, which he

wouldn't have left on if he were sleeping, that we were having company this evening and that he should restock the fridge.

To add to my well-deserved state of euphoria, when I clicked on the "missed message" notice on my cell, I found that there'd been a call from Lucy. I was almost afraid to call her back, lest I break the spell. Following quickly on that thought was the brainstorm that I should find a way to get her to write a sentence for me.

20

Bruce called me when I was about ten minutes away from home, caught in traffic from the late end of rush hour.

"I had my cell off," he explained. "I needed to sleep if I'm going to take the late security shift here tonight. I hope there's overtime pay in your budget."

Cute. "Where are you?"

"Supermarket. Any special requests?"

"A couple of six-packs." Bruce laughed, knowing my average consumption was one beer a year at the Franklin Hall summer picnic. "I'm serious," I said.

"Virge is coming over?"

Smart guy. I replayed the last hours of my day for him, emphasizing the pluses. "Pick up some snacks, too," I said. "And one of those cook-it-at-home pizzas. With pepperoni. And olives. Lots of both. Thanks."

"Buttering up, are we?"

"To the nth," I said. "Did you leave

through my garage?"

"Yeah, why?"

"Just wondering if the boxes were back."

Another great laugh. "See you soon."

Halfway through his first slice of extra pepperoni, extra olives pizza, Virgil asked, "I hope you don't mind if we eat first, then get to the other matter. No lunch today. And breakfast wasn't so hot. Only four doughnuts." Bruce and I raised our eyebrows. "Kidding."

"Take your time," I said. "Have some more chips." As long as the "other matter" was on the agenda for the evening, I was fine.

Bruce led the dinner conversation. A good thing, since despite my declaration otherwise, I was too distracted to think about anything but the crime scene photos. I glanced at Virgil's briefcase periodically, tempted to whisk it away to the den while the boys ate and talked.

First up from Bruce was asking about Virgil's family. Virgil had lost his wife to cancer a few years ago; his son was in summer school at a Southern California college where he'd start freshman year in the fall. It occurred to me that pizza was not necessarily a treat for a bachelor and I should have cooked him a meal.

Bruce and I exclaimed how great Ronnie looked in his high school graduation picture, and again holding his basketball trophy, and again with his date for his senior prom. The photos were for my benefit since Bruce and Virgil met every other week for card games with other guys in their clique — though maybe family pictures never came up during those sessions.

"What's new up in the air these days?" Virgil asked Bruce.

"*Up In The Air.* Good one," Bruce said, an acknowledgment that Virgil knew the title of one his favorite recent movies.

"I'm not as out of it as you think," Virgil said. He performed a neat trick with a long string of cheese that wouldn't detach from the slice. Using his chin deftly, he didn't miss a calorie.

"We've got competition," Bruce said. I'd heard the story: a new air rescue business had set up shop across the road from MA-star. "It's a for-profit company where one of the VPs is a Henley councilman."

"Isn't that what we call vested interest?" Virgil asked.

Bruce gave him a "what else is new" look. "What's good is we signed a new contract, with Oceanview Hospital, to do all their transport."

"Apparently the competition isn't creating a problem for MAstar."

"Not at all. We're spinning it like it's good for us. We can use it to make a case for some updated equipment and a facility upgrade."

"You're going to upgrade the double-wide?" Virgil asked.

We all laughed, maybe a little too hard on my part.

At long last, Virgil pushed his crumb-free plate away. "Let's get to it, Sophie," he said.

I took a deep breath. "Are you sure you don't want dessert first?"

Both men broke out in the kind of laughter that ends in coughing.

It was strange, and not in a good way, to see the coffee table in my den covered with crime scene photos. Virgil had spared me anything truly disturbing, but any reminder of Keith Appleton's murder was unwelcome.

Keith was the only faculty member in Franklin Hall to add an area rug to his office. A queasy feeling came over me when I saw a close-up of the blue oriental design carpet strewn with office supplies and crumpled yellow sheets of paper. The paper clips, pens, and pencils scattered over the floor might as well have been bloody daggers.

I must have shivered, because Virgil had a worried look on his face. "Are you okay with this, Sophie?"

I asked for it, didn't I? "I'm good," I said.

Bruce stuck his head in. "I'll be in your office, Sophie, hacking into your email, if you need me."

"Knock yourself out."

Virgil gave us a look. "I forgot how you guys go at it."

The close-ups of the papers were incredibly clear. However else the Henley PD might be strapped for money in the forensics department, they had an excellent camera and photography crew.

Virgil spread out more than a dozen views of Keith's office floor, encompassing the yellow sheets, each in a different wrinkled stage. On some sheets, only partial phrases showed.

"We've smoothed out the pages, of course," Virgil said, laying out another set, where the writing was more visible, but still not completely. "I think you can fill in the blanks."

I picked up each photograph in turn and took my time reading the red handwriting. I saw "(illegible due to creasing) is rubbish" on one, and "Your Awful Data . . . (illegible due to tear)" on another. Visible in full were "Use your brains" in the margin of one sheet and "Flaky reference" at the bottom of another.

"These comments don't even sound like Keith," I said. "He never says 'rubbish,' or 'flaky,' and what scientist says 'awful data,' and capitalizes the words at that? I've heard him use 'worthless,' for example, but never 'awful.' He'd refer to data as inadequate or spurious or skewed."

"Of course he would."

"And look how close together the letters are in each word. That indicates a person who lacks self-confidence, has low self-esteem, and is uncomfortable with himself. That was not Keith." I cleared my throat. I seemed to have been channeling Ariana.

"Sounds like you've been taking a class on handwriting analysis."

"Maybe."

"When did you fit that in?"

"I'm a quick study."

"That you are."

"What if you could get, say, a dozen members of the faculty and administration to vouch for the fact that that is not Keith's handwriting? Would that convince you that the markings on these pages are fake?"

Virgil shook his head. "Too subjective."

"What is your plan for checking the handwriting?" I asked, as sweetly as I could.

"I need to run it by a few people, but most likely we'll be going back in and asking for handwriting samples from students and faculty."

"But the killer would obviously know why you were on this track and alter his handwriting in some way."

"Experts say you can't do that. There's always a tell, something that gives you away, unless you're a professional forger, I guess. Didn't your teacher tell you that?"

"I left early."

I knew that would get Virgil laughing and buy me some time. Enough for me to come up with an idea.

"Let me get you the samples."

"And how would you do that?"

"I have years worth of notes or cards from just about everyone in Franklin Hall, and that's your main suspect pool, isn't it?"

Virgil didn't say "yay" or "nay" to my supposition.

Instead he asked, "Doesn't everyone email or text these days?"

"On the whole yes, for immediate communication. But a student will often slap a handwritten note on a stickie when she submits a paper or a problem set."

"Something like, 'Here's my paper'?" Virgil asked.

"More like an apology for being late or telling me there's a reference missing that she'll bring me tomorrow."

"The modern version of 'My dog ate my homework,' " Virgil said, pleased with himself.

"Exactly."

"Speaking of emails," Virgil said. "The techs have been at work on Appleton's computer."

Uh-oh. I'd been waiting for this. Rachel's nasty email, sent to Keith the day before he was murdered, had been on my mind. "Is that why Rachel was first in line again in Interview Two this afternoon?"

"Interview Two?"

"I think of it as the torture chamber."

Virgil smiled. "Archie's a good guy."

No comment.

"I know Rachel sent one that was a little out of line, but —"

"But it turns out, so did quite a few others. Not a popular guy if you'll forgive my saying so."

I felt a wave of relief, followed quickly by one of guilt over my delight that Rachel wasn't the only one bombarding Keith with harsh words.

"He wasn't as bad as it looks," I said. "The janitor loved him and it turns out he was some kind of benevolent uncle to his family in Chicago. We just never got to see that side of him." Here I was again, defending Keith in death as I'd never defended him in life.

"Most people aren't as bad as they seem," Virgil said, and I knew at that moment we were both thinking of Archie.

Back to work. "On the handwriting samples? I have loads of holiday and birthday cards and thank you notes. I could pull together quite a set that we . . . you could compare with the comments on Rachel's thesis pages. That way whoever did this has no warning that we're on to him."

Virgil sat back and took one of the whistling breaths that he and Bruce seemed to have a patent on. I waited not so patiently, my mind racing ahead with how to gather the promised postcards, greeting cards, and notes from various corners of my house.

"Okay," Virgil said. I nearly hugged him. "Tomorrow morning. Give me your best shot."

Then I did hug him. "Thanks, Virgil. Next time, dinner will be New York strip steaks and potatoes."

"And beer," he said.

"And lots of beer."

Virgil left around ten o'clock. Bruce had picked up enough of our meeting to get the gist of what was ahead of me. He and Virgil spent a few minutes in my driveway before Virgil took off in his old Malibu. He had flung his jacket over his shoulder, his wide profile dwarfing Bruce, who was in his longish khaki shorts. I could only imagine that conversation.

"Where did you find *her?*" Virgil might have asked.

"Up in the air," Bruce might have answered.

"I suppose there's no chance you're going to sleep tonight," Bruce said, when he reentered the house.

I'd already pulled a box of greeting cards onto my lap in the den. I saved cards until I had a large enough stack and then gave them to Ariana who used them in the grade school where she volunteered as an arts specialist. She and the kids made small gift boxes out of the cards. She'd show them how to fold the card so the design on the front became the top of the box. Ariana was expert at using scorers to get the edges clean and crisp. Lucky for me, I'd been negligent in handing over the cards and now had a wealth of potentially useful handwriting samples for Virgil.

"I'm not tired," I said. "And I'm sure you're not, since you had that nice, long nap."

He took a seat on the couch, one pillow over. "Okay. Hand over a bunch. What are we looking for?"

I shifted the box from my lap to his. "While you look through these, I'll search some other places for cards. We need anything with handwriting from Keith, Hal, Pam Noonan, Liz . . . oh, make it any student or teacher whose name you recognize from Franklin Hall. Plus Dean Underwood."

Bruce raised his eyebrows at the dean's name. "Plain Phyllis?"

I shrugged. "Why not?"

"You're the boss."

Bruce ran his hand across his brow, as if I'd asked him to dig a ditch. "You'll owe me."

"Sure, sure."

I got up and began my sweep of all the odds and ends spots in my house, all the places I put things on their way to where they belonged.

On a rack with computer peripherals I

found a small pile of birthday cards from April that hadn't made it to the stack I was gathering for Ariana. I usually sifted through them first, including only designs I thought were workable, and also to be sure some seven-year-old didn't end up with too personal a message among her art supplies.

In the knife drawer in my kitchen were postcards from Hal and Gil, who'd been to Bermuda at the end of June to celebrate his degree, and one from Fran and her husband, Gene, who'd taken their yearly cruise to Mexico. I hoped the scrawled "see you soon" and "the buffets are great" were enough to make some decent comparisons.

The odds and ends drawer in my bedroom dresser was a gold mine of more postcards and thank you notes stretching back to Christmas. Embarrassing, but serendipitous.

In an end table drawer in my den were recent invitations, including one from Hal to attend his graduation. It was a professionally printed card, issued by the school, but he'd handwritten a note about how Bruce was welcome, too.

Dean Underwood, true to form, always handwrote her holiday greetings to her faculty. I never dreamed I'd be putting the note to this unpleasant use.

I had more samples of Rachel's handwriting than of anyone else. I included several pieces so the set would be complete, though I didn't agree with Virgil that Rachel was devious enough to have framed herself in order to look innocent.

I returned to the den with a grocery bag half full of relevant correspondence. Bruce had arranged his possibles in stacks, one for each student or teacher.

He pointed to the array. "I should have read these a long time ago. It tells me a lot about how you interact with your students." He picked a note card off one of the piles and read. "Dear Dr. Knowles, Bijillion thanks for listening the other night. I was ready to give up totally and now I know I can do it. Yay. You rock! Love, Tanya." He put it down and pulled another. "Dr. Knowles, you're the best. I never thought I'd pass that test, and could never ever" — those words are underlined, Bruce noted — "have done it without your extra tutoring and encouragement. Franklin Hall needs a statue of you!"

He reached for a third, but I put my hand on his. "I get the idea."

"I didn't realize how involved you are outside the classroom."

"What did you think I do all day?"

He shrugged. "You know, just teach for an

hour and fifteen minutes then take off for the pool, and go back the next day for another hour and fifteen minutes."

I held my hand to my head, palm out. "Where shall I begin," I emoted.

Bruce drew me into a hug. "You rock," he said.

Bruce turned in around midnight. By the morning, he'd be back on a regular sleep schedule for the next seven days. A good thing, too, since he had to be up early for his yearly physical, verifying among other things that he wasn't diabetic, depressed, or prone to seizures. A drug test was also required. All to keep his license. Good to know the skies were safe with MAstar's PICs.

I was satisfied that I'd gathered enough handwriting samples for Virgil. I wished he'd left the photos so I could get started now vetting the phrases on Rachel's thesis pages. It was impossible for me to get anywhere from memory. I needed the pages with their gruesome bloodred marks in front of me. But Virgil had been firm about taking everything away with him, even though he'd be missing a chance to profit from the expertise of Ariana Volens, a professional.

"I've met Ariana," Virgil had said, as if

that explained why he wouldn't let me give her copies.

The most I could coax out of my new (again) favorite detective was that I could stop by the office with my samples at ten in the morning.

"That late?" I'd remarked.

He gave me that look, before he realized I was kidding.

Nothing better to do than go to bed. I knew I'd sleep better with Bruce in the house, but I didn't like that loss of my own confidence. I'd lived alone for many years and not been afraid. The only reason I had an alarm system in the first place was because of my mother. When she became disabled I wanted her to have a way to call for help, so I'd had a security system installed, with a panic button on every pad.

Another reason I'd felt safe had to do with the Henley crime statistic — no murders in recent history, let alone in Franklin Hall where I spent many hours a week.

All bets were off now, and I wondered if I'd ever feel completely safe again.

For tonight, I could relax. I fell asleep counting I-dots and loops and the relative weight of T-bars in fine penmanship.

21

When Lucy quickly agreed to meet for coffee at Back to the Grind on Tuesday morning, I was mildly shocked. From the way she'd stormed out of the faculty meeting in Franklin Hall yesterday, I'd expected her to hole up somewhere until after Labor Day. I wouldn't have blamed her if she withdrew and ended her career at Henley before it began.

I felt bad that I'd never invited her for lunch or even a girl-to-girl chat until now, when I needed her. How did I let myself get so busy that I couldn't reach out to a new teacher in my building? Granted she was in the chemistry department, not math, but a distance of three floors was no excuse.

I let myself off the hook a tad, recalling that I'd never sensed that Lucy needed anything. Students talked favorably about her. I'd heard that she'd landed a small research grant that would employ a half dozen chemistry majors during their free hours, doing calculations related to some kind of reactions. She seemed to be doing well.

I hadn't realized how well. Dating Keith Appleton! I was now convinced she was the woman Keith had spoken of to his cousin Elteen. In her short tenure, Lucy had achieved something no longtime faculty member could claim.

Lucy had arrived first at the small café where I'd met with Pam, Liz, and Casey a couple of days ago. If the baristas were listening in on my recent appearances here, I hoped they wouldn't think I was setting up shop. I ordered an iced cappuccino and a raspberry scone and left a big tip.

Lucy seemed forlorn, and not that much older than the freshmen she'd be teaching in a few weeks. She wore a knit sweater and hugged a mug of what looked like hot chocolate with a pile of whipped cream. To look at her you'd think we were in the kind of cold wave we'd had after Christmas, that had set teeth chattering and lasted for weeks. In truth, it was sweltering and all we had now was the weak fan of the coffee shop, barely adequate even at eight in the morning.

She half rose when she saw me. I felt old,

and to confirm it, my knees creaked as I sat down.

I looked around the shop, relatively empty this Tuesday morning. I recognized some Henley dorm students whom I didn't have in class, group studying, it seemed. I certainly understood why they might seek a change of scenery from the desolate campus.

It was clear that if Lucy and I were going to have a conversation, I was the one who'd have to go first.

"Thanks so much for coming, Lucy. I noticed how upset you were at the faculty meeting and I figured all those negative comments about Keith got to you."

Lucy bit her lip and nodded. "I knew he wasn't popular on campus. But he really was the coolest guy, you know."

"You two had something special, didn't you?"

Lucy's eyes widened and I sensed she was about to deny it. Then I saw a tiny shrug, as if she realized there was no point. "We just hit it off right away. It didn't matter that he's a little older."

What's twenty years? I thought. "I'm sorry you had to hear all that at the meeting yesterday. There's a lot of history you're not aware of."

"I know that, Dr. Knowles."

"Sophie, please."

"I'm just saying there was another side to him," Lucy said.

"I know."

Lucy smiled at last. "Keith had such a sense of humor. He'd find a cartoon on the 'net or in a magazine almost every day, something related to science or to school, and he'd leave it on my desk, so I'd start the day with a laugh. But mostly he had this sense of, I don't know, I guess you'd call it a duty to maintain high standards. Especially for premed students. He claimed he didn't want to be operated on by someone who barely got by in med school and he didn't want anyone to be taken care of by a C student."

Not a bad point. But I was here to see for myself whether I thought this sweet young woman was capable of killing her new boyfriend. The more we talked, however, the more the probability of Lucy as killer approached zero.

I was ready for another iced cappuccino. Lucy was fine with her hot chocolate, so I went to the counter myself. Only once did I look over my shoulder to be sure she hadn't fled.

As I waited for my iced drink, a jumble of

boxes on the other side of the counter prompted a new thought. The cartons were labeled "filters," "napkins," and "lids," but they might as well have said, "Keith's Stuff."

"Did Dean Underwood ask you to clean out Keith's office?" I asked Lucy as soon as I could reasonably broach the subject.

"Uh-huh, but someone else got there before me."

Imagine that. I tried to second-guess the dean's reasoning in asking Lucy to collect the material. Probably of all the faculty in Franklin Hall, the dean thought Lucy would be the least likely to be curious as to why the dean wanted the files in such a hurry. That would mean she didn't know about the special relationship between Keith and Lucy. Not that it mattered, since there was no rule against faculty dating each other. In fact, during my tenure at Henley I'd seen two full-blown courtships that ended in marriage, one between fine arts and history and the other between biology and phys ed.

"I wonder why the dean wanted the material so quickly after the police left?" I asked Lucy, all naïveté.

"She said there were some sensitive files in his office and she wanted to be sure they were secure. She was very upset when I had to call her and tell her the drawers were empty."

I'll bet. I made a mental note: check what's sensitive to the dean. "Did you ever find out who took the files?" I asked, wondering if everyone in Back to the Grind noticed how shaky my voice was.

Lucy shook her head. "Nope."

So the dean hadn't broadcast the fact of my little trick. The only questions that remained: Who retrieved the boxes from my garage? And what material did the dean consider sensitive? I knew Lucy wouldn't be able to help me with either.

It was time to do what Bruce would call fish or cut bait.

"Keith must have thought a lot of you," I told her. "He told his cousin in Chicago all about you."

Lucy's eyes brightened. "He did? Wow. Thanks for telling me. He wouldn't let me mention anything to anyone around here."

"That sounds like Keith. I hope you didn't argue too much over it."

Subtle. That was me.

"Oh, no, I didn't care, really. We loved the same things. We went to Boston most of the time. To the theater, the ballet, the MFA, the science museum. There's nothing like that in my little Down East town, believe me."

Lucy's eyes, fixed on a spot over my shoulder, told me she was traveling back a few weeks and reliving her excursions with Keith. I was amazed to hear that Keith had taken that much time to experience the arts and leisure Boston offered. Maybe all he'd needed was a companion who gave him a chance to show his better side.

I wished again that I'd tried harder to understand him. And, as current wisdom had it, I was his best friend. Except for Lucy.

"Lucy, did you see Keith on Friday at all? The day he . . . died?"

Lucy came back to the current reality. "No, I went to the party and he was going to come down later. When he didn't make it, I figured he was just too busy," she said, blinking back tears.

"Or, before Friday, did he mention anything unusual happening around him?"

"The police asked me that, too. I didn't tell them I was having a relationship with Keith outside of school, though. Do you think I should have?"

Not unless you had a big fight and killed him. "That's up to you, Lucy. If you think it will add to their ability to find his killer, then you should."

She shrugged. "I don't see how it could help them, and I don't think I have the energy right now."

So far I was batting zero on getting people to go to the police with what they knew of Keith or his death.

"You don't have to decide now," I said. "You might feel like going in the next day or so, or you might think of something that would help them."

"Maybe." Lucy looked at me and smiled, but once again she was smiling at the past. "Do you know how we started going out?"

"No, I don't."

"Actually our first date? I asked *him*. I had these tickets to the special Renaissance exhibit at the Gardner that my friends in Maine gave me as a going-away present. Everyone else I'd met up to then was married or in a relationship, so I asked him. I didn't know I wasn't supposed to, that he was mean and all. I just thought it would be nice to have a friend who wasn't hooked up either."

How simple it all sounded.

Lucy's eyes teared up. She brushed back her very straight, very shiny black hair. I could almost read her face: Now I don't have a friend anymore.

I couldn't bring myself to put her through

another minute of anguish. I took a small piece of paper from my purse and slipped it across the table to Lucy.

"This is the address for Elteen Kirsch, Keith's cousin in Chicago. In case you want to send her a note."

Lucy let out a little gasp. "Thank you very, very much, Dr. Knowles." She put her hand, warm from the mug of hot chocolate, on mine. "It's so good to have a friend," she said.

I felt like a heel.

It was now close enough to ten o'clock so I went to the police station to meet Virgil. I hoped he didn't expect me to simply hand over my bag of samples. In my mind, he and I sat at a table that was anywhere but in Interview Two and worked together, comparing loops and slants until one of us shouted, "Eureka!" And then Virgil would go out with handcuffs and an arrest warrant and bring in the killer. Bruce and I could go away to the Cape for a few days and I'd be back to prepare fall syllabi and lessons as I always did in August. I longed for reuniting with my steady, well-behaved math majors.

A girl can dream.

Once again I found myself in the waiting

area of Henley's police station. I tucked the paper bag of handwriting samples near my legs, checked my email using my phone, and replied to a few students with applied statistics questions. Then I resumed my practice of staring at the bulletin board across from me, with its wealth of memos and flyers.

Last time I'd focused on the fascinating stats about my hometown. This time I looked at the material around the charts. Wanted and missing persons flyers. A bicycle and pedestrian safety notice. A policy statement regarding abandoned vehicles. A bright orange "buckle-up" bumper sticker. I chuckled at a little cop humor: a cartoon picturing one policeman giving another the Heimlich maneuver while a doughnut pops out.

I remembered that two simple themed crosswords were due to one of my children's puzzles editors in a couple of weeks. Why not use the surroundings for inspiration? I whipped out a small pad and pen. My vast experience in waiting rooms like this during the past week told me I had plenty of time before I was summoned. Working on puzzles would be a good release of the nervous energy coursing through me.

For the first level puzzle I sketched out a

simple grid with four across and ten down and only nine common letters. I drafted simple fill-in-the-blank clues like "A (blank) is pinned to a police officer's uniform" and "A policeman's car is often called a (blank)." The next level would have a much larger grid. I'd use my standard fifty across and fifty down. I started making a list of words I'd fit into the intermediate level grid. Beretta. Miranda warning. Canine. Search warrant. I looked at the bulletin board for ideas. Mug shot. Home security.

The background noises of chatter and ringing phones didn't bother my concentration. But a sudden burst of screaming startled me. Two officers had entered the front door. The inordinately loud yelling came from an old man with a leathery face and a long, unkempt gray ponytail being dragged between the uniformed men.

"I know my rights. Check your own laws. I did nothing wrong," I heard between yelps of "police brutality."

Virgil came out of the office area at the same time that the old guy was spitting out terms like "fuzz" and "pigs," epithets I thought had died with the sixties. The man himself was a throwback to photos I'd seen of "the good old hippie daze," as my mother called them, spelling out the last word for me each time.

"It's Dweezil," Virgil said to me. "He's harmless."

"I take it this is a repeat performance?"

"Oh, yeah. There's a little settlement on the west side of town. A bunch of people who were in college in the sixties and haven't quite adjusted to real life. They have their own little pot farm out there."

"I thought marijuana was decriminalized a couple years ago."

"They go back and forth, the state legislature. Right now a small amount of marijuana is just a ticketable offense, except Henley passed a town ordinance prohibiting smoking it in public. The state law is so complicated and basically unenforceable that most uniforms ignore it, unless someone makes a nuisance of himself."

"Like Dweezil."

Virgil nodded. We walked back to the office area where it was significantly quieter.

"Funny how different people turn out," Virgil said. "My dad has newspaper photos on his office wall of himself and his buddies with their arms locked, protesting this and that. You can tell they're yelling at the cops and you know my dad must be pretty proud of his past or he wouldn't be displaying the pictures. But probably a couple of years after the pictures were taken he goes to law school, then he marries my straight-arrow mom and ends up a prosecuting attorney. He's probably the same age as Dweezil."

"It was an interesting generation," I said, my mind wandering to my own mother and her political activism in her heyday.

Then my renegade mind wandered farther from home. To Dean Phyllis Underwood. There had to be some important reason why she wanted whatever was left in Keith's office. Could her motive have to do with a crime that Keith found out about? She did, after all, belong to the generation that was known for activism that sometimes led to violence.

I ran the numbers. How old was she, other than the one hundred and ten years old she seemed to most of us? I remembered a discussion at a faculty meeting about extending the mandatory retirement age for administrators. I wished I'd paid more attention. My best recollection was that the dean, a case in point at that meeting, was in her early sixties, making her now about sixty-five or -six. That put her smack in the late sixties as a college student. The college website would give her year of graduation.

What if she did something back then that wouldn't look so cool now for a college dean? Something she wouldn't be proud of or want shown off as Virgil's dad did? I pictured the young, if she ever was, Phyllis Underwood. Smoking pot, protesting, maybe even getting arrested. I would have laughed hysterically if I weren't surrounded by cops who might misunderstand my behavior and carry me away.

Virgil and I took seats at a small table in Interview One. Whew. My ex-student Terri had been right about the difference between this room and Interview Two. Interview One was air-conditioned, even cooler than the outside areas, and the chairs stood even on four good legs.

"Are arrest records available to the public?" I asked Virgil.

He raised his eyebrows. "Anyone in particular?"

"Just curious." I pointed to my bag of cards and notes. "It's about another matter entirely." Maybe, maybe not, I said to myself.

Virgil sat back. "On the arrest records, yes and no. You have to have a 'need to know' such as the press would have, but your average citizen would not. The press is entitled to the report for factual information, like name, age, date and time of the arrest, but we can limit what else they can see." He gave me a questioning look. "Does that help?"

"A 'yes' would have been more help," I said.

"Well, there are some exceptions, like with Megan's Law where you can find out if someone has been arrested for certain sex crimes. In fact, you can check that on the Internet. But if your car is stolen and the police recover it being driven by someone they arrest, you're entitled to the theft report but not to the arrest report. Once the case was charged by the DA's office for a criminal prosecution, it used to become a public record, but not anymore. There's this thing called 'probable cause' —"

I held up my hand. "Thanks. Any more is too complicated."

"And you teach math."

"Trust me, the Chi-square test is much simpler."

It flashed by me that breaking into a police department or courthouse records office would be harder than slipping into Keith's office in Franklin Hall. I'd have to come up with another way to dig into the dean's past.

22

I couldn't fault Virgil for his pleasant co-operative attitude. He'd mounted the crime scene photographs on a small bulletin board that he'd propped up on the table. We sifted through card after card and note after note. Some were easy to dismiss.

I'd found only one sample of Lucy's handwriting, on a sign-up sheet for the picnic potluck in the middle of June. Why the month-old sheet was stuck between other notes, I had no idea, except to guess that I'd scooped up and moved a pile of pages to be filed from my campus office desk to my home office desk, making the latter even messier.

What Lucy had written was: "LUCY BRONSON — MEDIUM SIZE MACA-RONI SALAD." Lucy had capitalized all the words describing her offering, with great flourishes for the Ms and the Ss. Like both Casey Tremel and Liz Harrison, Lucy had used tiny circles to dot her Is. None of the three samples were even close to the red markings on Rachel's thesis pages.

Fran Emerson had a tiny scrawl of a style. No match. Robert, Keith's chairman, had such widely spaced words in the sample that I made a note to check with Ariana about what it meant, besides the fact that Robert Michaels hadn't tampered with Rachel's yellow pages.

Dean Underwood's handwriting checked out also as "no match." If she did have an embarrassing blot on her resume it wasn't enough for her to kill him. But maybe enough to snatch away what was in his files about her while she had the chance.

And so it went, with biology chair Judith Donohue and student leader Pam Noonan, and others who frequented Franklin Hall on a regular basis.

Until we came to the samples from the newly anointed Dr. Hal Bartholomew. Virgil and I agreed that of all the samples, Hal's was closest to the markings on the sheets strewn over the crime scene. Besides the overall appearance and slant to the letters, Hal's strangely curved capital A on his postcard with "All's well in Bermuda" looked like a perfect match to the A in "Awful Data," written on Rachel's thesis. This, combined with a couple of other unique strokes, caused us to set aside Hal's samples and create a new pile. When we'd gone through every card and note, Hal's were the only samples in the pile.

"Don't get your hopes up," Virgil said. "Neither of us is a professional, and we might be way off base."

I wasn't exactly hoping that Hal was a killer. What had I been thinking anyway, isolating all my friends as potential murderers? Now that it seemed one of them might actually be guilty, I was devastated.

I forced myself to skip past the high probability that Hal might have killed Keith. Whatever it meant, I was more than ready to see an end to the investigation. No matter what Virgil had said about how long he spent on a murder investigation in Boston, four days were enough for me.

Hal's motives were legion. Over the years, Keith had ridiculed him, voted against a bonus for him, and challenged his eligibility to take a turn as physics department chair, to name a few affronts. Even Hal's glee over receiving his doctorate was sullied because of Keith's constant reminder of how many times Hal had had to redo the experiments his dissertation was based on.

I breathed a long, heavy sigh. "What's

next?" I asked Virgil. I meant "for Hal."

"I'll get our expert to look at this. I don't see any reason to give him the whole bag, but I'll pick a couple out of the pile and add them, just as a kind of control."

"It sounds very scientific," I said.

"Don't tell anyone, okay?"

"I'd never want to spoil your image."

I stuffed all the "no" votes back in the grocery bag and headed out to my Fusion. I turned on the A/C and sat for a couple of minutes with my phone, checking emails and messages. The most exciting news was a "thumbs up" text from Bruce about his medical tests. I texted back, "Good 4 U. CU."

On par with that was a text from Rachel: "Home again. THX." Maybe the handwriting angle convinced Virgil who convinced Archie that Rachel was innocent. I was tempted to call and say THX to Virgil, too, but I didn't want to be presumptuous. I did keep my phone on in case he called me with his expert's results. I wondered if the turnaround time for handwriting analysis was as long as Virgil claimed it was for fingerprints and DNA evidence.

I hoped both Rachel and I had seen the last of the Henley police building.

Hal Bartholomew's handwriting seemed to be scrawled across the heavy, humid sky over Henley, Massachusetts. I couldn't imagine the mild-mannered physics teacher planning out a murder. And it was clear that Keith's murder was not a spontaneous crime of passion. You didn't just happen to have a needle with a lethal dose of poison in your pocket and use it in a moment of anger.

I thought of Hal's family — hard-working Gillian and five-year-old Timmy, who adored his father — and the effect Hal's conviction would have on them.

Maybe I was jumping the gun. I secretly hoped our amateur handwriting analysis was way off, like a data point on a graph that misses the average curve by orders of magnitude. It would mean back to square one, however, which might be where Rachel was standing. It seemed a no-win situation.

A few more minutes and I'd have been able to convince myself that the handwriting expert would tell Virgil he'd never seen a poorer match in all his years of experience. I stopped short of thinking what that would mean for Rachel or for finding the real killer.

What to do next?

With the afternoon free for research, a

good mathematician would immerse herself immediately in her field. Follow-up papers weren't expected sooner than eight to nine months apart, but even that schedule required steady application to the work. I told myself I could afford a short break, having mailed my latest differential equations paper so recently. And what better way to keep research skills sharp than to comb through decades-old newspaper articles?

One part of me admonished: The dean is right; this obsession with the kind of investigating best left to the police was distracting me from what it took to be a full professor. Nonsense, said the other part of me, you're smart; you can do it all. And what if the dean wants you off the trail of Keith's killer so you won't find her own involvement under the next rock?

I pulled out into traffic and headed home, stopping on the way for a veggie sandwich to go at a deli. The tantalizing smells distracted me and I spent a couple of minutes shopping for a good aroma to take with me for dinner. A container of mushroom sauce and a package of handmade pasta seemed perfect for a non-cook to create a special meal for Bruce tonight. Last night's pizza feast with Virgil, while an information windfall for me, interrupted our

tradition of a nice dinner on Bruce's first
night off shift.

I'd made my decision about the afternoon.
I'd spend two hours on the Internet looking
through archives to see what I could unearth
about the dean's past. If nothing surfaced,
I'd drop that line of inquiry.

Arguments were so much easier to settle
when it was Sophie vs. Sophie.

While I chewed on cucumber slices, sprouts,
avocado, Monterey jack cheese, and very
thick wheat bread, I finished the police-
themed children's crosswords I'd started in
the PD waiting room. Later I'd print out
my standard cover letter and send them off
to New York.

I brushed crumbs from my shirt and
headed for the computer in my office.

I was about to vet our dean. I blinked
away the vision of her pinched face and for-
ties hairstyle, and her reproachful eyes. I
knew why she was wagging her finger at me.

The good news was that the dean had
gone to college in New York, where there
was an excellent chance that the newspapers
maintained archives as far back as I needed.

Whenever it came up that Dean Underwood's alma mater was in Manhattan, many
of my colleagues and I wondered how she'd

managed to come away from that experience with such an unimaginative, stale outlook on life. Now I entertained the idea that she was a reformed hippie and, like many from that era, rued her reckless youth. I considered it my job to find evidence of any chinks in her straightlaced armor.

I clicked away and found newspaper archives back to the eighteen hundreds. I smiled. "She's not that old," I said to my computer screen.

I asked for a range of dates between nineteen sixty-five and nineteen seventy for starters. The dean never married. It was hard for any of us to think she'd even dated, so Phyllis Underwood would have been her name then also. Unless of course she was in the witness protection program. As fascinating as that would be, I hoped it wasn't true.

At the top of the list delivered by my search engine was an obituary for a Phyllis L. Underwood in nineteen thirty-three. A great aunt? Not important.

The Internet was a major source of diversion for me. I'd often start out looking for one item, say, casual shoes, click over to an article listed in the margin on how footwear has affected the progress of women's rights, and then stop to read statistics on clothing manufactured in the U.S. vs. in China. What should have taken ten minutes often took an hour. I'd once sat down to order plane tickets to Philadelphia for a conference and ended up a half hour later with new bedding for the guest room.

Today I tried to stay focused to meet my self-imposed deadline of three o'clock. I didn't know exactly when Bruce would come by, and there was always a chance Ariana would drop in. She'd been very solicitous through this ordeal, dropping sweet-smelling bath products and healthy baked goods at my doorstep several times.

Searching for the dean's name didn't get me far. Phyllis Underwood had apparently done nothing worthy of newspaper reporting in the range of years I'd plugged in. Typing her name in the general search engine, on the other hand, got too many hits. I'd have to open link after link to determine if any of the thousands of hits applied to the dean.

I needed a new tactic. My best guess was that like the majority of her peers during that era, the dean had experimented with marijuana. My not-very-vast knowledge of harder drugs told me that there would be more lasting effects and those users would have a much harder time entering the mainstream.

Good thing no student in my applied statistics class was looking over my shoulder and copying down my methods today.

I entered "marijuana" followed by the dean's alma mater and the date range.

Much better. The first hit was a link to an article on a survey taken at the school in nineteen sixty-nine. An overwhelming eighty-one percent of students had tried marijuana at least once. The profile was of a twenty-one-year-old social sciences major at the college. The dean had majored in sociology. So far so good.

I tried not to get caught up in all the graphs, a weakness of mine. I did stop to read the caption of a cartoon depicting a cop arresting a student. His partner says, "If pot gets legalized, we'll have to start chasing real criminals again." Not that the magazine was left-leaning at all.

I skipped down to an article on marijuana arrests and read an article excerpted from a nineteen sixty-seven issue of a liberal magazine. The editors decried the excessive number of "pot busts" as they were called and the travesty of smearing the records of respected professionals. The article specified, without naming them, an English professor in New York, a NATO diplomat's son, and a theology instructor in Illinois. I didn't see a mention of "a future college dean."

Rrring. Rrring.

For a moment, I thought I'd reached a file with sound. I'd moved to a photo search and it seemed one of the students being dragged away from a protest rally was screaming out at me.

I'd gone past my two-hour Internet limit and it showed.

I shook my head, rubbed my eyes, and clicked my phone on to talk to Ariana.

"What's new on the handwriting front?" she asked.

How rude of me. I should have called Ariana immediately after my handwriting meeting with Virgil. I excused myself on the basis that the probable result — that Hal Bartholomew was a murderer — was too hard to bear.

I gave Ariana a rundown without naming names. In case the FBI was listening. I promised details when we were together in person.

"Virgil said he'd give the project to their specialist."

I heard something like a "humph" and then, "Whatever."

"Right now I'm buried in my computer investigating my dean," I said.

Ariana listened through a briefing on my latest thoughts on why Dean Underwood was so anxious to have the material in Keith's office.

"You think she was arrested for something?"

"Yes," I said, in a voice weakened by the lack of evidence to support my theory. "It's just a guess. I don't think she posed for a centerfold, or anything like that."

Ariana laughed. "You mean she didn't make Miss January Nineteen Seventy?"

"Ha."

"Maybe she was a 'working girl,' " Ariana said, prompting a burst of schoolgirl giggles on both ends of the call.

Ariana let me whine for a couple of minutes, about how arrest records were not available to the public, the search engines had been no help, and I didn't have time or energy to hire a PI to track down all of Phyllis Underwood's college friends. Whine, whine.

"Bluff it," Ariana said.

"Excuse me? How do I do that?"

"I do it all the time. Not with you, of course. Tell her you know what she did in college and see how she reacts."

"It sounds like a horror movie." Bruce would have been able to give me the title.

"Why don't you come over? Mondays are always slow. We can role-play."

It was the best offer I'd had today.

On the way to A Hill of Beads, I queried myself. What would I do with information on the dean's past even if I had it? Confront her with it? Why? I no longer saw her strange behavior around the boxes as evidence of her guilt as Keith's murderer. To my distress, Hal seemed to have the lock on that. I was simply curious.

On the other hand, what if I could use the information to my advantage? I needed all the leverage I could get when negotiating with the dean.

This train of thought was beginning to sound like a reverberating blackmail scenario. The dean had said she'd hold up my promotion if I continued to investigate. Now I might say, if you don't hold up my promotion, I won't tell everyone about your sordid past.

It seemed I was taking over one of Keith's projects — find dirt on everyone and use it against them. I wasn't happy about it.

23

Ariana was with a customer when I arrived at her bright, attractive place of business. I stepped into the back to wait for her and noticed she'd changed the beaded curtain that divided the sales room from the rest of the shop. Today, if you took the long view, you could make out a large stem of purple irises springing from a background of many shades of green. I thought of the staggering number of small beads it must have taken to make up the design.

And Ariana thought it took patience when I worked through a mere six pages of mathematical proof.

Ariana's customer was an older woman in shorts that would have looked better on Lucy. She carried a small tray around the shop while Ariana helped her add selections to it.

"I need five small blue ones," the woman was saying as Ariana smiled "hello" to me.

"Five small blue ones," Ariana echoed, setting the beads in the woman's felt-lined tray.

"And one large purple," the woman continued.

Ariana plucked a large purple bead from a cloth-lined organizer on a table that held a set of them in different sizes. "There you go."

"Maybe I only need four small blue ones," the woman said.

Ariana removed one of the blue beads. "How's that?" she asked.

The woman frowned and shook her head. "Mmm. I'm not sure now."

I turned away. There was a reason I wasn't a shop owner. I'd have had choice words for this customer and sent her packing to some other bead store. Not good for business.

I did enjoy filling in for Melissa, Ariana's part-time employee, now and then, however. But even then, I preferred stocking inventory and wiping down cases to dealing with customers, probably because I was hopeless at offering design help unless the person was trying to model an arithmetic series in a bracelet.

I amused myself by looking around the shop. Ariana had sectioned off one area with a new line of crafts products, many related to scrapbooking and stamping. I turned rotating racks of two- and three-dimensional stickers, rolls of ribbon, glue cartridges, stencils, novelty rubber stamps and pads, and small cans of spray paint. I knew it had been hard for Ariana to make the decision to move away from a beads-only shop, but the need to diversify to stay in business had taken over.

About ten minutes and nine other changes of mind later, the woman left the store with a tiny bag of beads.

"You're so good with pesty people," I said to Ariana.

She smiled. "Lucky for you."

Whatever that meant. I poked her in the arm in case she'd just insulted me.

With the luxury, or maybe the curse, of an empty store, Ariana and I sat on folding chairs in front of a glass counter that held a more expensive inventory of gems and charms.

"I'll be you and you be the dean," Ariana said.

I was nervous already. "I'll give it a try."

"I found something very interesting as I was cruising online, Dean Underwood," Ariana said.

"I would say 'browsing the Internet' not 'cruising online,' " I corrected.

Ariana rolled her eyes. "Okay, browsing the Internet, but try to concentrate on the big picture, Sophie."

"Sorry. Can I get a bottle of water from the back?"

Ariana checked her watch. "Not for another ten minutes. We need to get this started."

"You're cold."

"As I was saying, Dean, I was looking up some examples of statistical surveys that I could use in class and I found many of them were carried out in New York City in the sixties. Studies of marijuana use, disorderly conduct, trespassing, that kind of thing, and I was so surprised to see your name come up."

"I don't know what you mean," I said, playing a thunderstruck dean.

Ariana gave me an exaggerated, skeptical look, then waved her hand dismissively. "It's probably a different Phyllis Underwood, a sociology major who graduated in nineteen sixty-eight. One of your classmates?"

She was good. "I give up," I said lowering my head and weeping.

"Wasn't that easy?" Ariana said.

"I see where you're going with this. I just let her tell me exactly what it was. And if I really am wrong, well, I won't be any worse off than I am now."

"You go, girlfriend," my mentor said.

If only the dean would follow the script, I'd be one happy mathematician.

A tinkling sound interrupted us. Two customers, a mother and teenage daughter, entered. I hoped they'd be easier to deal with than the old woman in shorts.

I left Ariana to her business and went through the sparkling curtain to the back. I grabbed a bottle of water from the fridge and sat down to check my emails and phone messages. Way too many emails for only about an hour and a half. I scrolled through them to prioritize. I deleted a few newsletters without opening them and flagged a couple from applied statistics students. I'd get to them later.

On to my voice mail.

I drew in my breath. A message from Virgil came in only a few minutes ago. I hoped no one was looking as I clicked on his voice mail before the one from Bruce and the three from Rachel. It might appear that I'd become a police groupie. One of the badge bunnies, as I'd heard Virgil refer to women who followed cops around.

Virgil's message was cryptic. "Heads up, Sophie," he said. "Our conclusion was correct. Give me a call."

I pressed the phone against my warm forehead. Virgil could only mean one thing: that his expert had submitted his analysis and the handwriting on Rachel's draft thesis pages was a match to Hal Bartholomew's.

I felt a wave of nausea and lowered my head, supporting it on the table with my sweaty arms.

How did the results come back so quickly? What happened to the underfunded, under-staffed police department where you had to wait three months for fingerprint analysis? I realized I was now angry at the efficiency of the Henley PD.

A callback to Virgil wasn't going to cut it. I had to get to the police station and see and hear for myself what Virgil had learned.

Ariana was busy with the mother and daughter pair. I was glad to see that they'd amassed a considerable amount of supplies. I blew Ariana a kiss and motioned with my hand to my ear that I'd call her, a lot easier than explaining anything right now.

Driving to the police station, I parsed Virgil's message. First, did "heads up" mean he'd told only me and not the rest of the Henley college family? Had he told Rachel? Her three messages might be shouts of joy that she was no longer in danger of losing

381

her freedom. I couldn't handle "joy" at the moment, not even Rachel's if that was the case.

And "conclusion" could have meant anything. Virgil and I had drawn many so-called conclusions, including the fact that the handwriting analysis might shed no light on the killer. I played the message again in my head. Aha, Virgil had not actually mentioned the word "handwriting." Also, Virgil had sent samples from others' along with Hal's. I asked myself would I be less rattled if the results had come back "Fran Emerson's handwriting is the match?" Or Pam's or Judith's? Of course not.

When Virgil ended the message with "Give me a call" he might have meant there's nothing new, just let's Bruce and you and me get together.

I reminded myself of my students, many of whom stayed up at night analyzing the last thing their boyfriends said that evening.

"Do you think 'see you later' means he will or will not call me back?" was a common question in the dorms.

I could hardly wait to hear what Virgil meant by his message.

Too anxious to walk at a normal pace, I jogged part of the three blocks from where

I parked my car to the police building, fast becoming home to me. The heat had let up by five o'clock, but not so much as to matter to me in my soaked shirt.

Mercifully, Virgil did not make me wait this time. I was ushered back to his desk by a uniformed officer as soon as I arrived, maybe because I looked scary. Or maybe the trick was to arrive unannounced.

I accepted a glass of iced tea, nothing so exotic as lemon zinger, and sat once again in front of Virgil's desk.

"How did you get the report so quickly?" was my first question. I knew it sounded like a reproof, that perhaps the analyst's work had been done too hastily, the results shoddy, therefore.

"We didn't. It is too soon for the results from our handwriting expert. But we don't need him. Your friend Dr. Bartholomew confessed."

I nearly choked on the generic iced tea. "What?"

"We called him and asked him to come down to answer a few more questions."

I wanted to ask if Hal were tortured. If so, I was sure it would have been Archie. I held back. "Just questions?" I asked. "He wasn't arrested or anything?"

"Not arrested, but we did have the thesis

pages handy and placed them so he could look at them. One 'does this look at all familiar?' from me and he broke down."

"And confessed to murdering Keith Appleton?"

Virgil nodded. "And confessed to murder."

"Why would he do that? He's smart enough to know that some scribbles on a few pieces of paper would be inconclusive, worth even less than a polygraph would be."

Suddenly my great faith in handwriting analysis was down the tubes, along with belief in psychics and palm readings. Ariana would not be pleased.

"You'd be surprised at how many people do confess eventually. Sometimes they can hold out just so long and then guilt takes over."

"Maybe it's a false confession. Didn't something like one hundred people confess to kidnapping the Lindbergh baby?" I was reaching.

Virgil gave me a patient smile. "Yeah, it was more like two hundred, as a matter of fact. Because they wanted to be famous. That happens a lot with high-profile crimes." He aimed an index finger pistol at me. "Your friend Dr. Bartholomew is not going to be famous for this, trust me."

"There must be some reason —"

"What's up, Sophie? I thought you wanted this case solved, like yesterday. It turns out you helped a lot. You found the samples. We went over them. I thought we were on the same page."

"I didn't want it to be Hal. You weren't mean to him, were you?"

Virgil laughed. "We weren't mean to him."

"Is he here? Can I talk to him?"

Virgil shook his head, sadly I thought. "His wife is in there, and then, he's . . . off in the van."

Gil. Timmy. It came to me again how profoundly they would be affected by this turn of events.

When Gil appeared in the desk area moments later, I rushed over to her.

"I'm so sorry," I blurted.

Gil looked a wreck and seemed to want to avoid a hug of condolence. Not that she ever looked really made up, but this evening there was no sign of grooming or that she cared. "I have to go," she said.

"Can I help with Timmy? I could take him for a while."

"My sister is coming to pick him up." Gil seemed to stare past me, her voice on automatic. It occurred to me she might blame me for her husband's plight.

In a way, so did I.

I drove home slowly, not having the energy to push hard on the accelerator pedal. I'd noticed another voice mail from Rachel, but I had no interest in talking to her. *She's not the enemy,* I reminded myself. *It's not her fault that Hal was on his way to jail.* I still needed some time before I could show her the excitement she was due at not having to endure any more trauma.

I arrived home to rooms that were empty except for a note from Bruce.

"Out gardening. Dinner at eight?" it read.

"Gardening" was our code word for when Bruce brought me flowers. I wondered if he'd heard about Hal. If so, I hoped only through his friend Virgil and not because the news had already been broadcast to the twenty-four hundred Henley students and faculty and the entire population of the town. A better theory was that Bruce saw my empty vases and decided to fill them, as he often did. If he didn't know of Hal's arrest, we wouldn't have to talk about it and it might go away.

In any case, I didn't deserve flowers. I should have minded my own business, as the dean warned.

I'd wandered into my office and hit the

key to wake up my computer, a built-in response when I first got home in the evening. The last active screen came up — the newspaper archives from my research on the dean. My finger seemed to move on its own to the delete key, ready to put an end to all aspects of my preoccupation with the murder investigation and the sea change it had brought into our lives.

Hal's confession had given me no closure. Along with that unsettled feeling, Ariana's voice in my head nagged me, urging me to follow through on our role-playing game. Should I confront the dean? Did any of it matter now?

I decided I had to finish the job.

My computer clock read five fifty-five. There might still be time to catch the dean in her office. I picked up the phone and dialed. Courtney answered and I quickly identified myself.

"Good, you're still there," I added.

"You think so?" Courtney asked.

"Well, not good for you."

"Or my social life."

"I can understand that, but I need to talk to her." Naming Courtney's boss didn't seem necessary. "It's urgent."

"Quelle twist. It might even be worth hanging around."

"I can guarantee it."

"Now I'm really curious."

"Go on to your social life and I promise to tell you tomorrow."

"She's about to leave, but I'll put you through. You'll definitely have to tell me tomorrow, though, okay?"

"Promise."

The dean took her time getting to the phone. Being on hold was better than sitting outside her office, in any case, and I made use of the time by sorting through my mail and email and checked my calendar to see what was coming up the rest of the summer. I clicked on August and saw that because of my laxity the last few days, an important birthday had almost gotten by me. Bruce's niece, Melanie, would be turning ten years old in a couple of weeks, on August fourth, the birthday of John Venn. We needed to make plans for a significant present and a visit to Boston to celebrate double digits with her.

Bruce had laughed when I'd told him what a great start in life his niece had, born on the same day as the author of definitive texts on logic and the creator of the widely used Venn diagrams. As it turned out, Melanie was outstanding in math. I doubted my stream of math-related presents and my online tutoring of her had more to do with it than her birthday.

Lame music continued to pour in over the line. Where was the dean? Had she guessed what urgent agenda I had with her? Maybe she'd fled to Canada. I was eager to get the meeting over with and return to normal life.

Even my busiest class days during the regular semester were less hectic than today had been. I'd started out with an early breakfast with Lucy, made two trips to the police station, role-played at A Hill of Beads, and now one more errand before I'd let myself enjoy dinner with Bruce.

"What's this about, Dr. Knowles?" The dean's voice interrupted the so-called music. I didn't know which sounded worse.

My mind went blank, trying to make the transition from the mushroom sauce I'd be having soon, to the dean's shady past. I hadn't thought through how to get the dean to agree to a meeting where I could use the script Ariana and I had practiced.

"I need to see you," I stammered.

"What in the world is so urgent?"

"It's about what's in a box from Keith Appleton's office," I said.

The long pause told me I'd hit on something. I thought I'd been put on hold again, this time without music. Finally I heard the dean's voice, almost pleading.

"I can explain," she said.

I was beginning to like the concept of bluffing.

I pulled into the southwest gate, now fairly used to the deserted look of the campus compared to last week. As I climbed the front steps of the admin building, I wondered if I even needed to rehearse my lines, as modeled by Ariana. It seemed entirely possible that the dean would pour out an unsolicited confession. An easy mark. Who would have thought?

A bigger issue was whether the dean knew of Hal's arrest. I was sure she or Courtney would have mentioned it if the word had gotten to them.

I asked myself one more time why I was doing this, since the murder case was solved. There was no question that whatever Keith had been holding over the dean, it had not led her to murder him.

Was I trying to get even with Dean Underwood for all the small annoyances she was bent on dealing me? I sincerely hoped not.

On a positive note, I could show the dean what a good researcher I was, ferreting out her past, and therefore deserving of that promotion to full professor. The absurd reasoning made me smile.

I'd come to the realization that getting a promotion wasn't as important as many other things in my life. If it had been, I would have bowed to the dean's warning immediately and put my career above my commitment to helping Rachel and, even more important, figuring out who among us was a killer. I'd seen no compromise on the journey to uncover the truth of the event that would mark Henley forever.

The important thing for me now was a sense of completion. I'd done my best on a project and I needed to clear up loose ends, like wrapping up a geometric proof that was particularly sticky.

The dean was waiting for me this time. As Courtney would have said, quelle twist.

She was standing at her open office door holding a sheet of paper.

"I saw you pull in. Come, Sophie."

I followed the dean into her office where a pitcher of iced tea — lemon zinger, I guessed — stood ready next to two glasses. The dean poured tea and handed me a glass. Nothing about this meeting was as usual. Even if it was Courtney who'd pre-pared the tea before she left, here was the dean serving it to me. Not your ordinary Tuesday evening.

Witnessing the dean's dejected state clouded my delight in maybe figuring out the dean's secret and her need to get her hands on the material in Keith's office.

The dean held out the sheet of paper. "This is what you were looking for."

"I don't really need to see it."

"I need to tell you."

It appeared Virgil was right. Once people got on a path to confession, it was impossible to stop them. "I was a college student, and I tried to do the right thing. I think about my decision every day of my life."

That was quite a bit of regret for a little hash.

I took the paper and saw immediately what it was. A birth certificate.

"This is —"

"Yes, that's the birth certificate. I assume you found out about it another way. Maybe Dr. Appleton told you? It's not unlikely that he'd bring a partner into his schemes."

I started. "What? No, he didn't. Make me a partner," I said. I was still trying to process the new information. The dean had a child. The simple sentence sounded like the start of a riddle.

"I'm sorry I suggested your complicity,

Sophie. I should have known you wouldn't resort to something like this. You never have. You've always been open and honest with me."

After all these years, was this a compliment from the dean? "I . . . uh . . . I've tried."

"You've given me every reason to trust you." She smiled. "Except for the story about the boxes."

I returned her smile and hung my head. "Sorry."

"That's the copy from Keith's files on me. It was in an envelope, along with family birth certificates and licenses and such, marked 'Appleton Family History,' as a security measure against an unlawful rifling of his desk by an intruder."

Or by the police in the event that he was murdered.

"So you were fairly confident the police wouldn't single it out as relevant to this case."

"I hoped not."

I had to be clear. I held up the paper. "This is your baby." I tried to make it sound like a statement, consistent with the bluff that I'd known all along.

The dean took a long sip of tea and came back slowly. "I had a son out of wedlock. I was a few months from graduation and had my life all planned out, plans that didn't include motherhood." She sucked in her breath. "I gave him up for adoption."

"And Keith found out."

She nodded. "I think he was always looking for ways to discredit me, not for the sake of it, or to be mean, but to gain some leverage for the changes he saw as good for Henley College. And as we know, in today's new computer world" — here the dean's expression said she'd liked the old world better — "it's easy to find just about anything if you're determined."

I went back to "out of wedlock." Who even used that phrase anymore? I thought it had gone the way of "love child."

"But surely if this came out, it wouldn't threaten your career," I said. "Would the board of trustees really care about something so far back in your past? It's hard to see how Keith could have used the information as a bargaining chip. You did nothing criminal." Like smoking pot, for example.

"Keith knew the technicalities didn't matter to me. It was the attention and the embarrassment it would cause me after my firm stand on —"

"Everything," I said, without thinking.

Was that an audible laugh coming from

Dean Phyllis Underwood's mouth?

"I know I've been hard on you, Sophie, and there's no reason you should give me any consideration. You can keep that copy and do what you want with it."

I tore up the certificate and handed her the pieces.

To make this a truly memorable Tuesday, Dean Underwood and I shared a silent embrace.

24

I rolled down my windows and sat in my car in the parking lot for a few minutes, letting the new information gel. I'd learned a lot, and not just that Dean Underwood had a son out there somewhere. I couldn't imagine her having to make a decision like that, and living with it for the rest of her life. It might account for a measurable percent of her overall disgruntled outlook on life.

I drew a huge red X around the picture I'd created of Phyllis Underwood lying around with her scraggly-haired friends in an orange-fringed caftan snacking on brownies laced with marijuana.

If I were writing an essay about what I did this summer, I'd title it "Research Gone Wrong."

There were so many more lessons to be learned about the complexity of people I thought I knew. The picture of Keith Appleton unfolded with more twists and turns than the most difficult metal twisty puzzle. I envisioned his calendar: Ten A.M., offer Woody the janitor a generous condolence gift. Noon, wander the second floor physics labs in Ben Franklin Hall and find a way to insult Hal Bartholomew. One P.M., send Delia the niece an unsolicited financial aid package for a private high school. Spend the rest of the afternoon digging into the dean's past for leverage and thinking of ways to thwart Sophie Knowles's policies and procedures recommendations.

Then there was Hal himself and the side I never could have predicted. And three cute young things, college chemistry majors, who were unethical and bold enough to sit at a computer and change their grades in the very room where their teacher lay dead. Granted, according to Rachel, only his feet were clearly visible, but they knew about the rest of him.

I thought of another favorite von Neumann quote, "If people do not believe that mathematics is simple, it is only because they do not realize how complicated life is."

Enough said.

My next creative venture was to think of something to tell Ariana about the dean's dark past. I figured the best bet was to let her assume that we'd been right. The notion that an authority figure had been a pothead in the sixties would make her happy and keep her quiet.

For Courtney — why had I built up my urgent meeting in her mind? — I'd cover that tomorrow. I'd wait until tomorrow also to talk to Rachel and the rest of my colleagues. I might even be ready to address the Big Three junior chem majors and find out how they fared at the police station.

For tonight, I wanted to focus on a quiet, crime-free dinner.

I called Bruce. As I expected, he respected my wish not to talk about Hal's confession and arrest. Instead, I explained the logistics that would eventually end in my serving him dinner.

"Where are you?" I asked.

"Goofing off in your house."

"Doing what?"

"I'm having fun with a little mental arithmetic."

Funny guy. "No, really. Did you finish your gardening?"

"I did indeed. You'll see the results this evening. And now I'm watching an old Hitchcock."

"That I believe."

"Sounds like there's something you want

me to be doing," Bruce said. "Can I pick up something?"

I reminded him of his niece's tenth birthday. "You could start rooting around in my box that has new greeting cards and pick one for Melanie. We should get it mailed soon."

"You want me to write it out?"

"You're her uncle; I'm sure she'd prefer to have it be in your handwriting."

"I don't think she's ever seen my handwriting. You're the one who always takes care of that."

That was Bruce. Ask him to take out the trash twice a day and he wouldn't balk, but writing out cards, whether Christmas, sympathy, birthday, thank you, even to his own family — that was my job.

Wait. That was my job. And probably the woman's job in nine out of ten relationships or marriages.

Blat blat.

I heard a loud noise in my head, like the sound my computer threw out when I made a wrong move during a math game.

Blat blat. A loud noise battered my brain.

Hal didn't write the cards Virgil handed over to his expert. Gil did.

"Sophie?"

Had Bruce heard the blatting, too, or was

he wondering where I'd gone? I tried to process this new insight. Gil, a nurse, and also a murderer? Didn't nurses promise to do no harm, like doctors? If not, they should.

"Never mind Melanie's card for now," I said. "New topic."

"Shoot."

"First, would there be handwriting samples of the staff at MAstar? Do you guys ever write notes to each other?"

"We don't exactly write notes to each other, but we do have to keep logs and occasionally we handwrite reports on what happened during the shift. The computer goes down a lot or someone might be in the middle of a game, and if your shift is up you just want to get everything down as quickly as possible while it's fresh. You know, there might have been a particular challenge up there or on the ground and you need to get it on paper."

"What about the flight nurses?"

"Same thing. Plus the nurses sign daily logs. They have to leave a handwritten count of all the controlled medications." He paused. "Is any of this helpful?"

"Immeasurably."

My mind raced. I needed two handwriting samples, one we could be sure was

Hal's, and one we knew was Gil's. I could take care of the first. I had many notes from Hal in my desk on campus. Unfortunately, all the samples I'd taken to Virgil had been from home, the personal cards that Gil most likely had written. I'd never thought to pull samples from campus correspondence also.

Bruce broke into my thoughts. "I assume you're going to tell me why this matters to you?"

I gave him the short form of my reasoning. "I think it was Gil Bartholomew, not Hal, who killed Keith and Hal is taking the rap."

"The rap? I knew it. You've been hanging around Virge too much."

"Please, Bruce."

"I'm just saying."

I appreciated the levity, but continued past it. "It makes so much sense. Gil always reacted more strongly than Hal when Keith insulted her husband. And according to you and the other rumormongers, she suspected Hal and Rachel of having an affair."

"That was more than a year ago."

"That kind of thing doesn't go away, Bruce."

"You sound like you're speaking from experience."

"I'm a girl. That's all the experience I

need. By framing Rachel, Gil's actions get rid of two ugly people in her life."

"Man, I am put on notice."

"Believe it."

"For real, I'm with you on this theory. I can see that Hal, good guy that he is, would rather be punished himself than have his wife pay the price," Bruce said. "But it's very hard for me to think of someone I thought I knew well as a killer."

"I'm sure it is. Hal must have realized it was Gil as soon as Virgil brought him in and showed him the marked up pages. Virgil said he confessed immediately. Why else would he do that?"

I didn't wait for or expect an answer. I was out of breath with excitement. I tried to calm down and plot the course of the next couple of hours. While I was on campus, I'd walk over to my office and see what I had in my files. I knew I'd recently had a note from Hal about changing my statistics exam date for one of his physics majors, and I'd seen his greetings on a "Welcome to Math and Science" poster Rachel was putting together for the incoming freshmen. She'd planned it for the display case. I hoped Keith hadn't signed it yet. It would be too gruesome a reminder.

"What can I do?" Bruce asked, barging in

again on my dizzy train of thought.

"If we had a couple of new samples, one from each of the Bartholomews, that would do it. Can you go to MAstar and get me a couple of samples of Gil's handwriting?"

"Yeah." Bruce stretched the word out. Suspicious. "What are you going to do with whatever I find?"

"Give it to Virgil."

"Can I trust you to do that?"

"Yes."

"You have to promise me that you won't do anything yourself. You'll turn over whatever we have to Virge."

I was happy to hear the "we."

"I promise," I said, meaning it. I longed to get back to where the puzzles didn't involve real humans and life and death.

It was almost pleasant this evening, still in the eighties, but with a slight breeze wafting across the Henley College lawns as the sun descended. There was talk that the heat wave was coming to an end. At least until the next one.

Near the library were a few students who must still have been living in Paul Revere dorm, but there were no cars to speak of. Even the lot nearest the admin building had emptied out. My car was near the tennis courts, only a short walk to my first-floor office in Franklin Hall.

I entered the building through the basement. It was hard not to relive my last trip through this door, the clumsy red dolly at my heels. The memory prompted a question in my mind. If Gil was Keith's killer, as I now firmly believed, it must have been she who took the boxes from my garage, and then returned them here. The only reason I could think of was that Keith had secreted another incriminating letter or photograph — birth certificate? — that would be embarrassing to her or Hal or both. I wondered how he'd buried that one. In a file labeled "Christmas Lists" or "Facebook Friends"?

Come to think of it, did Keith have a file on me? Maybe I should have bargained with the dean to let me look through the material in the boxes.

The basement was as creepy today as it had been on Saturday. I wished I'd taken the front steps to the first floor, but this seemed quicker and cooler than a lumbering trip up the long outside flight. The sounds of the generator and fans and the accumulated musty smells of waste and chemicals dominated the hallway. I hurried to the elevator.

More than any other year, I couldn't wait

for school to start, when generator sounds would be replaced by student footsteps and chatter and the smells would be of perfumes and lunches. Well, maybe not the lunches.

I got off on my floor and nearly ran to the far end where my office was, three floors below Keith's. I unlocked the frosted glass-front door and stepped in for the first time since the day of the murder. With a strange reflex, I glanced at the floor behind my desk. Clear. That was one hurdle down.

The office seemed musty after four days of being closed up. Though I didn't plan to stay very long, I opened a window onto the campus. I noticed a dark sedan parked next to mine but didn't recognize it. It appeared to be empty, as did the campus around it. I walked back to the door, closed and locked it. I didn't dwell on why I thought this was necessary.

I sat at my desk with my back to the window, enjoying the fresh air without benefit of cross ventilation. It didn't take long to find what I was looking for. I pulled two notes from Hal from exam folders, and a page of notes from a recent Franklin Hall faculty meeting.

What I also needed was the handwriting binder Ariana had showed me. I wanted to present the most comprehensive case possible to Virgil in the morning.

Another day I might have enjoyed the peace and quiet and lingered a while to leaf through the journals stacked on a shelf in my bookcase. Not today. Nor did I allow myself the luxury of turning on my computer and posting to groups I belonged to.

I stuffed the notes in my briefcase, closed the window, and left. I made a quick on-the-run call to Ariana to alert her that I'd be stopping at her shop to borrow the binder.

"No need for you to go back," I said. "I have my key. I'm going to collect the binder and zip back home."

"Take as long as you want with the notes and let me know if I can help."

"You've already helped a lot."

"Keep me in the loop, okay?" she said, her tone expressing her delight at having been of assistance.

I assured her I would and hung up.

I exited through the basement, without mishap. The sedan was gone, thus eliminating the trepidation I'd felt over having to squeeze in next to it before I could drive away.

Once I had a chance to study the new samples from Hal and Gil, and the material in the binder, I'd take the package to Virge.

It would be hard to wait, but I wanted to be sure this time.

I hated to admit that as much as I was looking forward to seeing Bruce tonight, I was also eager to see what he'd been able to round up from the various handwritten pieces around the MAstar trailer.

Some romantic girlfriend I was.

25

A little after seven thirty I let myself in through the front door of A Hill of Beads. I punched in the alarm code on the wall pad, reminding myself first not to use my own code, but Ariana's, a numerology sequence pertaining to her birth date.

It was still light out, but thanks to the semi-transparent solar window shades Ariana had had installed, the interior of the shop was dark.

I was tired of wandering into unlit, spooky spaces and hoped this was the last of them. At least this one smelled nice. Sage, I thought. I was also tired of being frightened of every little creak, like the sound of the rotating rack of stickers when I bumped into it. I wasn't used to the new layout with added crafts supplies.

It wasn't only the new nooks and crannies that got to me, however. How many times had I seen the row of dressmakers' forms above the counters? The velvety necks and chests sporting beaded necklaces had been there for as long as I could remember. This evening the sight of the headless, bejeweled women sent a ripple of fright through my body. Familiar baskets holding sale items made spindly shadows against the wall, which was crammed with beads, in plastic packages, on strings, and in small glass jars.

I'd decided against turning lights on so as not to attract attention or give would-be customers false hope. Now I questioned that decision, but I was more than halfway to my destination and I was determined not to give in further to irrational fear.

I dug my phone from my purse and hit "favorites" on the screen. I leaned on a counter and clicked on Bruce's number, ostensibly to let him know what time I thought I'd be home, but mostly to have company in the store, if only in the form of a friendly voice.

I waited while the phone dialed. Or whatever these smartphones did.

Hal would know. Besides being a physicist, Hal was a techie and tutored everyone in Franklin on our latest i-purchases, doing a much better job than the manuals that accompanied them. I cheered myself with the fact that Hal's ruse would soon be revealed and Timmy would have his father back, if not his mother.

I walked toward the new beaded curtain that led to the back room where I'd last seen Ariana's binder.

I stepped over the threshold and into a loud noise.

Crash!

Gillian Bartholomew had smashed the window and entered the shop by the back window, the better to avoid being seen, I imagined. Even in my shock, I had to admire her agility as she climbed over the low sill.

My heart seemed to stop; my throat tightened to the maximum as I pretended not to scan her body for signs of a weapon. Both her hands were visible and empty, but she was wearing a khaki fisherman's vest with many pockets. It couldn't have been for warmth, so I imagined the worst. A knife in the top right pocket, a gun in the lower right, a venomous needle in the lower left, and a bomb strapped across her chest.

I hoped I was wrong and she was packing only lipstick and tissues, like a normal woman.

I slipped my phone into my own pocket, ruefully empty of weapons. I didn't have "speaker" selected and couldn't tell if Bruce had picked up or if it had gone to his voice mail.

"Gil," I said, loudly, in case Bruce was listening. "What are you doing here?"

As if I didn't know.

It didn't surprise me that "breaking and entering gracefully" might be part of an army reserve soldier's skill set.

"Why, Sophie, why?" Gil asked, a sad look on her face.

Wasn't that a more appropriate question from me to her? Not the time for technicalities, however.

Gil had a good four inches on me, and more than a few pounds. Moreover, she'd spent her life building up strength in physically demanding jobs, whereas, except for the occasional bike ride and kicking the exercise ball out of my way in the garage, the most athletic thing I'd done this summer was sharpening my puzzle pencils.

It was lighter in this area since the back window had no shades, and now, no glass either. I thought of running to the window and waving and screaming madly for help, but Gil was between me and the window, and the alley seemed deserted anyway. I could turn and run out through the sales floor, but I had a feeling she was quicker than I was. Wrong or not, I envisioned emergency workers like Gil able to run at the speed of light.

I saw that Gil's eyes were tear streaked, her face a map of despair. She inserted her hand into one of the vest pockets. I clutched at my shirt and swallowed audibly. She pulled out a tissue and wiped her eyes. I relaxed. Sort of.

"We should talk, Gil," I said.

Good luck with that, I added to myself.

Gil shifted from one leg to the other, nearly hopping off the floor. "The funny thing is I knew I blew it, going back, moving the cake inside, adding those thesis pages. Overkill." Poor word choice, I thought. "But when I saw that Rachel was going up to his office" — this came out as a hiss — "I couldn't resist. I knew I should leave well enough alone but I wanted to be sure the little tart was suspect number one."

"Tart? You think Rachel and Hal —"

Gil stopped hopping and began rocking on the heels of her heavy athletic shoes. She seemed to be warming up for . . . I didn't want to think what.

"It doesn't matter if they did or they didn't. Rachel wanted it and Hal's weak. God, is he weak. He took it on the chin for years from the great Dr. Appleton. The slights, the public insults, and then the let-

412

ter, the final straw."

Except for Gil's deranged look and the smashed window, a passerby might have thought she was witnessing two girlfriends talking things over, albeit one more agitated than the other.

I began to relax. Maybe Gil actually had come to talk. She hadn't threatened me physically. Yet. I checked the alley for a dark sedan, but the broken window was too narrow to provide much of a view from where I stood. Most likely she'd followed me here from campus, or she might have been on my tail all day for that matter.

Ergo, I reasoned, if she'd wanted to do me harm she'd have taken one of a wealth of other opportunities.

I was safe. Gil needed to talk; that was all.

Gil had mentioned a letter as the final straw. I went into the bluffing mode Ariana had taught me and that had served me well with the dean.

"You needed to remove that letter from the files in Keith's office."

Gil threw up her hands; her face took on an angry expression, directed at me.

Not safe anymore, if I ever was.

"See, you had to butt in and take those files away, Sophie. I was there, you know, parked right around the corner. I was on my way to go through his office but you got to it first. I knew immediately what you'd done. There just wasn't time the day before to stand there and sift through all his poisonous correspondence."

Another nice choice of words. I needed Virgil's advice on how to deal with a crazy killer. Actually I needed Virgil's gun. With neither at my disposal, I chose the sympathetic route, at the same time looking around for something I could use as a weapon if the need arose. I held on as long as possible to the delusion that the need hadn't already arisen.

Ariana's back room served as a storage area, among its many uses, with boxes and bits of inventory everywhere. The workshop table held unfinished projects and sharp tools — scissors, pliers, even a wrench — but none longer than a few inches. I'd have to close the gap between us to grab one, and even if I could bring myself to attack her at close range, it would be child's play for her to take me down. I longed for a remotely operated weapon. The only one I had was my brain and it was currently on hold.

I woke it up and tried my skills at communication.

"I know you absolutely had to get that letter from Keith's files," I said, now a master of the big bluff.

Gil's face sank into a deeper frown and she stood still for a moment. "The all-powerful, well connected Keith Appleton drafted a letter to the doctoral committee at Massachusetts University requesting a review of Hal's thesis and asking them to revoke his degree."

I was genuinely shocked. "Why would he do that?"

She gave me a screwy look. "You know how much he wanted to discredit my husband. He had no respect for MU, for one thing. Thought Henley should have as few faculty as possible from a state college. Hal and I think he had a physicist friend from some stupid Ivy League school that he wanted Fran to hire in Hal's place."

"That sounds awful." Agree with the captor, that was my plan.

"Keith researched some archaic standards about how many words you're allowed to cite from another work and claimed that Hal had violated an old guideline. He showed Hal the letter, offering not to send it if Hal withdrew his name as a candidate for the degree."

Gil bit her lip. Her eyes stared beyond me while her feet beat to an inaudible rhythm.

"I'm so sorry," I said, wondering too late how smart it was to keep reminding her of my presence.

"We thought he'd changed his mind. We told him how much Hal needed this job, with Timmy headed for private school. Without the degree, he'd be so limited . . ." Gil threw her hands up. She'd made the best case she could. "But once Hal graduated, Keith brought the letter out again. I knew the police wouldn't find it because he stuck it in a file labeled 'Graduation Speeches.' He had the nerve to show us where he was burying it."

Keith's office was a veritable hot bed of material for a tabloid, all in plain sight under innocuous labels. I was more certain than ever that somewhere in those boxes I'd ferried out of Franklin Hall was a piece of paper with research on me that he'd been keeping for leverage, should he ever have needed it.

Hal wasn't in Keith's department. Why would he bother vetting Hal's thesis unless Gil was right and he simply wanted to hire his friend? Lucy's defense of her boyfriend, that Keith wanted all medical workers to be from the top of their class, didn't work here. Physicists didn't do open heart surgery. But then, what did giving a baby up for adoption have to do with Dean Underwood's academic credentials?

I was back to labeling my deceased former colleague "ruthless."

"That was a terrible thing for Keith to do," I told Gil.

"See, I knew you'd understand all this, Sophie, and I wish there had been a way to get your support before all this happened."

Nothing had "happened." Gil had killed Keith by her own hand. But once again I felt guilty — not only had I not befriended Lucy-the-new-girl, but I'd missed a chance to be pals with Gil and therefore have a chance to prevent Keith's murder.

It was a lot to bear for a simple math teacher.

While keeping up my end of this life-and-death conversation, I'd been keeping up my search for a potential weapon. I knew there were knives in the drawer under the microwave oven. And there was always the flame from the small gas stove. And spray paint on a shelf in the sales area. Nothing I could reasonably reach or use. I'd already stopped fiddling with the phone in my pocket afraid that, instead of contacting help, I'd set off a ringtone and anger Gil beyond her current red-faced state.

My best chance was if my call had gotten

through to Bruce and he'd heard what was happening. Unfortunately no police sirens accosted my ear.

I tried another bluff: Assume Gil was through with me. She could go back out the window and I could be on my way. I took a breath and started toward the table with the binder and handwriting material.

"Well, I need to pick up something —" I said.

Gil grabbed me by the arm.

It was worth a try.

She put her other hand in her pocket. This time she came out with a needle.

"If only you'd minded your own business, Sophie," Gil said, seeming honestly broken up about the fact that she had to kill me.

With great effort, my adrenaline winning temporarily over Gil's muscle and skill, I twisted my arm and pulled away. The un-natural movement sent my shoulder into a spasm. Small price to pay for freedom.

I backed up as far as I could in the crowded space, aiming for the beaded curtain. In the brief tussle, Gil had moved between me and the curtain and I found myself practically sitting on the worktable I'd sat at such a short time ago, blithely stringing beads into a little key chain.

Gil held the needle as if it were a dagger,

waving her arm, ready to thrust.

"What would killing me accomplish?" I asked, holding my arms tight across my chest. "Bruce knows all about the handwriting and Hal's false confession. And it's going to be so obvious if you use that needle."

What was I saying? Was I asking Gil to shoot me or stab me instead?

Gil didn't bother to answer my question. It was clear that she'd lost it and wasn't thinking past the moment. She lunged at me. I swung away and the needle ended up stabbing a large bag of cotton balls meant for the crafts section. I hoped it could be that easy; that the poison threat was over. There were still two pockets in her vest with unknown weapons, however, and even a weaponless Gil could knock me out in a heartbeat.

She lowered her arm. Had I managed to talk a killer out of a second murder? I didn't trust her.

I revisited the idea of making a run for it, through the curtain, through the shop, and out the front door.

The curtain.

At last, I had a way to slow Gil down.

I knew I'd suffer Ariana's wrath if my plan worked, but it was my only chance of survival.

I took a breath and made a sudden dash for the beaded curtain. I arrived there with my arms up. Ignoring the pain in my shoulder, I crossed the threshold into the sales area. I turned quickly to face the curtain and pulled down with all my might, grabbing the strings of beads and wrenching the heavy curtain from its mooring at the top of the doorframe.

As I hoped, the curtain came crashing down, the strings broke, and thousands — a million? — of tiny purple and green beads rained behind me.

By the time Gil could react to my flight, she was fighting off an avalanche of beads. I heard her slip and fall and crash into a counter, knocking more beads to the floor. The sound as the beads splattered behind me was sweeter than that of a cool summer rain.

I was almost at the front door. I heard Gil scramble behind me to regain her footing. I opened the door to the sounds of police sirens and the screeching brakes of two Henley PD squad cars outside.

Bruce had figured it out. Who said cell phones were an unnecessary luxury?

A moment later a female officer caught me as I fell into her arms and the other three ran into the store.

When the officer patted my back to assure me I was safe, tiny purple and green beads fell out of my shirt, onto the ground.

26

The romantic dinner for two turned into a midnight potluck with Bruce and me joined by Ariana and Virgil. We stretched the pasta and mushroom sauce with a large salad provided by Ariana and an extra large pizza ordered by Virgil.

"I really like pepperoni better than steak," Virgil said, reminding me of my promise to cook him a better dinner some day.

"What a relief," I said, swiping my hand across my brow.

We ate as though we'd been lost in the desert for a week, which, in a sense, was true.

As hard as we tried to avoid conversation about what had put Henley College on the front pages of Boston newspapers and YouTube, we strayed now and then.

We talked briefly of the tortuous route Gil Bartholomew had traveled on the weekend of the murder. She had to take measures to get what she needed for a lethal dose of a chemical that otherwise was stocked in small medicinal quantities. She had to murder Keith at a time when everyone else was busy partying. She worked hard to frame Rachel, then deepen the frame by adding to the crime scene. Who knew how long ago she'd retrieved yellow pages from the trash. She had to track down the files from Keith's office, steal them, remove what she wanted, and take them back to Franklin Hall.

"Why did she return the boxes, again?" Ariana asked, confused by the timeline of people in and out of the deceased Keith Appleton's office. "And what happened to Sophie's usable discards?"

Virgil shrugged. "I'll bet you'll see those discards down at the Main Street Thrift Shop. As for the boxes of files, she probably just didn't want to get caught with them. Otherwise she'd have to destroy all those files and boxes and that would take time, and also attract attention. A midnight drop at the school was an easy disposal method. One time, back in Boston, this bank robber took a briefcase —"

"Virge." Bruce interrupted his friend in an attempt to get us off the crime tack.

"Never mind," Virgil said, grabbing a few

circles of pepperoni from the pizza, still in its box.

I couldn't help apologizing over and over to Ariana about the mess I'd left in her shop. Between the undoing of the beaded curtain and the counter of bead trays Gil had knocked over, it would be many days before the inventory at A Hill of Beads was back in place.

Ariana waved away my mortification. "I've been wanting to reorganize anyway," she said. "And I'm going to order this neat velvety, shimmery curtain that I've had my eye on for the back room."

I felt a little better.

I checked my email before going to bed. I read one from Rachel with the subject, "Confession."

"In police custody," it read. "Kidding. But I'm happy to be assigned to community service all next semester."

I smiled as I opened similar messages from Pam, Liz, and Casey, with the same general sentiment.

The community would be well served next semester.

By the end of the week, the heat wave had finally ended and cool breezes blew through the campus and the town of Henley. The weather was even better on Cape Cod when Bruce and I finally checked in to a cottage at a beach in Hyannis for a long weekend.

Bruce eventually stopped beating himself up for being miles away while I was being held hostage. Reminding him that he was exactly where I'd sent him that evening — looking for samples of Gil's handwriting — and that he had sent the Henley PD to the shop, helped a little.

"A lot of good I was, camping out to protect you."

"You could sign up for more shifts," I said.

By Monday I was back in my office, filing some and tossing other material from the summer program. One thing I passed through the cross shredder was the difficult puzzle Gil had solved and returned to me. I wanted no reminders of the deadly weekend.

All my students had turned in their papers early. I guessed they were as eager as I was to put the summer session behind us.

Courtney called right before lunch. "I've been trying to reach you."

"I took a few days off."

"I know what it was."

"You know what what was?"

"You know, the urgent matter you had to talk over with the dean the other night."

I'd nearly forgotten and now I started. "You know?" Had the dean told Courtney about her son? That surprised me. Who else knew?

"Yeah, she came in the next day with the agenda for the faculty meeting. I'm not supposed to tell anyone. Big LOL here, 'cause I know you know you got your promotion. Full Professor. I'm so excited for you."

In what corner of the world, academic or business, were administrative assistants not the first to know the latest news?

"Oh, that," I said, containing my own excitement.

"So, of course that's what your meeting was about the other night," Courtney said, triumphant.

"Of course."

"Awesome!" she said.

I had to agree.

BRAIN(TEASERS)

Sophie Knowles doesn't expect that everyone will be able to unwind with arithmetic, but she feels that doing puzzles and mental arithmetic keeps you sharp, and improves your memory and your powers of observation. Here are some samples of puzzles and games that exercise your wits.

Browse in your bookstore and library, and online for more brainteasers and have some fun!

Math Riddles
1. *Why is 6 afraid of 7?*

ANSWER: Because 7 8 9.

2. *Try solving this classic riddle.*

As I was going to St. Ives
I met a man with seven wives
Each wife had seven sacks

Each sack had seven cats
Each cat had seven kits
Kits, cats, sacks, wives
How many were going to St. Ives?

ANSWER: Only 1, the narrator. There's no indication that the others were going to St. Ives.

Another interpretation, that all were going to St. Ives, requires a considerable amount of arithmetic:

1 narrator
1 man
7 wives
49 sacks (7 × 7)
343 cats (49 × 7)
2401 kittens (343 × 7)
Total = 2802

Mental Arithmetic
Multiplying a 2-digit number by 11

There are several shortcuts for this case. Here's a two-step device for multiplying a 2-digit number by 11 without using paper.

1. Take the number (we'll use 52) and imagine a space between the two digits:

5_2

2. Now add the two numbers together and put the sum in the middle:

$$5\_(5+2)\_2 = 572.$$

That's it!

If the numbers in the middle add up to a 2-digit number, just "carry 1 over" — that is, insert the second number in the middle, and add 1 to the number on the left. For example, for 99×11, the steps are:

$$9\_(9+9)\_9$$
$$9\_(18)\_9$$
$$(9+1)\_8\_9$$
$$10\_8\_9$$

1089 is the answer!

Another way to multiply by 11 is to multiply the number by 10, then add the original number:

$$52 \times 10 = 520$$
$$520 + 52 = 572$$

For the second problem, 99×11:

$$99 \times 10 = 990$$
$$990 + 99 = 1089$$

The correct answer, again!

Wordplay Puzzles

The doublet, attributed to Lewis Carroll, involves transforming one word into another by changing only one letter, with each intervening change being a word.

Example: Transform HEAD into TAIL.

ANSWER: (the letter in bold is the letter changed on the way to the final word):

HEAD
HE**A**L
TEAL
TE**L**L
T**A**LL
TA**I**L

Try turning WHEAT into BREAD!

The employees of Thorndike Press hope you have enjoyed this Large Print book. All our Thorndike, Wheeler, and Kennebec Large Print titles are designed for easy reading, and all our books are made to last. Other Thorndike Press Large Print books are available at your library, through selected bookstores, or directly from us.

For information about titles, please call:
(800) 223-1244

or visit our Web site at:
http://gale.cengage.com/thorndike

To share your comments, please write:
Publisher
Thorndike Press
10 Water St., Suite 310
Waterville, ME 04901